Calvin's Chronicles

Volume 1

SONG W. ERETSON

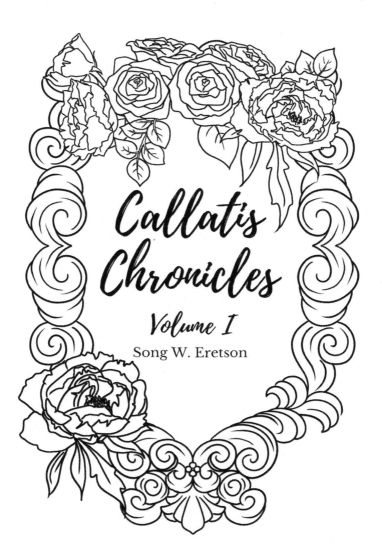

Callatis Chronicles

Volume I

Song W. Eretson

Thank you to my Ko-fi supporters, for helping to make this possible

TABLE OF CONTENTS

The Black Rose

16th day of Aurostra, 1544

Callatis, Cardea

Ducking into the alleyway had been a mistake, Heather realized. She had hoped to lose the guards, but had been too slow. And now she was fully exposed.

Four days before the Summer Solstice, Callatis bustled with preparations for the upcoming celebrations. Banners emblazoned with Aurora's sun sigil had begun to appear throughout the city, while flower pots around the city had been replanted with new, colorful blooms. The sweet scent mixed with rosemary, basil, garlic, cloves, and roasting meat in the market.

It all created a heady cacophony, which she had been in the midst of just a few minutes before.

Merchants haggled and hawked their wares, while customers purchased supplies, or placed orders ahead of the festival. Commoners and nobles intermingled, shopped, and gossiped. A few people schemed in the shadows, if not right in broad daylight.

A cool breeze blew off the sea, past the merchant, and pleasure vessels moored in the harbor. Warding off some of the early summer heat, so the crowds weren't too uncomfortable.

Heather had decided to take the day for herself—no pickpocketing, or canvassing. She had planned to enjoy the preparations; instead, she had five guards hot on her heels as she ran down an empty alleyway.

Not for the first time, she cursed Caspian as she ran.

Up ahead of her, she saw an open door into one of the shops on the main avenue. A couple was pressed against the wall, tangled in a deep kiss that blinded them to the world.

They jolted apart in surprise when Heather jumped onto the steps beside them. Before they could react, she ran inside and closed the door behind her with a resounding slam. It would buy here mere seconds, but those seconds were precious.

She found herself in an unlit storage room, but didn't slow down. Just enough light came through a half-opened door to let her see the wooden shelves against the walls, and the crates and barrels stacked on the floor.

In the doorway, she nearly ran into a young woman, who cried out in surprise.

Heather felt a twinge of guilt, but dodged around her and kept running. She burst into the front of the shop, surprising a merchant, and the four or five customers gathered there.

A marble counter blocked her way to the door.

An oil and vinegar shop, she realized, finally noticing the strong, tangy smells that permeated the air.

Behind her, Heather heard the guards force the door open. Their steps were heavy as they stormed into the shop.

Thinking fast, she vaulted over the counter. Ignoring the startled customers, she ran straight for the door.

Once out in the street, she was frustrated to find herself no longer in the heart of the market. Instead, she had moved north, into the more affluent, less crowded area of town.

To her left, a block and a half down, she could see the memorial fountain, and the market beyond that. Behind her came the sound of the guards reaching the door, pressing her to keep moving.

She veered right.

A merchant with a heavy crate suddenly turned into her path, and she barely dodged to avoid him. He cried out in surprise, then shouted at her to watch where she was going.

The guards calling for someone to grab her was a far more pressing issue.

She ignored the burning in her lungs, and pushed herself to run faster. Without a crowd, the scattered people around her became more of a threat than a protection.

Reaching the next corner, she turned left. Relieved to see that there was no one there.

One of the shops caught her attention.

Above the door, a carved wooden sign hung from a wrought iron bar. Intricate knotwork reminiscent of the northern lands framed the words *Thorinson's Curiosities and Consultations*, painted in black and violet.

The name set off a bell in the back of her head, though she was sure she had never seen the shop before. And she didn't have time to consider why.

With a shaky breath, she decided to take her chances inside.

✲ CHAPTER 2 ✲

As soon as she stepped inside the cool air of the shop, Heather found herself face to face with a wolf.

Her breath caught with a whimper, heart pounding in her ears as she looked into the intense blue eyes of a large, gray wolf on the wall.

She blinked as her thoughts realigned, and she came back to her senses.

The wolf wasn't real. It was only a beautifully painted mural on the top half of the far wall, above dark wood wainscotting.

A scene of what she thought must be the northern forests, with a pack of wolves among the trees and ferns.

Heather gave a small sob of relief as she collected herself. Then took a deep breath, and looked around.

The shop front was small, about ten feet across, and sixteen feet wide. To her right, a bookshelf was built into the wall, filled with books and knickknacks. To her left were two wingback chairs, an end table between them. There didn't appear to be any wares for sale.

In front of the mural was a polished, dark wood counter carved with knotwork, with a polished marble surface.

The rest of the space was similar dark wood, and the scent in the air was of paper and wood polish - a delightfully simple smell after the market, and the oil shop.

"Search the shops! She's here somewhere!" The cry was accompanied by the clatter of armor, and boots on the cobblestone street outside.

Heather's eyes darted around, searching for the best place to hide. But with such sparse decor, there were few options. There was the counter, and a door next to the mural that she only noticed on a second look. But the door had no knob.

She knew better than to try opening locked doors without knobs.

So instead, she ducked behind the counter. The back was as much a work of art as the front. The drawer and the cupboard were beautifully carved... but neither had a knob or handle.

Panic surged through her.

If the guards searched thoroughly, hiding behind the counter wouldn't save her. And as aggressively as they had pursued her, she had no doubt they would be thorough.

Gripping the counter's edge until her knuckles turned white, Heather sobbed as she rested her forehead against the cupboard door. Tears welled in her eyes, spilling down her cheeks.

How had it come to this?

Once more, she cursed Caspian. The egotistic, self-righteous bastard. All of this was his fault.

Just as she began to sink into self-pity, she heard footsteps.

But it wasn't the clatter of guards in armor. And it wasn't coming from the door.

Looking to her left, she blinked in surprise at the arched doorway, and a staircase she could have sworn hadn't been there before.

A man's charcoal leather boots appeared on the chair. Very nice leather boots, according to her trained eye. As he continued down the stairs, she saw dark pants, and a blue jerkin.

Even in her current situation, her heart fluttered when she saw his face.

He was in his early twenties, handsome, in an unassuming way she found incredibly charming. His chestnut hair was lightly tousled, but not messy, and his blue eyes reminded her of the wolf on the mural behind her: shrewd, and intelligent.

He looked her over, expression carefully schooled. There was no sign of surprise as he looked at her, but she did see his expression flicker.

"Please," she said, throwing herself at the man's mercy. "Hide me."

He looked towards the front of the shop, where they could hear the guards on the street. There were far more than the original five now.

"I'll expect an explanation," he said.

"I'll give you one," she promised. "Just don't let them find me."

He nodded, coming down the last few steps and behind the counter.

Heather flinched as he came closer. But he walked past her, opening the drawer in the counter and withdrawing a large book.

She looked up at him in confusion.

"Stay there," he murmured, and rested a hand on her head.

At first, she was offended at the touch, which seemed condescending. But he murmured something under his breath, and she felt a tingling sensation down her spine.

Magic.

That sent a different kind of chill down her back.

She tried to look at him without being too obvious. Her eyes fell on the boot next to her. Just as she had thought, the leather, and workmanship, were of the highest quality. A bulge in the side caught her attention.

A knife, she realized. Another one hung from his belt. Unobtrusive, but easily accessible if needed.

Her memory finally found what had been nagging her since she first read the sign above the door.

Thorinson.

Her heart stuttered in her chest.

The Thorinsons were a family from the north, as the decor suggested. Their history stretched back to the Aurellian Empire, if the stories she had heard were true—stories of merciless battles, rivals who disappeared, and women who fell under their savage spell.

They were also one of the most powerful families in the republic, with connections to the ruling families. Important enough that she had heard the name repeatedly over the past few years, even when she didn't bother paying attention to politics.

Heather shuddered, wondering if she hadn't entered an even more dangerous situation.

CHAPTER 3

Hammond was in his study when he heard the commotion in the street. He had left the windows open to let in the sea breeze, and the sounds of life from people going up and down Laurel Avenue. Sounds that were suddenly overtaken by loud clatters and calls.

He looked up from the grimoire he had been studying, and listened as they approached his shop.

Standing up, he went to the window to look down at the street. But before he got there, something else drew his attention.

The security spells he had carefully laid downstairs alerted him that someone had entered the shop. His head turned away from the window, and looked toward the staircase.

He didn't have any appointments that afternoon. And midday wasn't usually the time for people to drop by unannounced. Even the market would be closing down while people went to lunch, and waited for the heat of the day to pass.

"Search the shops!" someone called from the street. "She's here somewhere!"

With a frown, Hammond turned to the oval mirror that hung on the wall to his left. A gesture caused the glass to cloud over for a moment, before giving him a view into the shop.

A dark-haired woman stood inside the doorway, looking around frantically for a place to hide.

He looked down at the street again, and saw city guards gathering. They had begun to search the shops along the street, pushing doors open, and pounding on those that were locked. There were already ten of them, with another group arriving.

All of which seemed rather excessive for one young woman, he thought.

Turning away from the window, and the mirror, he went downstairs.

As he reached the first landing, another spell went off. Alerting him that the intruder was trying to open the cupboard in the counter.

The doorway at the bottom of the stairs appeared as he neared it.

The woman looked over as he approached, her eyes wide. And Hammond found himself momentarily distracted.

Her black hair was pulled up in a braid crown, but some had come free, framing bright, cat-like green eyes that glistened with desperate tears. Full pink lips quivered as she looked at him.

She was beautiful, and desperate. His two weaknesses.

"Don't look anyone in the eye," he said, lifting his hand from her head. He withdrew a glass quill and inkwell from the drawer, and began to review the notes in his ledger. "The spell can't hold up to eye contact."

Simple spells always had limitations.

As the spellcaster, however, he could still see her as she hugged her knees to her chest, back pressed against the cupboard door. He felt a pang of sympathy, but wasn't sure how to reassure her.

Before he could think of something to say, he realized the guards had gone quiet.

He could still hear them searching the other shops on the street. But something had changed.

Finally, the door to his shop opened.

But it wasn't with the force of city guards storming in to raid the shop. Instead, it was opened aggressively by a single man, who stalked inside with irritating arrogance.

Hammond pretended to look up from the ledger, careful to hide his annoyance.

"Caspian," he said. "To what do I owe the visit?"

⋙ CHAPTER 4 ⋘

Hammond felt his teeth set on edge as Caspian Graves entered the shop.

The captain of the guard was around Hammond's height, with olive-toned skin, brown eyes, and black hair that he wore slicked back. He wore a black cape over his armor, to ensure no one could forget his position.

A position Hammond still wished someone else had gotten instead.

In the several years Hammond had known Caspian, he had concluded that the man was full of himself to an absurd degree. He was so focused on his aims, and perceived success, that he refused to see his own failings.

He had been the Prefects' Council counselor when the position for captain of the guard had opened. But despite his allies' best efforts, Caspian won the position. And never let anyone forget it.

Hammond sometimes wondered if it was the greatest failure of his career.

Caspian's upper lip curled slightly as he looked around the shop. "I'm looking for a criminal."

"That sounds serious," Hammond said, feigning interest.

"A thief," Caspian elaborated.

Hammond resisted the urge to mirror his disgusted look. But for a very different reason. "Did you want me to see if I can locate her?"

"My men told me she came down this street," Caspian said. "So she must have come into one of the shops to hide."

"No one's come in here," Hammond said.

Caspian gave a dismissive hum, stalking around the room like an animal in a cage. His dark eyes swept the room, before he came to look behind the counter.

Hammond didn't dare look at the woman next to him. But he quietly willed her to remember what he had said about not making eye contact.

He did look over when Caspian reached for the cupboard door.

Sure enough, she moved like a thief, slipping out of the way to the other side of Hammond's feet.

"The cupboard is sealed," Hammond said. "Only I can open it." That wasn't quite true – a handful of people did access to it. But he felt no need to explain that to Caspian.

Still, to appease the man, Hammond opened the cupboard. Even if it weren't sealed, there wasn't enough space for her to hide. There was a shelf in the middle, filled with ink bottles, paper, and various other stationery supplies.

Caspian gave the interior an annoyed look, before slamming the cupboard closed.

Hammond couldn't stop himself from glaring. But, fortunately, Caspian had already turned his attention to the door next to the mural.

"I wouldn't touch--"

He was too late. Caspian had already pushed the door with his gloved hand. Only to gasp as he was shocked by the warding spell.

"That's sealed as well," Hammond sighed, unable to keep the annoyance out of his voice. "And protected."

"So I see," Caspian said, through gritted teeth. "I could almost be suspicious of how tightly you keep this place locked up, Hammond."

"You know the people I work for," Hammond reminded, hoping the man would also remember his place. "I'm hardly going to leave their papers lying around unsecured."

Caspian might be captain of the guard, from a moderately respected military family. But Hammond was a Thorinson, with connections to the ruling families.

"You're sure no one could get in there?" Caspian asked, still rubbing his shocked palm.

"You tell me," Hammond said, with a pointed look.

But he reminded himself that he should maintain a polite façade. Antagonizing the man wouldn't get this over any faster.

Instead, he reached for the door. The wrought iron knob appeared under his fingers, and turned easily.

"I assure you, whoever you're looking for couldn't get in."

Caspian still stepped inside, looking around.

While Hammond had the chairs in the front room, he conducted appointments in the back room.

It was more than twice the size of the front room, set up as a parlor. Bookshelves lined the walls, while couches and armchairs created a comfortable sitting area, with a locked desk against one wall. But as Caspian looked around, the only thing that seemed to interest him was the wood and glass liquor cabinet.

"Who are you looking for?" Hammond asked, wanting to keep Caspian focused. The sooner he could be convinced there was nothing there, the sooner he would leave.

But Caspian's face darkened as he looked around again—more than Hammond had anticipated.

"The Black Rose."

Hammond barely stopped himself from looking over at the woman.

The Black Rose was one of the best thieves in the city, having worked her way up the ranks of the Thieves Guild in a few short years. And while she was rumored to be beautiful, Hammond hadn't put much stock in that idea. People tended to romanticize what fascinated them.

And rumors of the Black Rose certainly fascinated people.

But in this case, they hadn't done her justice.

"She was spotted in the market," Caspian went on.

"I wasn't aware anyone knew what she looked like," Hammond said.

He might have been wrong... But he could have sworn Caspian's face turned red.

The reaction only piqued Hammond's curiosity more. But he already had the promise of explanation from the Black Rose herself. He had no need to get it from

Caspian. And no interest in having the man in his shop any longer than necessary.

Finally satisfied that the parlor was empty, Caspian returned to the front room with an irritated look.

Hammond closed the door, the knob disappearing again as soon as he let go, and looked around the room.

It took a moment to find her, crouched in the corner behind one of the chairs at the table. Out of the way, but still able to watch, and listen. As Caspian looked around, she hid her face behind the chair, avoiding accidental eye contact.

Caspian gave an annoyed huff, glowering at nothing in particular.

"Insolent hussy," he muttered.

"She probably went into one of the other shops," Hammond said. "There aren't many places to hide in here."

That earned a glare from Caspian, who didn't like being spoken down to. The man seemed constantly looking to take offense at anything said to him.

"Probably," he said with a scowl. "I blame my men for being inept. It shouldn't be so hard to catch one girl."

"A will to live is a powerful thing." Hammond ran a hand over his ledger.

Trying to get across the hint that the shop was empty, and he wanted to get back to his work.

"What's that supposed to mean?" Caspian asked, face still twisted in a scowl.

"I just mean to say that, if she doesn't want to be caught, she'll fight to avoid it," Hammond said. "It's impressive how far some people will go to stay alive."

Not that Caspian seemed at all impressed. With a final glare around the shop, as if convinced he had missed something, Caspian turned back to the door. "If you see her, let me know."

"Of course," Hammond said, without meaning it in the slightest. He had no intention of telling Caspian anything.

The captain of the guard nodded, then finally left.

When the door closed behind him, Hammond took a moment to breathe deeply, and calm his agitation. This was far more excitement than he had expected from today.

Once he had regained his composure, he glanced over at the woman. She looked at him with wide, beautiful green eyes, as she stood up in the corner.

"I think it's time for that explanation."

⊰ CHAPTER 5 ⊱

Heather's heart had pounded in her ears the entire time Caspian had been in the shop. It was the first time she had seen him in months. While her anger had stewed that entire time, it was still eclipsed by fear.

She felt like a fox hiding from a jackal.

"Are you alright?"

She jolted. "Y-yes. Yes, I'm fine. Just a little overexcited."

He nodded in understanding. "What's your name?"

She hesitated for a moment. But then decided there was no point in trying to lie to him. "Heather Moore."

"Hammond Thorinson."

The name sounded vaguely familiar, but she wasn't sure where she might have heard it.

"I'd say it's nice to meet you, but that would be an understatement," she said. "I don't know how to thank you."

"You did promise me an explanation," he said. "And I admit, I'm even more curious now."

She tried to think of how to explain it, since she wasn't sure where, or how, to begin.

Before she could, the grandfather clock in the corner chimed, announcing midday. Hammond looked at it, almost as surprised as she was.

"Why don't you join me for lunch?" he suggested, returning the ledger to the drawer under the counter.

That wasn't an invitation Heather could refuse. "Alright."

Hammond gestured for her to follow him.

When Hammond had first appeared on the stairs, she had been confused that she hadn't seen them before. It made her feel better to realize it simply hadn't been there. Like the doorknob, the arched doorway to the staircase appeared at his touch.

For a moment, Heather hesitated, one foot on the bottom step. The last time she had followed a man upstairs... Well, that was precisely how she had ended up in this situation. And her mind reminded her of all the whispered stories about Thorinsons, and how they were as wild as their wolf sigil.

She glanced at the mural on the wall again.

Ahead of her, Hammond paused, glancing over the banister. "Are you coming?"

Too late to back out now, she decided. It wasn't as if she had much left to lose.

Instinct told her he wasn't like Caspian. So she followed him up two flights of stairs to the second floor.

Another set of stairs led up to a third story, but she barely noticed them as she entered the drawing room. The space was wide open, brightly lit by the windows that looked out towards the sea. Like downstairs, there were polished wooden floors, with exposed dark wood beams in the whitewashed walls. And unlike the sparse shop front, this space was tastefully furnished.

On the right was a sitting area, with bookshelves, a liquor cabinet, a sideboard, two sofas, and several armchairs. While on the left was a dining table that could seat eight people comfortably. That was where Hammond led her.

Lunch was already on the table. Grilled salmon on a wooden serving dish, garnished with a twist of lemon. There was a glass pitcher of water, a bowl filled with peaches, plums, pears, and grapes, and a basket of bread rolls with melted butter to dip them in. Only one place was set, at the head of the table, but Hammond went over to the hutch in the corner.

"I have unexpected guests often enough that I try to be prepared," he said, setting out a plate, silverware, and water glass for her.

people drop in often enough that I make sure I have enough prepared." He set the place to the right of his seat, before pulling out the chair for her. "Have a seat."

"You're awfully polite, considering you know who I am." It was hardly the kind of welcome she was used to.

"Because you're a thief?" The corner of his mouth twitched in a half-smile. "My cousin is the Wild Wolf."

Heather blinked in surprise.

She had met the Wild Wolf once. Briefly. They had both been wearing masks and hoods, so it hardly counted. While she had known, at least from rumors, that he was well connected to the controlling powers of the guild, she hadn't suspected he was a Thorinson.

When she considered the wolf iconography, perhaps she should have guessed.

"Sit," he said again, a polite invitation.

Once she was seated, he took the seat at the head of the table, confident and at ease in a way that she envied. He seemed so secure in himself, his position, and his home.

Heather watched as he served himself a cut of the salmon. The rich smell made her mouth water, and she was hit with just how hungry she was. Initially, she had planned to eat lunch in the market, and had been looking forward to some of the grilled lamb from one of the food carts. Before the guards had ruined that plan.

Hammond took her plate, serving her a generous portion of the fish, and one of the rolls.

"Help yourself to the fruit and water," he said, setting the plate in front of her again.

"Thank you." It was all she could say.

This was the most anyone had done for her in... longer than she could remember. And she wasn't sure how to handle how nice it felt.

She waited until he took a bite of fish before taking her bread roll and delicately tearing off a piece. The taste of lemon and garlic filling her mouth. It might just have been because of her hunger, but it was the best food she had had in a long time.

"Thank you," she said, glancing over at her host.

"For harboring you, or for the food?" he asked, giving her a small, wry smile.

"Both," she admitted, dipping another piece of bread into the butter.

"I certainly didn't expect Caspian himself to come after you," Hammond said. He turned a roll of bread in his hands slowly.

Heather stilled for a moment.

"What happened?" he asked.

She picked up her fork, taking a moment to think as she took a bite of the salmon. The meat seemed to melt on her tongue. "A few months ago, Caspian started to raid guild meetings, and important jobs," she said.

Hammond nodded. "The informant. I remember."

"They offered a reward to find out how he was getting information." She sighed as she cut off another bite of fish. "I hadn't planned to do anything. I've survived by avoiding attention. But one day, I was in the Mother's temple, and noticed him watching me. It seemed like an opportunity I shouldn't pass up."

"Deceit in a temple isn't recommended," Hammond pointed out. "Especially the Mother's."

"I didn't talk to him until we were outside," she said, a little defensive. But they had been in the temple circle. And sometimes, she wondered if that was why things had gone so wrong.

She took another bite before continuing, but her thoughts made it difficult to enjoy the food.

"I spent two weeks fawning over him." She scowled, stabbing at her fish. "Two weeks listening to him complain about officers who didn't respect him, and nobles he resented."

"That probably included me," Hammond said wryly, as he took a drink of water.

"Good," Heather said. "He's insufferable."

She paused, realizing that might be why his name had sounded familiar when he introduced himself.

"Don't I know it," he muttered. "Did you get the information?"

"Technically. He wouldn't tell me anything important - not directly. But one day, I saw him reading a note he said was from his informant, setting up a meeting the next day." She sighed, frustration from that day coming back. "I knew it might be my only chance, but he just wouldn't turn his back for a minute."

"What did you do?" There was no judgment in Hammond's voice, just curiosity.

But Heather found she didn't want to admit it. She didn't want it to color his opinion of her.

"He's a terrible kisser," she said, almost before realizing she had opened her mouth. "He has no skill or finesse."

Hammond nearly choked on a bite of bread, coughing to clear his throat. "I can't say that's something I ever thought about." He actually seemed to blush a little.

"You're not missing anything," she said. "But it let me drug him and shackle him to his bed. I stole some gold, and other papers from his desk to cover up the letters. But I couldn't pretend it wasn't me."

She would be lying if she said that hadn't been satisfying—a small comfort in the situation.

"He must have been humiliated when his men found him. I wish I could have seen his face." Hammond smirked, but it soon turned to a frown. "It certainly explains why he hates you."

Heather nodded. "The guild caught the informant, and I was rewarded. But I didn't think things through, so now he, and about half the guard, know what I look like."

Hammond nodded thoughtfully. "Caspian is making things difficult for the guilds, so they can't protect you as they usually would."

She nodded. Things had undoubtedly become more difficult in the last few years, ever since Caspian had become captain of the guard.

Hammond swirled his glass slowly as he thought, and Heather took the time to eat. While sneaking glances at him through her lashes. The sight of him certainly helped clear away his negative thoughts of Caspian.

He was clean-shaven, with a square jaw and straight nose. And she liked how the sunlight through the window shone on his chestnut hair, highlighting hints of red.

"Did you grow up here in the city?" Hammond asked after a moment, changing the subject, but looking at her curiously.

Heather nodded as she swallowed another bite of fish. "I was a street thief as a child. Just another orphan trying to survive."

"The guild's favorite kind of recruit," he noted.

She nodded.

The guild preferred to find children on the street with few attachments, who already displayed an inclination for the work. Heather had been fortunate enough to catch the eye of a Thieves Guild member who had brought her in to be cleaned up and trained.

"They decided I was worth teaching etiquette, but not enough to be a con," she said. "I'm a better cat burglar."

"Even some of the best cons didn't dare get close to Caspian," Hammond pointed out.

"They were smarter than I was," Heather said.

A properly trained con artist would have thought through being so obvious when stealing from the captain of the guard.

"What about you?" she asked, after taking a few more bites.

He seemed genuinely confused by the question. "What about me?"

"Did you grow up here in the city?"

He shook his head. "No. I grew up in Ulfvard, on my family's estate. It's about a day and a half north of here. My mother didn't want my sister and me growing up in the city, though I came with my father often enough."

The image of a young Hammond following his father around the city made her smile.

"Where's your sister now?" she asked curiously.

"Eydis?" He shrugged. "Wherever she wants to be. She's not the type to do what people expect of her."

"I always wondered what it would be like to have a sibling," she admitted. "Probably a pretty common fantasy for a street orphan."

"In my case: trouble," he said.

Heather couldn't help but giggle, and earned a wry smile from Hammond as he took a drink.

As he swallowed, though, his expression turned thoughtful. "The guild can't offer much protection right now. But my family could."

It took her a moment to process the words. "Are you offering me patronage?"

He nodded. "I would have to speak with my father. And even Richard."

"Richard... Galloborne?" she asked, just to be sure.

The Gallobornes were among the most powerful of the ruling families in Callatis. Richard was the notoriously handsome, but intimidating, head of the family.

Hammond nodded. "If you'd like."

"Why?" She asked, suddenly feeling a bit wary.

As he had said, the guild could do little for her. But even when the situation was ideal, patronage was a goal for every thief - to work directly in the employ of a powerful family. And he was offering not one, but two of the most powerful families in the republic.

"I've been looking for someone with your set of skills," he said. "And I know others who have as well. As I said, I would have to speak with my father before I can make an official offer."

Heather's heart fluttered, almost unable to believe the offer. "I would appreciate it."

He considered for a moment. "I'll be busy with the solstice celebrations for the next few days. Why don't you come back on the 22nd, at noon? We can make a lunch appointment to continue this conversation, once I've had a chance to discuss details with them."

She smiled. "If the food is as good as today, I won't argue."

Hammond chuckled. "I'll make sure my cook is in top form."

It occurred to her that she would see him again in just a few days. And that excited her almost as much as the idea of patronage.

"Thank you," she said, hoping her voice expressed how much she meant it.

"You're welcome." He seemed a little embarrassed.

With her fish gone, she looked towards one of the windows before her. "Do you think they're still looking?"

"Most likely," he said, looking towards the window as well. He considered for a moment, before looking back at her. "Are you familiar with the catacombs beneath the city?"

"Well enough to get around." She didn't use the catacombs as often as some thieves did, but could use them to get to specific points in the city.

Hammond paused again. "There's an entrance to the catacombs in my basement. You could use it to get far enough away that they wouldn't be looking for you."

She hesitated a moment. Some areas in the catacombs were safer than others, and she wasn't familiar with this one. But then she nodded, since it did seem like the best option.

Hammond led her down the backstairs, and passed the kitchen that was half underground. What appeared to be a stone wall revealed a heavy wooden door when Hammond touched it, and he unlocked it with a key that appeared in his hand.

Her first impression of the basement was that it was surprisingly spacious. But when she looked around the dimly lit room, she realized it was much smaller than she had thought. Several trunks were stacked in one corner, and she could feel the subtle hum of magic all around her. The air was cool, and a little stale, but there was no smell of must or mildew.

Next to the door on the far side of the room was a locked wooden cabinet.

"Do you have a light?" Hammond asked.

She shook her head. "I didn't bring one today."

He unlocked one of the doors on the cabinet, and she caught sight of what looked like a full leather satchel inside. He opened the flap, and pulled out a polished blue gem the size of her palm.

He murmured a word, and the gem began to emit a glow, which grew stronger as he handed it to her.

"Thank you," she said. "I'll bring it back next time."

He shook his head. "No need. You can keep it."

He unlocked the second door, and a rush of cool air blew through the door.

On the other side, Heather looked down the long, dark passage of the catacombs.

"If you follow this tunnel, there's an exit behind The Golden Hare tavern," Hammond said. "Do you know it?"

She nodded. The tavern wasn't far from the bridge that would take her back to her home in the Rat District.

"Good. The door is marked with the knotwork hare on the tavern's sign," he said.

"Straight ahead, about twenty minutes walk?" she guessed, based on how far away she knew the tavern was.

"Exactly," he said, holding the door open for her.

She stepped into the catacombs, holding up the vial to see the tunnel around her.

The tunnels were old, from when Callatis had been a port city in the Aurellian Empire, the arched roof held up with wide, solid columns.

"I'll see you on the 22nd," Hammond said.

"Without Caspian, hopefully," she said, turning to face him.

"Hopefully," he chuckled, giving her a sheepish smile.

When she saw that smile, she wondered how she could ever have been afraid of him. Thorinson or not.

She was struck again by how handsome he was, even in the light from the gem in her hand. And she didn't want to leave. Between his looks, and how he had protected her, she found herself drawn to him. So she lingered, trying to think of some reason to stay.

"I'll see you in a few days, then," she said, unable to find any excuse to stay.

"I look forward to it." It was said with that shy smile.

"Do you mean that, Hammond?" she asked, tilting her head to give him a flirty look.

"I do."

She wasn't sure if he was flirting back. She couldn't read his expression. But it seemed genuine, so she decided to enjoy that for what it was.

Stepping closer, she rose on her toes to kiss his cheek. "I do, too."

He even smelled good, she realized. Clean, but with a hint of paper, leather, and musk. She had to fight the urge to inhale deeply, to fill her senses with the smell.

When she pulled back, he gave her a stunned look.

"I'll see you then," she said, giving him one last smile before she turned into the catacombs. Holding the gem above her head to light her way.

Looking Down

CHAPTER 1

19th day of Aurorstra, 1544

North of the Callatis city proper, across the Silver River, lay the Aurellian District—the most affluent, and beautiful, of the five districts.

When the Aurellian Empire to the east had fallen, a few of the wealthier families had remained in Callatis. Merchants, in particular, as much of their trade had been based along the coast. Five centuries later, they still thrived in the area they had built for themselves.

Her brother could talk for hours about the fall of the empire - the wars and politics that had caused the fall, and led to the establishment of Cardea. But unlike Hammond, Eydis was bored to tears with history.

She knew the empire had fallen, while the conquered tribes had reclaimed their land. And the imperial remnant had established a district of wealth, art, academia, and a veneer of civility that masked a cut-throat hierarchy. All wrapped up in only the finest silks, bedecked with intricate, flashy gold jewelry, and stained with purple dye. It was home to palatial manors along the river, and a luxury market that was the envy of the western coast.

It was also home to the Di Antonio Arena. And the gladiators who fought there.

Which was what drew Ella to the Aurellian District. And Eydis let her friend drag her across the bridge, and through the Aurellian streets—a familiar path after the last year and a half.

They passed the Temple Circle, with its massive fountain in the center, surrounded by statues of the gods. The two largest, to the east and the west, depicted Aurora and Selene, the Titan sisters that ruled the pantheon.

East of that was the library, and the university. Both architectural works of art - towering marble pillars and intricate gilt work. Sponsored by the families within the district.

Then they moved into the market, where Aurellian merchants - and a few elves - hawked their wares.

Preparations for the Summer Solstice were in full swing. But Ella led her down a less crowded side street, attention fixed on their destination.

They passed a bakery, the smell of baked goods making Eydos' mouth water. But she knew better than to suggest they stop.

"Come on," Ella said impatiently, grabbing her hand to pull her along.

"I don't know why you're in such a hurry," Eydis said. "We both know Lucius won't be here today."

Unofficially, the arena had been open for the past month or so. Ever since the spring rains had passed. But the season didn't officially begin until the Summer Solstice.

The whole city buzzed with excitement for the celebrations. But in the Aurellian District, there was heightened anticipation. Waiting for Lord Marcus Di Antonio to oversee the opening ceremonies, and the first official tournament of the season. With all appropriate grandeur, of course.

Not that the unofficial status of the skirmishes had stopped even Di Antonio's gladiators from participating.

"He might," Ella insisted. She was a little shorter than Eydis, red hair framing her deceptively innocent face, with lively green eyes, and full lips painted dusty pink.

"But why not wait until tomorrow, when we know he will be?"

Ella had dragged her into the arena several times in the last few weeks, without any guarantee that Lucius Gaspari would be there.

Eydis enjoyed the games, so she didn't usually complain. But she doubted there would be much in the way of sport today. Not when any gladiators worth their weight in salt would be resting for tomorrow.

"Because I'm bored," Ella said. "And optimistic."

Champion's Way was lined with vendors setting up and decorating for the next day, just as they were in the market. Including the bakery they had passed earlier.

The smell of baking bread overwhelmed Eydis, making her mouth water. She paused and handed over a coin in exchange for a couple of slices of bruschetta flavored with olive oil and herbs.

Ella paused, waiting for her to catch up. With an impatient look as she did.

Other stalls included trinkets they claimed came from the gladiators - everything from shirts to tokens.

One, in particular, had glass vials of perfume. Or so they called it. Eydis had never understood the Aurellian tradition of making perfume from the sweat of gladiators. Personally, she found it repulsive. But the women of the Aurellian District didn't seem to think so.

A group of young noblewomen stood around the stall, blushing and giggling as the merchant insisted his wares came from this or that champion.

"Do you think it's made from his sweat, or his horse's?" Eydis asked, munching on her snack.

Ella wrinkled her nose at the thought. "Hopefully the horse's."

Eydis laughed as they continued through the massive gate, and the tunnel that led into the arena.

Gladiator sweat perfume wasn't the kind of thing a simple vendor outside the arena would sell. It was far too valuable a commodity for that, and was instead controlled by the gladiator's patron. None of them would license it to a snake oil salesman lurking outside the gates. Simple tokens, yes. But not their sweat.

The Di Antonio Arena was massive, with stone pillars and walls intricately carved with reliefs of animals and heroes. Around the top, Eydis could see the rolled-up banners of the gladiators. Waiting for the next day, when they would be unfurled to announce the games.

The arena, and the games, drew people in from all the districts to see the fights, which gave the champions notoriety throughout the city. A reminder of just how thin the Aurellians' civilized facade was.

Alcoves around the first level of the arena held life-sized statues, representing the titans, the gods, and heroes of the past. Not the gladiators, ironically. Save for one in the arena itself. Statues of arena champions were scattered around the district.

Numitor the Warrior, god of bravery, justice, and righteous warfare, was separate from the rest. He stood ahead of the gate, in segmented, Aurellian-style armor, his spear held aloft in victory. While at his feet stalked his wolf companion, Faolan.

As the path split to flow around the plinth, Ella went to the right. Eydis went to the left, brushing a hand over Faolan's marble leg. She smiled up at the wolf, before reuniting with her friend.

A few people trickled into the arena, in groups and pairs, though it was the smallest audience Eydis had seen in the past few weeks. With the official games starting the next day, most people were waiting for the real show. Just as she suspected Lucius would be.

They passed a group of tittering noble girls as they entered the arena. Eydis only made out a few words of their conversation, but could guess that they were giggling about the gladiators.

It was what drew most women to the arena.

Ella shot them a condescending look, and Eydis couldn't help but giggle.

"What?" Ella asked, glancing over at her.

"You're here for the same reason!" Eydis accused. "You have a favorite gladiator, and you want to see him shirtless, glistening with sweat in the arena. That's the whole reason you drag me here!"

Ella's only response was an indignant huff.

Her crush on Lucius had proven to be a treasure trove when it came to teasing her, and Eydis never got tired of it. It was usually so hard to make her flustered, but one mention of the gladiator did the trick.

Despite the lack of a crowd, Ella still found opportunities as they made their way up into the stands. Twice she bumped into the more affluent-looking people they passed, then gave sweet, seemingly earnest apologies for her clumsiness. All the while slipping coins and valuables into the pouch on her belt.

A skirmish was already happening in the arena, but it was hardly worth the name. The fighters in question were both unskilled, with a complete lack of showmanship.

"How can you want to be a gladiator without understanding what it truly means to *be* a gladiator?" Ella sighed, glancing at the skirmish with apparent disdain as they took a seat in one of the middle rows.

Eydis shrugged, having heard this opinion more than a few times already. "We definitely won't be seeing them tomorrow."

She and Ella could have put on a better fight with just their knives, and quick footedness.

But plenty of young people in the city dreamed of gaining fame and fortune in the arena. Since the skirmishes were open to anyone who wanted to join, aspiring fighters entered, hoping they would catch a wealthy sponsor's eye.

"Not a chance," Ella said. "Lord Di Antonio would never be so humiliated."

Eydis giggled at how Ella named one of the most powerful men in the city so casually. "Have you ever even met Lord Di Antonio?"

Ella blushed, her fair cheeks turning bright pink. "Once."

"What's this about Marcus?"

⊰ CHAPTER 2 ⊱

Both of them started at the interruption, looking over.

"Kat!" Eydis couldn't help but grin as she recognized the woman who had crept over unnoticed.

Katherine Fischer gave her a cat-like smile. "Hello, Little Wolf."

She was a tall, lean woman in her late twenties. Her low-cut bustier, and the high slits of her skirt showed off her bronze skin, and toned limbs. Brown hair curled down her back, smoldering hazel eyes enhanced by dark sweeps of kohl. Her perfume, a scent of dark liquor and rich vanilla, no doubt enhanced with magic, filled the air around her.

"Is this a thieves-only party, or do you mind if I join you?" Katherine asked.

"The more, the merrier," Ella said, gesturing to the bench, which was empty to either side of them.

Further down, Eydis saw a couple of boys craning their necks to watch Katherine as she took a seat next to Eydis. Moving with a feline grace that Eydis wished she could emulate.

"Now, what were you saying about Marcus?" Katherine asked.

"You talk like you know him," Ella said, glancing over at her.

"I do," Katherine said. "I served with him under Reinhardt, before and during the war."

"I keep forgetting he serves the Starks," Ella admitted.

"I keep forgetting that Kat serves the Starks," Eydis said, glancing over at the older woman.

"Why?" Katherine's ankles were crossed on the bench below them. Her muscles were toned, but it was hard to think of her as a soldier. "Aren't I intimidating enough?"

"Oh, you're intimidating," Eydis said.

"Very," Ella interjected.

Eydis nodded. "But you sell lingerie and romance novels."

"Ropes and handcuffs, too," Katherine reminded, with a satisfied smirk. "Among other things."

Eydis and Ella exchanged amused glances.

"Oh, now you two are judging me," Katherine said. "I don't like being on the receiving end of that."

"You're not what I first think of when I imagine a Stark soldier," Ella said.

The Starks were the ruling family charged with Cardea's protection against outside forces. They, and those that served them, tended to be hard to miss. Usually because of their weapons and armor, rather than long legs and cleavage.

Katherine just shrugged. "Don't forget, I met your brother during the war."

"Of course," Eydis murmured. But sometimes she also forgot that her brother had fought in the Cymbrian war.

Hammond and Katherine's friendship didn't make sense. Her uptight, bookish brother, and the flirty former soldier who now sold romance novels and sex accessories.

"What are you doing here?" she asked, keen to change the subject.

"I had an appointment that wanted to meet here. I was just leaving when I saw you two, and decided you needed adult supervision."

"From who?" Ella asked.

Eydis quirked an eyebrow. "You?"

"You're the one who needs a chaperone," Ella said. "Why are you even allowed to walk around freely?"

"Friends in high places." Katherine smiled. "What brings you here? Tomorrow would be much more profitable for a couple of pickpockets."

Eydis leaned towards Katherine, seeing an opportunity. "Ella's hoping to see a certain gladiator. He's probably not going to be here, but she doesn't want to miss him if he is."

Katherine giggled, scooting closer to Eydis. A very un-soldier-like action. "Ooh, does our Ella have a favorite fighter? Which one? No, no, let me guess. You were talking about Marcus. You said 'he', so it's not Aelia. It must be Lucius. Though I certainly wouldn't question your judgment either way."

Eydis glanced over, seeing that Ella's cheeks had turned bright pink. She tried to hide her face behind her hands, but it was impossible to miss.

"Lucius," Eydis confirmed.

Katherine nodded approval. "Excellent taste, Eleanor. And this way, you're only competing with a third of the city, rather than half of it."

"Oh, shut up," Ella whined, face still buried in her hands.

"No, I mean it," Katherine said, tone a bit more serious. "He's a proper gladiator, obviously. Muscles, ego, and all. But those looks weren't bought from a mage."

That got Ella to lift her head. "I knew it," she almost squealed.

Eydis glanced over, interested.

Many gladiators went to mages in the city to improve their appearances. They would get unsightly scars healed, teeth straightened, and jaws strengthened. As long as a gladiator was attractive and charismatic, he didn't necessarily need to win in order to be popular.

Katherine grinned. "The ego is a bit much, but that's part of being a gladiator. He's just as good on the battlefield as he is in the arena, though. And he's loyal to his brothers-in-arms. I can't give higher praise than that."

Ella was hanging off every word, scooting closer to Katherine as she listened, eyes focused intensely on the woman.

"You haven't actually met him, have you?" Katherine's voice was amused as she correctly interpreted Ella's hungry expression.

"I have," Ella said, too quickly. Then she looked away sheepishly. "Once."

"Briefly," Eydis clarified. "She was on a job, and got into one of Marcus' parties."

"When was this?"

"Last summer," Eydis said. "They haven't even had a real conversation."

The teasing was good-natured. And Eydis knew her friend wouldn't be really upset by it. But that didn't mean Ella was the kind to lay down and take it.

"Have you decided if you're going to the ball tonight, Eydis?" Ella asked. Her tone somehow managed to be both pointed and innocent at the same time. Her wide green eyes blinked sweetly. But the curve of her painted lips quickly turned vindictive as she saw that the question had served its purpose.

Eydis swallowed, and turned her attention back to the arena. The current fighters were more skilled than the last, and showed potential. But they weren't as fascinating as she tried to pretend.

"Eydis has a crush on Graham Galloborne," Ella told a very curious Katherine. "She has since they were children. Which is why she won't go to the Galloborne ball tonight."

Katherine was a fickle ally, who turned on her at the prospect of amusement. "Really? Interesting choice, but I approve."

Ella's false innocence faded to satisfaction, knowing the attention had been successfully redirected. And she was going to enjoy her turn at sharing gossip. "Hammond invited her, but she won't go!"

"I don't need my brother to invite me! I'm a Thorinson. I don't even need an invitation." That was an exaggeration, but she wasn't about to walk it back.

"You don't act like it," Ella reminded. "When was the last time you appeared in society? Let alone in the gossip pages."

"I like it better that way."

Ella rolled her eyes. "And does Graham remember who you are?"

"Of course he does!" Eydis' cheeks grew hotter. "I just saw him a few months ago." He had been visiting her brother's shop when she stopped in.

"That's not much better than one conversation last summer," Katherine said.

"He'll be at the ball tonight," Ella said. "Unlike me, she has a legitimate opportunity to go see him. She could get all dressed up, and make a grand entrance to get his attention. But she won't go, because she's scared of seeing him."

"I'm not scared!" Eydis insisted. "The ball is going to be full of grand entrances, I would hardly be able to stand out."

"But you would, because you're a Thorinson," Katherine said. "A beautiful, scandalous she-wolf from the north would certainly get everyone's attention."

Eydis had no interest in everyone's attention—just Graham's.

Katherine hugged her shoulders. "Aw, poor little wolf. Not brave enough to tell a boy she likes him."

Eydis tried to argue... but found she couldn't. Not when it was true. So instead, she leaned into the hug, resting her head on Katherine's shoulder.

Ella rolled her eyes. "Well, now you're just coddling her."

"You're supposed to be my best friend," Eydis reminded her.

"I am your best friend!" Ella insisted. "That's why I'm trying to get you to go!"

"No," Eydis said. "If I do, Hammond will insist that I play Lady Thorinson more often. That would be awful!"

"What? Being Lady Thorinson isn't good enough for you?" Katherine smirked. "You'd rather be Lady Galloborne?"

Ella giggled. "I had no idea you were so ambitious, Eydis."

"It's not ambition!" Eydis insisted, her cheeks burning in embarrassment.

She'd had a crush on Graham long before she had understood their family positions.

Since he had just been a boy tumbling and wrestling with her brother in the grass, or drawing in the first with a twig.

"I should hope not." Katherine scoffed. "He's a Galloborne, but he's the fourth child."

"He still outranks her," Ella said. "The Thorinsons aren't a ruling family."

"Yet," Katherine murmured. After a moment, she smiled and changed the subject. "Well, if she did make a dramatic entrance, it would distract the gossips. I have it on good authority that there will already be at least one surprise guest at the ball tonight."

That got both their attention. "Who?"

Katherine held a finger to her lips, which did nothing to hide her satisfied smile. "It's a surprise. But summer hasn't even started yet. So maybe the lost Lady Thorinson should wait for another time to make her entrance."

The title made Eydis uncomfortable each time she heard it. It was like a poorly fitting dress made for someone else.

"The Gallobornes throwing a ball is news enough as it is," she said, not wanting to think about her title, or her family's rank. "I can't remember the last time they did that."

"Marcus isn't even throwing a party tonight," Katherine said. "He's going to the Gallobornes' instead. I tried to get Hammond to take me, but he said Richard forbade it." She rolled her eyes in exasperation.

Eydis looked down at the arena again.

Part of her was tempted to go. Out of curiosity, as much as an interest in seeing Graham. For a moment, she considered changing her mind. If she left now, she might have enough time to get ready.

But as soon as the thought crossed her mind, she remembered that she didn't have a dress appropriate for a ball. She shook her head. "I already agreed to look after Vetr tonight. The gossips will have to wait for my return."

The Lion, The Wolf, & The Eagle

⊰ CHAPTER 1 ⊱

On the banks of the Silver River, in the heart of the city proper's most affluent district, sat the Galloborne's palatial manor. Even amongst the houses of other ruling families, eager to flaunt their wealth and position, the grandeur of the house itself, and the immaculate gardens, refused to be ignored, much like the family themselves.

It was a four-story work of art in pale marble and gold, with columns reminiscent of the Aurellian style. The stairs up to the tall double doors were flanked by two lion statues, while a growling lion relief presided above the door.

Servants were still putting the final touches on the garden decor when Hammond arrived. Scurrying around to ensure the house was ready before the guests began to arrive.

A red and gold carpet had been unrolled along the path leading up to the door. But Hammond chose to walk across the lawn, not wanting to mat the carpet with any dirt from his shoes.

Two large red banners with the Gallobornes' growling gold lion hung on either side of the double doors.

The garden itself was filled with carefully manicured plants and trees. With flower garlands and colorful ribbons strung between them - the traditional Solstice decorations. Glass orbs floated in the air just above eye level, their glow not yet visible while the sun was still up. Hammond had enchanted the orbs himself, and was confident they would be more than enough to illuminate the courtyard and gardens.

The servants bowed as he walked into the manor, none of the guards making a move to stop him. They all recognized him, knowing he could come and go.

The first floor glittered, showing off the family's wealth and status. Finer carpets had replaced the daily ones, while every piece of wood and metal had been polished until it gleamed. Vases bursting with colorful flowers were in every corner, and on every surface, filling the room with their heady scent.

It had been years since the Gallobornes' hosted a ball. Not since before the death of Lady Annabelle, more than twelve years earlier. Even then, it had been a rare occasion. While they hosted regular dinner parties, a ball was an entirely different creature. Elizabeth, the youngest of the five siblings, had spent months planning the affair.

On the second floor, once he got past the bustle of the mezzanine, and made his way into the family's quarters, Hammond sighed in relief. Since no one would be coming into the family's area of the house, it had been deep cleaned and polished, but not decorated, aside from the fresh flowers set in alcoves that weren't occupied pieces of art.

He made his way to Richard's chambers - the master suite of the manor. After John Galloborne's death, Richard hadn't waited long before making it his own.

His knock on the door was answered by Richard's valet, who opened the door for him without hesitation.

Richard was in his dressing room, sitting in an armchair by the window as he read over a sheet of paper. He was shirtless, wearing only black pants, and highly polished dress boots. His shoulder-length, jet-black hair was untied, and not yet combed back.

He glanced up as they approached, beckoning Hammond in. "Come in. I'm taking a last look at the seating chart for dinner."

The dressing room alone was larger than Hammond's bedroom above his shop, tastefully decorated in the Galloborne black, red, and gold colors.

Hammond went over to the black lacquered sideboard, pouring himself a glass of water from the pitcher. He was dressed in blue-gray silk, embroidered with silver wolves along the hem, his chestnut hair brushed back.

Richard made a couple of marks on the seating chart, before handing it to his valet. "Take this to Elizabeth."

The valet nodded. "Right away, my lord."

When the valet had left the room, Richard rose from his chair, stretching his neck and shoulders.

"Any important changes?" Hammond asked, pouring another glass and holding it out.

Richard hummed as he accepted the glass and took a drink. "Nothing serious. I separated a few of the prefects, and put William next to the Lofgrens."

Richard was a couple of inches taller than Hammond himself, and three years older. His eyes were slightly off-putting, both from their intensity, and their pale blue color.

"You've decided on pushing him towards Birgitta, then?" Hammond asked, turning around to brace his hips against the sideboard.

"Yes." Richard returned to the armchair, sitting back down. "At least for now, I'm fairly secure with the Gartners. And Geoffrey has been spending more time with Thomas Lofgrens." He scowled. "But enough business for tonight. So whatever you want, it will have to wait."

Hammond started. "How did you know?"

"You're not subtle, Hammond." Richard took a drink of water. "I can see it in your eyes. You want something."

"It's not business," Hammond said. But was immediately forced to admit that it was a lie. "Alright, it is business."

"I've been looking forward to tomorrow for months," Richard reminded him. "Don't bring me bad news, Hammond. Not today."

"It's not bad news," Hammond assured. He took a seat in the second armchair by the window. "But I have something of a proposition for you."

Hammond knew Richard wouldn't be able to resist at least hearing the proposition. And he had spent the last three days deciding the best way to sell him on the idea.

Richard didn't respond immediately, but Hammond could almost see his thoughts churning—his desire to avoid distractions at war with his need to know.

"Alright, what is it?"

Hammond fought back a smile. "You've heard of the Black Rose, correct?"

"The one who caught the Thieves Guild's snitch, as I recall."

"Correct," Hammond said. "Humiliating Caspian in the process."

"I should thank her for that."

"My father is offering her patronage," Hammond said. "I thought you might be interested in doing the same."

Richard eyed him suspiciously, clearly trying to find what angle he was playing.

Hammond did his best to keep his expression neutral.

"I just made a sizable investment," Richard reminded him. But he rubbed his jaw, so it was clear he wasn't dismissing the offer.

"You'll make it back twice over in no time," Hammond said.

"And yet I notice you're not asking this tomorrow, after the fights."

"I thought about it," Hammond admitted. "But I decided not to let that decide how I do business."

Richard nodded, expression thoughtful.

"You did just say you should thank her," Hammond reminded.

"I meant a bottle of brandy. Not a townhouse and a living."

"Half a living," Hammond countered. "And we can put her in one of our houses."

Before the war, the Thorinsons had already owned several townhouses in Callatis. Afterward, during the rebuilding, his father decided to invest in more. He hadn't expected several of them to be immediately claimed by family members moving to the city, but they had still earned back their investment by renting out the others.

"Having a thief on staff could be beneficial," Hammond added, getting back into the pitch he had worked out over the last few days. "The guild would certainly appreciate the gesture."

"A thief that Caspian has a vendetta against," Richard countered.

His voice wasn't harsh, but Hammond still winced slightly. He had hoped Richard wasn't aware of that detail, but realized immediately that he should have known better.

"Why not put Throthgar forward?" Richard asked, taking another drink. "If you're going to try and sell me on patronizing a thief we both know I don't need, why not someone from your family?"

This was a line of questioning Hammond had prepared for.

"Throthgar doesn't need it," he said. "We both know he doesn't even need to be a thief. When he's had his fun, he'll return to his estate."

Richard nodded, leaning back in the seat as he considered the idea.

"I certainly wouldn't mind a chance to spite Caspian," he said eventually.

Richard had put forward his own nominee for the Captain of the Guard position - his second cousin, Gerulf Solberg. Hammond didn't think Richard would ever forgive Roland Selelon for casting the deciding vote in Caspian's favor.

He looked over at Hammond. "The idea does have its advantages. I'll consider it."

"That's all I ask."

It was the answer Hammond had expected. He knew as well as anyone that Richard never made a decision without thinking matters through. But he also knew how Richard's mind worked, and was reasonably sure he would agree.

It would help if the next day went well, of course.

Richard stood up again, going over to where his black silk shirt and doublet hung on his wardrobe door.

"In the meantime, have Katherine look into the Black Rose." He pulled his shirt over his head. "I trust your judgment, but I want more information before I make an investment."

"I stopped in to see her this morning," he said. He had known Richard, and his father, would want that at least.

Richard nodded as he shrugged into his doublet. The garment was embroidered with gold thread, with a roaring lion on the back.

As Richard reached for his belt, there was a knock on the door to the suite. They heard the valet open the door, then footsteps coming towards the dressing room.

Henry Gerrod walked in like a soldier, with a strong, confident stride. His short, dark blond hair and beard were well-groomed, green eyes sweeping the room instinctively. The beard covered most of the scar that ran from his right temple, down to his jaw. It surprised Hammond a little that he didn't opt to wear the formal brigandine cuirasses the Stark family wore to formal events. But instead, he wore brown silk, with gold eagles embroidered on his chest.

Richard's back straightened as the older man entered the room, and he smiled. "Henry, come join us."

"You two aren't discussing business before a ball, are you?" Henry asked, looking between them as if he suspected some scheme.

"Just a few loose ends," Richard said, waving as if to brush the suspicion away.

"It can wait for one night," Henry insisted. "It's a ball, Richard. Enjoy it. Enjoy being young, and in love."

Richard didn't blush. It wouldn't be in character if he did. But his expression did change. A mix of embarrassment, and excitement as well. He tried to cover it by polishing the gold buckle of his belt, despite the fact it already shone in the light.

"Is Phillipa here yet?"

"I don't think so," Henry said. "Vera and I are early."

"She'll probably come at the last minute, to make an entrance," Richard nodded.

"Have you seen her since she arrived in the city?" Henry asked.

Richard shook his head. "Not since the dinner at the Selelons. I think she's been keeping busy to make me wait."

Hammond and Henry exchanged amused glances.

Two months earlier, while on business in the south, Richard and his brother, William, had stayed several nights at Summer Grove, the Bellerose family seat.

Hammond almost wished he could have been there. Over the years, he had seen Richard occasionally take note of some of the women who tried to get his attention. He wondered what Phillipa Bellerose had done to succeed where so many others had failed.

"It is nice to finally see Richard find a situation he's not completely in control of," Hammond said, grinning.

Henry chuckled. "I thought that was your job. To make sure Richard keeps everything under control."

Hammond shrugged. "I try. But even I can't keep everything in line."

"Imagine when you meet a woman who turns your world upside down."

The thought almost made Hammond shudder. As much as he joked about having things under control, most of the time, he felt as if it was all precariously balanced, and could fall at any moment. The idea of having it all flipped upside down sounded like a nightmare.

"I think that would do him good," Richard agreed.

Hammond scoffed. "Do you really want to share my attention with someone else, Richard?"

It was hard to imagine having time for a lover in between everything else.

"I'm sure you could make it work," Richard said with a shrug.

Hammond rolled his eyes, but only once his friend's back was turned. And he gave Henry a bemused look.

Henry smiled as he shrugged.

"Well, if you can't control the situation, you've certainly pulled out all the stops to impress," Henry said, turning back to Richard. "That is why you're throwing this ball, isn't it? To impress her?"

"She's a part of the reason, yes," Richard said, unashamed to admit it.

"Do I want to know the other part?"

"You won't disapprove," Richard said, rather than answering. It didn't stop a satisfied smirk, though.

Henry looked to Hammond. But he simply shrugged. Far be it from him to spoil Richard's surprise.

"That only makes me more suspicious," Henry said.

"We should head downstairs," Richard said, before Henry could ask any more questions. "I shouldn't neglect my guests."

Henry shook his head in amusement, but fell into step with Hammond as they followed Richard out.

Wine & Roses

◦⊰ CHAPTER 1 ⊱◦

Cardea had fourteen ruling families. Each of them governed a territory of the republic, where they had an estate for their family seat, as well as a manor in the city. While all of it remained the property of the republic itself, they were free to remodel the houses as they saw fit.

The Bellerose house was rarely opened, as they preferred to stay in their territory, Bourlet. So they had done little to renovate their home in Callatis.

Unlike the Gallobornes, who had become a ruling family in 1492, roughly fifty years ago. While researching the family, Phillipa had learned that Richard's grandfather, Henry Galloborne, had set about remodeling the house extensively as soon as it was in his possession. But he hadn't lived long enough to see his vision completed.

Only a few renovations had taken place under John Galloborne's rule. Perhaps because he had less ambition than his father. Or because he'd had other things to worry about.

But as soon as the Cymbrian War had ended, Richard set about completing his grandfather's plans for the house. With a few of his own touches, of course. Creating a work of art that flaunted the Galloborne wealth and identity.

A Galloborne footman, in a red and black livery, helped her down from the carriage, and Phillipa stepped up to the open wrought iron gate accented with gold. Her gray eyes were fixed on the house in awe.

When she arrived in Callatis, she had been unable to resist having the carriage drive past to catch a glimpse of it. A glimpse that hadn't done the house justice. The beauty and grandeur of it exceeded her expectations.

And her expectations had been high.

Now it was decorated and lit for the ball. The gardens were in full bloom, their natural beauty augmented by the traditional Summer Solstice decorations of streamers and garlands.

And it was for her.

Richard had other reasons, of course–she was well aware of that. But if she succeeded - if she could keep his attention... this could all be hers.

Behind her, her cousin Carolyn stepped down from the carriage, and came to take her hand.

"I think he loves you," Carolyn said, sighing dreamily as she looked over the house and gardens.

"He's infatuated," Phillipa clarified, not letting Carolyn's romanticism distract her. Still, she couldn't help but smile as she squeezed her cousin's hand. "I am working on it, however."

If this ball was any indication, she was succeeding.

Behind them, she could hear Carolyn's parents bickering already. Aline Bellerose complained about something, while Roland

Selelon brushed her off. After a fortnight of staying with the family, Phillipa had grown accustomed to that.

Two additional carriages pulled up in turn, carrying Carolyn's three brothers, and their wives.

Beside her, Carolyn busied herself with smoothing the full skirts of her violet gown. Her long black hair was in a half up-do, while the rest cascaded down her back in soft waves. She wore an intricate silver and amethyst necklace that Phillipa had given her as a birthday present two years earlier - a piece of Dark Elf workmanship that drew attention to both the graceful curve of her neck, and the cleavage perfectly sculpted by her corset.

Phillipa wore a wine-colored gown, the full skirt draped so the gathers and tucks fluttered as she moved. Her honey-blonde hair was styled up, held in place with gold, ruby, and pearl ornaments. She had brushed gold glitter on her bare shoulders and chest, while she wore a set of gold and ruby jewelry on her neck and wrists. One way or another, she would have Richard's eyes fixed on her tonight. And if that meant draping herself in gold, she would do it.

"Oh, Phillipa, isn't it beautiful?" Aline rested a hand on her shoulder.

She was the younger sister of Phillipa's father - tall and fair, still beautiful, though Phillipa always thought she looked tired. Her constant irritation with her husband might account for that. But she smiled as she touched Phillipa's hair, ensuring it was in place. "And you look right at home. I'm so proud of you."

Carolyn stepped away from them, into the garden to admire a rose bush in full bloom. Phillipa glanced after her, but Aline hardly seemed to notice.

"Thank you, Aunt Aline." She forced herself to smile, hiding the bitterness in her mouth.

Before Aline could say anymore, they heard the commotion of Regis, Quinten, and Gratien Selelon coming over. In particular, Gratien's wife, Evangeline. A tiny, blonde woman with a voice nearly twice as large as she was, who immediately set about fussing over everything in sight.

"Such a pretty garden," Evangeline cooed. "Oh, Gratien, it's so elegant. We should have a garden like this when we have our own house."

"As if they could ever afford it," Carolyn whispered, as Phillipa approached her. She had never been very good at hiding how she felt - especially her sisters-in-law.

Even as a ruling family, the Selelon fortune would hardly be enough to allow all five of their children to have their own lavish houses. Certainly nothing like the Galloborne's.

"Could she be any more crass?" Phillipa sighed, glancing back at where Aline and Evangeline fawned over the property.

"I'm afraid to ask, for fear she'll get worse," Carolyn whispered back. "Do we have to go in with them?"

"How would that look?" Phillipa asked.

"How will it look if we go in with her exclaiming how grand the house is? Caitlyn Galloborne is here. Never mind Elizabeth and Matilda." Carolyn shivered at the last name. "Is that the impression you want to make?"

Phillipa hesitated a moment.

But as Roland and Aline began to disagree over something petty again, the idea became more appealing. She hadn't met any of the Galloborne women, and Carolyn's descriptions made it clear they wouldn't take well to Evangeline's chatter.

"Carolyn and I are going inside," Phillipa said. "I want to greet our hosts." Before anyone could argue, she squeezed Carolyn's hand and led her up the steps.

Her excitement grew as they got closer, eager to see the manor's interior. And to meet Richard's sisters.

A pair of marble lions flanked the stairs that led up to the open double doors, which were attended by two liveried footmen.

"Are you ready?" Carolyn asked.

"I'm not sure," she admitted, feeling herself tremble.

Carolyn giggled. "It's so strange to see you nervous."

"It feels strange to be this nervous," Phillipa admitted. It wasn't a sensation she was used to. But so many of her plans hinged on this ball being a success.

The footmen at the door took their invitations, bowing as they ushered the two women into the entryway.

Inside, the manor was brightly lit, every surface polished until it shone. Dark wood furnishings were accented with gold leaf. Vases full of cut flowers and blossoming branches added color, and a sweet, heady scent.

"I'm not sure I wore enough gold," Phillipa noted, as she saw how much of the decor in the house was gilded with the precious metal. Even on the marble statues of animals, heroes, and maidens in repose.

"You don't need it," Carolyn assured her, as they were led into the drawing room.

☙ CHAPTER 2 ❧

As the daughter of a ruling family, Phillipa had come to appreciate the privileges of her position. She liked the respect and influence, and the luxuries it afforded her. But with two older brothers, she had little chance of inheriting more than her allotted sum, and the relatively Bramble Wood Cottage.

She was smart enough to know that she would need to marry into another ruling family to maintain her lifestyle and influence. Marrying down simply wasn't an option.

She had considered trying to marry into a royal family in one of the neighboring kingdoms. But Vestra's royal family had been replaced by Breanna Ravine, Richard's second cousin, after being decimated by civil war. And now Cymbria was a vassal state, its royal family gone.

She would prefer to stay in Cardea, anyway. With thirteen other families, she had options. Some of which wouldn't require much sacrifice on her part.

Then Richard had come to visit. From the moment she had seen him ride up to their home, she knew she had found her mark.

She had caught his attention by drawing on all her mother's lessons in flirtation. Mostly by making herself scarce, and rationing the attention she gave him. Just enough to flatter his ego, and make him want more.

Richard was attractive, which was undoubtedly an advantage. Love wasn't on her list of priorities, however. Mutual respect, compatibility, and an appreciation of her skills, yes. That was vital. But romantic love wasn't necessary.

As she took in the splendor of the manor, with its ostentatious but elegant decor, she became all the more determined.

In the drawing-room, she noted that a few people had arrived so far.

For a moment, she thought she saw Richard. But realized quickly that it was his cousin, Byron Galloborne. While they looked similar, with the same shoulder-length, jet-black hair and pale blue eyes, Byron was taller, with broader shoulders. More so than you would expect in a man known to prefer his library and studies. Phillipa knew he was a mage, but didn't know what kind of power he possessed.

Byron's younger sister, Caitlyn, was on his arm, in a fashionable, ivory satin gown accented with black lace. Her black hair was elegantly swept up, held in place by gold combs and pins.

They were in conversation with Richard's brother, William, and a young woman with light brown hair, in a soft pink dress, that Phillipa didn't recognize.

"That's Richard's sister, Elizabeth," Carolyn whispered to her.

Phillipa nodded in appreciation.

The other guests she did recognize.

Geoffrey Randell, an older man with graying dark hair, immediately stood out. He was still a powerful presence, his gray doublet perfectly tailored.

His son, Morten, and daughter, Vera, were close by, as was his wife, Priscilla.

Vera wore a modestly draped, nightingale gray gown, her brown hair elaborately coiled up. She glanced expectantly towards the door as they came in, but her look turned to disapproval as she looked Phillipa over.

The Randalls were one of the older ruling families, while Vera's husband, Henry Gerrod, was descended from one of the three families that had established Cardea. Facts they were incredibly proud of.

The Belleroses were a newer family. And her mother, Marguerite, was from a lesser noble house. One that had gone bankrupt and been lost not long after Marguerite married Nathaniel Bellerose. Which some of the older families never forgot. The Bellerose name earned her respect, but the more snobbish families - the Randells in particular - snubbed her.

Phillipa had hoped that she might find a way to connect with Vera if they were thrown together often enough in the city. But in the past fortnight, she wasn't sure there were enough dinners or garden parties to make that possible. If anything, Vera had become colder since their arrival.

There was already a heady amount of power in the room, Phillipa noted, as she continued to look around.

She felt the weight of everyone's eyes on her, and knew she was being judged by the Gallobornes in particular.

They were the ones she had to impress tonight.

Phillipa squared her shoulders as she and Carolyn moved into the drawing room. Even her tutors would have been satisfied with her posture and grace.

Elizabeth stepped away from the others, coming to meet them with a sweet smile.

"You must be Phillipa," she said, with a gentle, melodic voice. The delicate scent of roses surrounded her, while her light brown hair was curled to frame her round face. "It's such a pleasure to meet you at last."

"Elizabeth, I presume." Phillipa smiled, leaning in to kiss the woman's cheek. "The pleasure is all mine."

She did her best to hide her surprise. There was nothing of the Galloborne look about the young woman. Her face was soft and sweet rather than noble, her eyes a light blue.

"Come meet the others," Elizabeth said. "Henry and Hammond are still upstairs with Richard."

The Triumvirate, Phillipa thought, delighted at the opportunity to see Richard,

Henry Gerrod, and Hammond Thorinson together.

"We're waiting on most of the others," Elizabeth said. "You know Lord Randell, and his children?"

Phillipa and Carolyn both curtsied.

"Of course." Phillipa smiled politely. "It's wonderful to see you both again."

Polite, albeit untrue.

Geoffrey Randell looked them over, nodding politely. "Lady Bellerose. Lady Selelon."

"We've already met," Caitlyn Galloborne said, leaning in to kiss Phillipa's cheek. "And we all know we have you to thank for tonight."

"I'm sure I don't know what you mean," Phillipa insisted. But she didn't even try to sound sincere as she said it.

Caitlyn gave her an approving smile. And compared to that, Vera's look didn't concern her.

William chuckled. "Well, I'm certainly glad. We should have had a ball years ago." He turned to his younger sister. "You've outdone yourself, Elizabeth."

Elizabeth basked in the praise for a moment, before they were all distracted by the arrival of the Selelons. They were hard to miss, with Evangeline fawning over the grandeur of the house.

Phillipa was very glad she had entered separately.

Carolyn didn't even try to hide her exasperated sigh, ignoring her family as she turned to compliment Caitlyn's gown.

Roland quickly joined Geoffrey, the two men taking seats in armchairs near the window.

Other guests began to trickle in, arriving in all their finery. Phillipa made the rounds, greeting the families she knew, and being introduced to those she didn't.

But the next members of a ruling family didn't require an introduction.

Runa Sorensen, heiress of the Sorensen family, swept in. Beautiful and fair, with dark red hair in soft curls down her back, smelling of roses and vanilla. The bodice of her dark blue gown hugged her hourglass figure, while the full skirt was made from layers of frothy silk. She earned her Highland Rose nickname.

Her escort, however, was the one who truly captured people's attention.

"It's Godric," William grinned.

Phillipa looked at the man next to Runa again. She vaguely remembered meeting

Godric Sorensen when she was younger, but it had been long ago. Like his cousin, he wore dark blue silk, which suited their similar coloring. They looked more like siblings than cousins, and it was easy to forget.

"Godric has been serving in the Stark forces for the past eight years," Caitlyn told Phillipa. "I don't think he's been in Callatis in all that time."

The Sorensens were the newest of the ruling families, and a polarizing one at that.

While the Randells had looked down on Phillipa, they didn't even look at Runa. Save for a short glare from Geoffrey. Just as he had at a garden party they had all attended the week before. The Sorensens had chanced into the position thanks only to a convenient marriage, and unfortunate loss.

Runa gave no sign of noticing the Randells, gaze sliding past them as she looked around the room. Something that had to infuriate Geoffrey.

The cousins went straight to Elizabeth, greeting their host with apparent intimacy. Runa clasped her hands, speaking animatedly as they kissed each other's cheeks. Godric seemed less enthusiastic, but soon fell into conversation with William.

Phillipa and Carolyn moved towards them, and Runa gave her a familiar smile.

"Runa and Godric grew up with Richard, and his siblings," Caitlyn whispered helpfully.

Phillipa gave her a grateful smile. Well aware that the information was an offering of friendship.

"Until Richard decided he was too mature to waste his time with us," Runa said, with a teasing glint in her green eyes.

"Runa, you know Carolyn Selelon, of course," Elizabeth said. "Have you met Phillipa Bellerose?"

"I have," Runa said. "We visit the Bellerose estate whenever my mother and I are in the south."

"And we always look forward to it when you do," Phillipa said, kissing Runa's cheek. "Are your parents coming tonight?"

"They just returned from a trip to Sapphire Bay today," Runa said. "They send their compliments, but wanted to rest after their travels. My mother and I agreed that Godric's return to the capital would more than make up for it."

Godric grumbled. "You didn't give me a choice."

Runa just smiled, her eyes sparkling with satisfaction.

A young man entered the room in a rush, dressed in black silk embroidered with gold, his curly brown hair disheveled.

"Graham..." Elizabeth sighed as he came over to them. "I told you not to be late!"

The fourth Galloborne sibling had darker hair than Elizabeth, gray eyes, and was two or three inches shorter than William. He was clean-shaven, save for a patch of hair on his chin that gave him a roguish look.

"I'm here before Richard, aren't I?" Still, he gave his sister a sheepish grin, ducking his head so Elizabeth could comb his hair down with her fingers.

Elizabeth sighed. "Phillipa, this is my brother, Graham Galloborne. You'll have to forgive his complete lack of decorum."

"He's an artist," Caitlyn said. "It's to be expected."

Graham gave his cousin a grin. Then he looked Phillipa over curiously. Not improper, but entirely without guile. "It's a pleasure to meet you, Lady Phillipa."

"The pleasure's mine." She was somewhat amused at how relaxed he seemed. He completely lacked the air of superiority that his brother and cousins wore with such ease. But he wasn't shy like his sister.

Seeing Graham, standing between charismatic William, and shy Elizabeth, it was easier to see a connection. William's hair was lighter than Richard's, but still darker than Graham's. At the same time, Graham's eyes were somewhere between the Galloborne's icy blue, and Elizabeth's brighter ones. As if the family coloring had faded a little with each child. It seemed a safe guess that the younger two took after their mother, though she would need to see a picture of Annabelle Galloborne.

"You're still late," Elizabeth murmured.

Graham had the decency to look apologetic. "I got caught up with the painting."

"I told you not to do that!" Elizabeth chastised. But it was affectionate scolding.

It was surprisingly genuine. And not something Phillipa had expected, from what she knew of the Gallobornes.

Before Elizabeth could scold him anymore, their attention was drawn once more to the doors.

Phillipa's breath caught as three men entered the room.

Richard was in the lead, in black with gold embroidery, and a scarlet sash around his waist. His pale blue eyes swept the room, and landed on her.

She had his attention. Good.

Behind him were Henry Gerrod, and Hammond Thorinson.

Three of the most powerful men in the republic.

Henry, the Defender of Callatis, who had led them to victory in the Cimbrian War three years earlier.

And Hammond. He had arrived in the city before the war, and established himself as a politician afterward. The unexpected dark horse who had brought his family to the very brink of a ruling seat. His term as counselor over the Council of prefects had ended a year ago, but no one seemed to doubt the sway he still held.

Together, they were an unofficial Triumvirate. When the three of them were in agreement, there was almost nothing they couldn't accomplish.

After an initial look of curiosity, Phillipa's attention was entirely on Richard.

And his on her.

⊰ CHAPTER 3 ⊱

Richard came straight towards her, barely pausing to greet members of the other ruling families as he did.

"Lady Phillipa," he greeted her with a smile that caused a surge of satisfaction in her.

Carolyn squeezed her arm supportively. But it was hardly necessary. She wasn't weak-kneed, or lightheaded. She was focused.

"Lord Galloborne." She dipped in a proper curtsy. "It's a pleasure to see you again." And it was the most sincere she had been all evening.

"You made me wait for you," he reminded her.

She had.

When she had prepared to come to the city, she and her mother had discussed her course of action. One of the first things they decided was to avoid seeing him until the ball. To build his anticipation for tonight.

And the intensity of his gaze told her it had worked.

"Absence makes the heart grow fonder," she teased, offering her hand.

He bowed, kissing the back of her hand. "An idea you seem to have mastered."

Phillipa was well aware that all eyes in the room were focused on them. And that was exactly how she liked it.

Richard guided her hand into the crook of his elbow, before turning to his siblings.

"You've exceeded my expectations, Elizabeth," he said, kissing his sister's cheek.

"That's very high praise coming from you," Elizabeth said. Her smile said that she appreciated the weight of the compliment.

"I mean it," he said. He then looked at Graham. "I'm glad to see you could join us."

Graham shrugged, with a muttered acknowledgment. Then turned to greet Hammond with an apparent familiarity.

On the other side of the room, Phillipa noted that Vera had slipped her hand around her husband's arm, rising on her toes to whisper something in Henry's ear.

Richard turned his attention to the Sorensen cousins. With a familiar greeting, he kissed Runa's cheek just as he had his sister's. "Godric. I didn't realize you were back in the city."

"I arrived yesterday," Godric said. "I hadn't planned to attend any parties, but Runa insisted I come tonight."

"What's the point of having a hero in the family if I can't show you off?" Runa asked.

"The honor of having a hero in the family?" he countered.

Runa rolled her eyes, and Phillipa suspected it was a conversation they'd had several times before.

Richard chuckled. "We'll have to catch up soon. I want to hear about your experience at the border."

"I'm at your service, Lord Galloborne," he said, with a slight bow. And there was a seriousness to the exchange that caught Phillipa's attention. But they quickly moved into shallower waters, and Richard continued to make the rounds among the guests.

After speaking with the Gartners, she noticed Richard kept glancing toward the door between conversations.

"Are you waiting for someone?" She did her best to keep her voice light.

"Marcus," Richard admitted.

Phillipa smiled, squeezing his arm as her jealousy eased.

According to Carolyn, this would be the first time in memory that the Di Antonios would attend a Summer Solstice celebration in the city proper. Usually, they hosted their own in the Aurellian District. So rumors that Marcus and his wife would be attending the Galloborne ball had created an added layer of anticipation.

"He'll probably arrive at the last minute, to make an entrance," she said.

"No doubt." Richard gave her a wry smile. "I'm a little surprised you didn't."

"I wanted to," she said, a hint of annoyance creeping into her voice. "But Evangeline convinced Aunt Aline we should arrive early."

She saw Richard's lip curl in what looked suspiciously like disgust. It would seem he wasn't particularly impressed with Evangeline either. But all he said was: "I'm glad you're here. I just hope I won't have to wait another fortnight before I see you again."

"We'll see," she said coyly. "I have to check my schedule."

Richard's shrewd smile told her he knew exactly what she was doing - but he didn't mind.

He started to say something, but stopped as another party arrived. His shoulders straightened, and he led her over to greet the newcomers.

There were three of them, all dressed in red, with white and gold accents. Phillipa didn't recognize them, but as they drew near, she saw that the two men wore formal brigandine, segmented armor plates covered in red satin brocade.

The Starks were one of the three founding families, along with the Gartners and Gerrods - the family who controlled Cardea's military.

Richard clasped wrists with the dark-haired man leading the group, greeting him with respect and familiarity.

Phillipa looked them over curiously, making eye contact with the woman on Jonathan Stark's arm.

"Lord Stark, may I present Lady Phillipa Bellerose," Richard said, drawing attention to her. "Phillipa, Lord Jonathan Stark."

Jonathan was a tall, broad-shouldered man with dark brown hair starting to gray at the temples, and hazel eyes. His manners were reserved as he bowed politely. "It's a pleasure to meet you, Lady Bellerose. May I present my wife, Maria Stark?"

Maria Stark wore a low-cut red gown, with decorative gold plates at the shoulder, but with no other armor or military elements. The color suited her bronze skin, while her black hair was styled into a braid crown woven with red ribbon.

"The pleasure is mine," Phillipa said, inclining her head.

Maria met her gaze with clever, dark brown eyes. While Phillipa might not have met the woman, she did know of her. Jonathan Stark marrying a merchant's daughter from Castile had been more than enough to send ripples through high society. Not just a commoner, but a foreign one at that.

"I've heard quite a bit about you," Maria said. She had a clear accent she didn't try to hide. But her manners were polished, her posture perfect, with no sign that she didn't belong at a Galloborne ball. "I'm sorry it's taken so long for us to meet."

"Better late than never, I hope," Phillipa said.

Maria's red-painted lips pulled in a playful smile. Giving Phillipa the impression she had the woman's approval. "Very true."

"We'll have to make up for lost time," Phillipa said. Already making a mental note to arrange a tea to invite Maria Stark to. Whether her aunt and uncle liked it or not.

"I feel like we should all be worried," Aksel said, quirking an eyebrow as he watched them. He looked like his cousin, but with a more open countenance.

Phillipa was pleased to see Richard smile in approval.

Runa and Godric arrived to greet the Starks, all clearly familiar with each other. As the men spoke, Runa and Maria exchanged kisses on the cheek, complimenting each other's dresses.

"Where's Nadine?" Runa asked Aksel.

"She sends her apologies, but didn't feel up to attending," he said. "My wife is expecting our first child in the autumn," he explained to Phillipa, with a look of unmistakable pride.

"Congratulations," Phillipa said.

Finally, as the grandfather clock in the corner struck seven o'clock - just when the invitation had said dinner would be served - the Di Antonio's arrived.

"Leave it to Marcus and Lucilla to make an entrance," Maria muttered, amused.

"Do you know Lucilla?" Phillipa asked, unable to hide her eagerness.

"Quite well," Maria said. "Marcus served in the forces with Jonathan, and they're still good friends. I might hate Lucilla, if I weren't in awe of her.

Marcus Di Antonio entered with all the pomp of a man who knew he was descended from emperors, and wanted to be sure everyone else knew it as well. He was tall and broad, in a sleeveless purple tunic that showed off the powerful muscles under his bronze skin. He wore fashion reminiscent of the old empire, a trend he had started in his youth. And he certainly wore it well.

As Phillipa's eyes slid to Lucilla Di Antonio, she understood what Maria meant.

Lucilla looked perfect on her husband's arm. Her bodice was sculpted with a modern corset, but the skirt was draped in the imperial style, in the same purple as her husband's mantle. And Phillipa suspected it was a true purple dye, not a less expensive replica made by magic. Both of them seemed to drip with gold. More than Phillipa had even considered wearing. But she carried herself so it didn't appear the least bit gaudy. Her brown hair was curled, braided, and twisted, held in place with gold combs and pins.

Just as Maria had said, there was an arrogance to Lucilla's statuesque beauty. But an elegance that demanded respect.

"Come," Richard murmured. "I want to introduce you."

Phillipa followed eagerly. Her interest in an introduction to the Di Antonios increased at the sight of them.

"Lord and Lady Di Antonio, welcome." Richard inclined his head respectfully.

Marcus gave a slight bow, Lucilla dipping in a curtsey.

"May I present Lady Phillipa Bellerose?"

Phillipa made eye contact with the woman, who looked her over with appraising hazel eyes. One corner of her painted lips pulled in a slight smile.

"It's an honor to make your acquaintance," she said, imitating Lucilla's curtsey. While she outranked both of them, she felt it right to show respect.

Marcus bowed, and Lucilla stepped forward to kiss her cheek.

"I've looked forward to meeting you for a while now," Lucilla said, her voice tinged with an accent.

"As have I," Phillipa said, sincerely.

"I am a bit disappointed your mother isn't with you," Lucilla added. "I would love to make her acquaintance."

"I'm sure she would be honored," Phillipa said, a little surprised. For someone so notorious for her snobbery, she hadn't thought Lucilla would have any interest in the daughter of an obsolete family.

Lucilla smiled, still as regal as an empress. "I look forward to getting to know you, Lady Bellerose."

"As do I, Lady Di Antonio."

"I'm glad you could make it," Richard said to Marcus, and it was clear to Phillipa that he meant the words.

"I wouldn't miss it," Marcus said.

❧ CHAPTER 4 ❧

On the terrace at the back of the house, a long table had been set up to accommodate the fifty or so guests who had been invited to dinner. Phillipa looked around in admiration as Richard escorted her.

The table itself was draped in a white tablecloth, with a scarlet and gold table runner that matched the placemats, ladened with impeccably arranged flowers, glowing glass orbs, and towers of fruit. The sun setting in the west glistened off the water of the Silver River, as well as the glass and gold on the table.

She felt Richard's eyes on her, searching for her approval.

"It's beautiful," she said, rewarding him with a smile.

"Elizabeth deserves the credit," he said, gesturing to where Graham led his sister down to the other end of the table.

"Not Matilda?" Phillipa asked, careful not to let too much curiosity show. But she had expected to meet Richard's twin sister tonight.

"Matilda isn't one for social gatherings," Richard said, his voice carefully schooled. "She's spending the evening with her son."

He pulled out the chair to the right of the table's head. Phillipa didn't hesitate to accept the honor, and allowed herself a moment of satisfaction.

From a few seats down, Vera Randell gave her a look of disapproval. But Phillipa took a leaf from Runa's book and ignored it.

When she glanced to her left, she found Richard looking at her, and she gave him a small smile.

"Encourage without confirming," her mother had taught her. "Promise nothing until you know how much someone else will give you in return."

Marcus was sat to Richard's left, while Hammond was on Phillipa's right.

Once they were all seated, the servants presented bowls of creamy soup, the appetizing smell making Phillipa's mouth water.

She looked around to assess the seating arrangement while they waited for everyone to be served. Carolyn was further down the table with her family, nearer to where Graham and Elizabeth presided over the foot of the table. Runa sat near the Starks, chatting easily with them, and the Gartners on her other side. She noticed Birgitta Lofgren was seated by William Galloborne, who was at the center of the table, near Byron and Caitlyn.

Richard and Marcus were discussing something, though Phillipa tuned most of it out. Lucilla was seated across from her, but not close enough to allow for a private conversation.

As she sipped a spoonful of the soup, she glanced at Hammond, who was surprisingly quiet next to her. Henry was on his other side, talking across the table to his father-in-law.

Hammond didn't seem to be listening to any of them. Instead, his gaze swept over the table. If she had to guess, he was assessing who was talking to who, probably picking up snippets of conversations, and taking mental notes.

He glanced over, catching her eye, and smiled. Friendly, but almost awkward. "We haven't met, have we?"

"We haven't," she said. "I don't think I've ever met a Thorinson, for that matter."

"Which is surprising, considering how many of us there are," he said. "But we do tend to stay in the north."

"And you're hardly known for taking part in society," she reminded. "There are only two of you here in Callatis."

Hammond shook his head. "Four, actually," he corrected, taking a sip of his wine.

She was a little annoyed to find her information was so far off. "I know of your cousin Adrian, but who else?"

"Adrian is my second cousin," he said. "My younger sister, and one of my first cousins, live in the city as well."

"'Beware the lone Thorinson leading you into the woods...'" Phillipa murmured, recalling the old saying.

"'For the pack is near, and hungry'," Hammond finished. "Yes." He gave a faint smile again, with no sign that the saying offended him.

"It doesn't bother you?" she asked.

"Why should it?"

"It is one of the most famous betrayals in history," she reminded him. "It still affects your reputation."

"History is written by the victors," he shrugged. "Or whoever lives to tell the tale. We tend to think of it as a victory."

Phillipa quirked an eyebrow. "I seem to recall my tutors calling it a massacre. What was it? Emperor Cymbrius's heir, and several legions that were killed?"

"His two eldest sons, and six of his finest legions," Hammond said, matter-of-factly.

"Is Hammond boring you with a history lesson?" Richard asked, his tone amused. "He knows not to do that at parties."

"Hardly," Phillipa said. "We were discussing Wulfgar Thorinson's attack on Emperor Cymbrius' forces in the north woods."

"We were debating if it was a victory or a massacre," Hammond said.

Richard hummed thoughtfully. "You're Aurellian, Marcus. What do you think?"

Marcus considered the question, leaning back in his chair. "Outside of Wolf's Rest, I think we're all taught that it was a massacre. But I have a certain level of respect for it.

Wulfgar led the Thorinsons, and a handful of elves, against highly trained Imperial legions, and was victorious."

"Didn't it lead to the fall of the empire?" Phillipa asked. She was a little hazy on the details, though she had long meant to return and read up on imperial history.

"The decline," Hammond corrected. "The entire continent was under the empire's rule when Cymbrius took the throne. But once Wulfgar revolted, others did as well, with mixed success. At least until Marcus Di'Antonius rebuilt the empire a few centuries later."

"My ancestor, and namesake," Marcus said, clearly proud of the connection.

"And the founder of Callatis," Richard said. "Were it not for him, we - and our republic - might not be here now."

Callatis itself had once been an imperial port city, used by Di'Antonius as his base of operations. But when the empire itself had withdrawn, the survivors had rebuilt, and established themselves as the Republic of Cardea. That part of history she did know well.

"Wulfgar's betrayal may have been an impressive military feat, but it was still a massacre," Geoffrey Randell said. Phillipa was almost surprised he had taken so long to step in.

"You say that as though he didn't bring it on himself," Lucilla said. "Cymbrius could call it fostering all he wanted, but he kidnapped Wulfgar, taught him all the intricacies of the Aurellian military, then expected him to be docile and obedient when he sent him back to the north."

Marcus gave his wife an approving nod.

"You talk as though it was Cymbrius that kidnapped him," Geoffrey said. "It was a legate that took Wulfgar as a hostage. Cymbrius himself saw Wulfgar as another son."

"And the betrayal broke him, as I recall," Henry added.

"Then maybe he shouldn't have threatened Wulfgar's lover," Hammond said, and there was an edge to his voice as he met Geoffrey's gaze. "But Cymbrius' hatred of elves was well known."

"Or maybe he should have kept Wulfgar in the south," Geoffrey countered. "Away from his siblings. You Thorinsons do seem to have a corrupting influence."

There was an accusation to the words, and Phillipa suspected he was referring to Hammond's friendship with Richard, as much as to Wulfgar's relationship with his family.

"You say that as if Cymbrius weren't notorious for his cruelty," Lucilla said. "How can you defend him?"

"It's a matter of perspective," Geoffrey said. "He was created by his father, who was a harsh disciplinarian."

"That explains it; it doesn't excuse it," Lucilla insisted. "Cymbrius made his bed, and had no one to blame but himself."

Marcus touched her hand. "Easy, My Love."

She scowled a little, but some of the fire in her eyes faded. "Of course. Forgive me."

If Geoffrey's expression was any indication, he forgave nothing. "As I recall, Marcus, your namesake, dealt with another murderous Thorinson, bent on putting the world to fire and sword."

"That's hardly fair," Hammond said, his spoon clanging against his bowl as he put it down. "Brynnja was trying to keep the family together as the world burned around them."

"She also became one of his closest allies," Marcus said. "Based on mutual respect for each other's strategy and leadership."

Geoffrey shook his head, taking a sip of his wine.

Phillipa saw Lucilla rolls her eyes as she also took a drink.

"I should remember not to bring up complicated details of history at dinner," Hammond said quietly.

"Do you study history in general?" Phillipa asked. "Or just your family's history?"

"History, in general, has always fascinated me," he said. "It tends to repeat, and the lessons it teaches can be invaluable."

"It's part of why I keep him around," Richard said. "Even if he doesn't always know how to behave at social functions."

Hammond smiled sheepishly. "Turns out my years of studying can be useful. But, as my cousin, Hannah says: you can never fully tame a wolf."

"Speaking of, where is Vetr?" Henry asked. "I half expected to see him here."

Geoffrey looked genuinely horrified as he glanced at his son-in-law. "I should hope not."

"He's at home," Hammond said. "My sister is one of the few people he listens to, so I asked her to watch him for the night. I had to pay her a pretty sum, but she is there."

Phillipa gave Richard a curious look.

"Vetr is Hammond's wolf," Richard explained. "The Thorinsons have a pack of wolves that live on Wolf's Rest, half-wild and half-domesticated."

"They like our warm houses and butchered game," Hammond chuckled as he took a sip of his wine. He then looked at Phillipa again. "Wulfgar's lover was an elven hunter named Ogin. As the legend goes, when she was hunting one day, she found an orphaned wolf pup in the woods. Its mother and siblings had died, but this one seemed determined to survive. Wulfgar had already taken the wolf as his sigil, so she brought the pup to him as a gift.

"He named the wolf Sjurd, which means victory in the old language, and it became his constant companion. Sjurd eventually found a mate, and established his own pack. Our wolves are descended from them, though I suspect they have become less wild. It became a tradition for each of us to have a wolf as a companion."

"Vetr is beautiful," Richard said. "Pure white, with blue eyes almost the same color as Hammond's. I wish I had a lion to follow me the same way."

"That might be a bit over theatrical, don't you think?" Vera said.

"I think it would be fantastic," Lucilla said. "I can just see Richard working in his office, a lion lounging by the desk, waiting for the order to bite."

"What sort of barbarian age do you think we live in?" Vera sounded almost horrified.

Lucilla rolled her eyes again, not bothering to even glance at Vera.

"It would be an impressive image," Phillipa said. "Imagine if the two lions flanking the front door were real."

Richard had been about to take a drink, but he lowered his glass as he looked over at her. "I quite like that idea. It would certainly inspire respect in anyone coming to the house."

"I thought our peacocks were impressive," Marcus said. "I like how you think, Lady Bellerose." He inclined his glass to her slightly before taking a drink.

"Indeed," Lucilla agreed.

"Ridiculous," Vera muttered.

"Careful, Lady Bellerose," Hammond said. "You're giving them both ideas."

Phillipa glanced at him again.

The Thorinsons had a reputation for being rough and wild. They rarely came to the city because they preferred the country, where they worked their own land, which was one of the most well-managed in the country. Until recently, they weren't known for playing political games. If they did, they might have risen to be a ruling family already, since they had the power to leverage.

Hammond had something of the wolf about him - she saw it in his smile. But he seemed in his element at the Galloborne table. Phillipa was having a hard time pinning him down. And she suspected there was more to him than she could see now.

"It would seem that, as with many things," she said, "your family started it."

Hammond chuckled, inclining his spoon to her as he took another sip of soup. "You're not wrong."

Enter The Wolf

CHAPTER 1

Fifty invitations to the dinner had been sent out, with only four of those allowing for guests that weren't explicitly named.

By contrast, there had been over a hundred invitations to the ball.

The remaining guests had already begun to arrive by the time they came in from dinner.

Hammond was momentarily overwhelmed by the sea of bright colors, the swish of full skirts, the buzz of conversation.

As he adjusted to the glittering pageantry, he recognized more of the new arrivals. He had gone over the guest list with Richard several times, so there were few surprises in the attendance.

"Hammond."

He looked towards Richard, whose face was wary. "Yes?"

Richard jerked his chin towards the guests. And Hammond felt a twinge of panic as he saw his cousin, Throthgar, talking to Aksel Stark.

He had dressed appropriately, in a dark, blue-gray vest, with his chestnut hair combed back and pulled off his face. But he stood out like a wolf in the sheep's pen, tall and broad with muscles visible under his silk shirt.

"Take care of it," Richard said, before turning to Sior Lewellyn.

Hammond nodded, cutting across the entryway, towards his cousin.

As he approached, Throthgar noticed and excused himself from his conversation. "Hammond," he grinned.

"What are you doing here?"

"What kind of greeting is that?" Throthgar's expression shifted from surprise to a wolfish grin. "I'd think you weren't happy to see me."

"It's a wary one," Hammond said. "What are you doing here?"

He chuckled. "Are you worried I'm here to rob the Gallobornes? I'm not an idiot."

The Gallobornes were allied with the Thieves Guild, so stealing from them was forbidden. A fact the Wild Wolf would know well. Even before considering the connection between their two families.

Still, this wasn't the kind of party where he expected to see his cousin.

"Relax," Throthgar said. "I'm here for the ball. Specifically, for Richard's announcement." He glanced towards where Marcus was speaking with a few city prefects who had just arrived. "I didn't miss it, did I?"

"Not yet," Hammond said. Then he frowned as he registered what Throthgar had said. "How did you even know?"

Only a few people knew that Richard intended to make an announcement. Even fewer knew what that announcement was.

"Kat," Throthgar said. "We saw each other at the arena earlier, and she mentioned it."

"How did-- Nevermind. It's Katherine."

No secret was safe from Katherine Fischer. Hammond appreciated the source of information, but the fact still unsettled him from time to time.

"She probably heard it from Lucius," Throthgar chuckled. "He gossips like an old woman."

"Maybe," Hammond said. It made sense.

Still, he couldn't help but suspect that Katherine had let it slip to Throthgar on purpose. Probably to punish him for refusing to bring her as his guest.

"Are you saying I'm not welcome?" Throthgar asked, brow arching. "I am a Thorinson."

"You are," Hammond said. "Of course you are. So long as you stay out of trouble."

"I have no interest in causing trouble," Throthgar said. "I just want to enjoy the party."

"I'm sorry," Hammond said. "Richard wants tonight to go off perfectly." He paused as another thought occurred to him, and he eyed his cousin again. "You're not here to harass Byron, are you?"

Throthgar's icy blue eyes flashed. But there was no hint of denial in his voice as he said: "And why would I do that?"

Hammond knew all too well that there was no arguing with that expression.

"I won't make a scene. I know how to behave in a ballroom." Throthgar paused, gaze caught by something through the open doors of the ballroom. "Who's that?"

Following his cousin's gaze, Hammond frowned.

"Don't."

"What?"

"Do you mean the blonde woman in the wine-colored gown? That's Phillipa Bellerose. Richard's guest."

"Not her," Throthgar said, gaze not wavering. "The black-haired woman next to her."

"Oh." Hammond had barely noticed the woman in the violet gown beside Phillipa. "Carolyn Selelon. Roland and Aline's youngest."

"Any connections I should know about?" Throthgar asked, his interest now clearly fixed on Carolyn.

Hammond felt a bit dizzy at the sudden change of subject. "Not that I know of."

"Good." Throthgar flashed him a wolfish smile. "Then I'm going to enjoy the ball."

Hammond stared at his cousin's back as he passed through the ballroom doors with the grace of a cat burglar. Seeing the liquid grace in a slender woman like Heather was one thing. In his broad, muscular cousin, it seemed out of place.

After a moment, he collected himself enough to move into the ballroom as well.

It was every bit as lavish and elegant as the rest of the house, made of limestone, marble, and gold gilt work. A massive gold and crystal chandelier hung from the ceiling, augmented by the glowing glass orbs that Hammond and Byron had enchanted for the evening.

Four sets of double doors on the far wall led out to a terrace, and the gardens beyond. Magic had been used to create subtle air currents to keep the air fresh and cool, even in the crowded ballroom.

On the southern wall, a mural depicted Numitor's Peak, the snow-capped mountain surrounded by green trees, and a lake that reflected the billowing white clouds in a blue sky. For a moment, Hammond forgot the ballroom. He knew that landscape well, having grown up with that same mountain range visible from his bedroom window. It was from the other side, but he still recognized the view from the Galloborne estate.

For a moment, Hammond felt homesick. Longing for the open fields of Wolf's Rest.

This would be his first time being away from home on the Summer Solstice, which was also his father's birthday.

But he shook the feeling off, and returned his attention to the ballroom itself.

He looked around, to see where Throthgar had gotten to, and to place others around the room.

"It's too early to look so confused," Graham Galloborne said, approaching Hammond.

Hammond shook his head. "I don't understand people. Sometimes I think I do, but then they surprise me."

"When they do something unpredictable?" Graham asked, with an amused quirk of his eyebrow.

"Exactly."

"Emotion, Hammond," Graham said. "You can't find it in books - you just have to accept that people aren't straightforward."

"I prefer books," Hammond admitted.

"And I prefer my paints," Graham said. He stopped a footman who was passing with a tray of glasses, and took two. "But here we are."

He offered one of the glasses to Hammond.

"Here we are," Hammond agreed, tapping his glass against Graham's before taking a sip of the sparkling wine. Imported from Vestra, no doubt.

He and Graham were the same age, and had been close friends as children. They had been educated together, until Graham had chosen to focus on his art, while Hammond had turned to history, and magic. He still considered Graham among his closest friends, but knew befriending Richard before the war had made Graham less willing to trust him the way he once had.

"Is your brother pushing you towards anyone the way he is with William?"

"You would probably know better than me," Graham said. "I've been avoiding him for the past few days just so he couldn't."

"I can hardly blame you," Hammond admitted. "But he hasn't mentioned it."

A footman appeared next to Hammond, bowing his head politely. "Lord Galloborne requests your presence."

Graham saluted him with his drink, before slipping into the crowd.

"There you are." Richard seemed slightly annoyed as Hammond arrived at his side. "Did you take care of Throthgar?"

"He's just here for the party," Hammond said.

Richard nodded. "Fine. As long as he behaves."

He decided not to mention that Throthgar's attention had been caught by Phillipa's cousin. There was no need to tell Richard unless something came of it. In which case, Hammond hoped he wouldn't have to be the one to explain it.

"Are you going to make your announcement now?" Hammond asked.

"Not yet," Richard said. "I want people to enjoy the party first."

"It seems to be going well."

Richard nodded, eyes sweeping the room to see where everyone was, and who they were talking to. His eyes lingered on Phillipa and Carolyn, who were speaking with Azalea Gartner.

Overall, the mood was relaxed and pleasant.

"William." Richard waved his brother over, bringing Hammond's attention back into focus.

"Yes, brother?" William asked, coming alongside Richard.

"Where's Birgitta Lofgren?" Richard asked pointedly.

William winced slightly.

"I expect to see you dance with her," Richard said.

"There she is." Hammond pointed to where Birgitta stood by her father, Frans Lofgren, who was talking to Geoffrey Randell.

She was a beautiful, elegant young woman with platinum blonde hair. Polite, but quiet and aloof. It didn't seem she had any input in the conversation, standing by her father while her hands were folded neatly.

"I don't think she's interested in dancing," William said. Trying in vain to avoid the command.

"I didn't ask you if she wanted to dance," Richard scowled. "I told you I expect to see you dancing with her."

"Do I have any say in this?" William asked.

All three of them knew the answer.

Richard shot his brother an intimidating glare. "No, you don't."

For a moment, it seemed William would argue... but he reconsidered. "Alright."

At a pointed look for his brother, he made his way through the crowd toward Birgitta.

Once he was gone, Hammond looked at Richard. "Are you going to ask Phillipa to dance?"

Richard tensed, and Hammond quirked an eyebrow in amusement.

"You know she's expecting it," Hammond went on, while they both watched Phillipa laugh lightly. A crystal clear sound that he could tell caught Richard's attention. "If you don't, she might start ignoring you for real, instead of just playing hard to get."

Hammond understood her game. At least in theory. He suspected it was the game she had been playing since Richard first met her at Summer Grove.

Most interested young women tended to throw themselves at Richard. Fawning over and flattering him, all but begging for his attention. Instead, Phillipa gave Richard just enough to draw him in. A subtle smile, a soft touch, a compliment to stroke his ego. Only to leave him wanting more.

It certainly seemed to be working.

"I doubt it," Richard said. "If I'm right, her interest in me is ambitious rather than romantic." Still, something in his expression as he looked at her told Hammond that didn't change Richard's interest in the socialite.

"It doesn't bother you?" Hammond asked.

Richard himself could certainly never be accused of romanticism. He was a pragmatist, focused on his goals. Still, Hammond would have thought that the game would turn Richard off.

To his credit, Richard did consider the question. "I would be a hypocrite if it did, don't you think?"

When he put it like that...

"I suppose."

"Besides, she's not silly or frivolous," he said. "She's intelligent, clever, and determined. With impeccable taste, and an understanding of what it takes to manage a ruling family. What more could I ask for?"

"So it would be mutually beneficial," Hammond said. "She's also on your level intellectually, but probably won't challenge you the way Runa would."

He couldn't resist the jab, and only chuckled when Richard shot him an annoyed look. But they both knew it was true.

"Go on," Hammond encouraged. "It would be a shame to waste all those dancing lessons."

"You're right," Richard said. "And who will you dance with?"

Hammond balked, the question taking him by surprise. "What?"

Richard gave him a toothy smile, clearly satisfied with his victory. "You had just as many lessons as I did. It would be a shame to waste them."

Not for the first time, Hammond wondered if Richard had plans for him, as he did with William. At the very least, he had ideas.

He swallowed, suddenly hyper-aware of the heartbeat in his ears as he cast his gaze over the ballroom in search of a safe choice.

Off to his left, he spotted a familiar head of red hair, and noticed that Runa was being talked to by Brenden Rathdrum. By the look of it, the young prefect had cut in on her conversation with her friend Elaine Howell. And failed to notice the look of disapproval both women gave him.

"It looks as though Runa could use a rescue," he said, sighing in relief.

Richard followed his gaze, and frowned at the sight. "You'd think Godric would be keeping an eye out for her."

On an educated guess, Hammond looked towards the Starks and saw Godric talking to Jonathan and Marcus.

"By all means, rescue Runa from her would-be suitor," Richard said, his tone amused. "Preferably before she loses patience. I'd rather not have young Rathdrum crying in the corner."

Hammond chuckled. He knew Rathdrum from his time on the council of prefects. And knew Richard's concerns were valid.

When it came to social climbers, he was the worst type. Neither intelligent nor charming enough to match his ambition, or understand that his position didn't open every door. All of which was proven by his attention to Runa.

Hammond watched Richard approach Phillipa, and he wasn't the only one interested. Several people nearby turned to watch.

As she spoke, Phillipa gestured elegantly, and Richard timed it perfectly so her hand landed in his. When she turned her head in surprise, Hammond thought he saw a flash of delight before she could school her expression. She gave Richard a subtle, approving smile as she greeted him, and Richard returned it as he raised her hand to his lips. Hammond almost envied Richard's easy, suave grace.

If he'd had even a fraction of that, maybe he wouldn't have been left dumbstruck when Heather had kissed his cheek. He might have known how to respond, instead of standing in the doorway, staring after her.

Phillipa pretended to consider when Richard asked her to dance... but no one in the ballroom believed she would say no. And a moment later, Richard led her onto the dance floor. The orchestra in the corner sprang to attention at the cue.

Satisfied, Hammond turned his attention, and his step, towards Runa. Just in time, as he could see from her expression that she was losing patience.

"Hammond." She smiled as he approached, stepping away from Rathdrum without a backward glance.

"Runa." He offered her his arm. "I'm sorry I didn't come to greet you sooner."

"I know you were preoccupied," she said. "We've known each other far too long to stand on ceremony."

Branden Rathdrum attempted to shoot Hammond a glare. But considering he had just shrugged off a glare from the

Galloborne lion, it hardly phased him. Hammond gave him a dismissive look - something he had done many times during council meetings - before turning back to Runa.

While she had grown into a beauty that turned heads wherever she went, Hammond could never see her as anything other than the young girl he had known since she was born. Before the Sorensens had become a ruling family, and she had found herself the center of attention because of her rank as much as her beauty. They were third cousins, thanks to a marriage between their families several generations back. But Hammond tended to think of her more as a sister.

"I wondered if you would do me the honor of a dance."

Her look was earnestly grateful. "The pleasure would be mine."

Rathdrum started to speak, but Runa shot him a glare that made the young man wither on the spot.

Hammond led Runa to the edge of the dance floor, where Richard and Phillipa began the first dance.

"They're certainly a handsome couple," Runa noted.

"Indeed," Hammond said, having been struck with the same thought.

Phillipa seemed to glow as the lights reflected off the gold dust on her shoulders and cheeks, while her sandy blonde hair shone in the light. She contrasted Richard in his black silks, while at the same time complimenting him.

"I know it's calculated," Runa said. "But in this case, those calculations were perfect."

Graham led Elizabeth onto the floor, now that the head of the family had been given a respectable amount of time to be the center of attention. William and Birgitta were a step behind.

"That one I'm less sure about," Runa murmured.

He glanced over to see her watching William and Birgitta shrewdly.

"You think so?"

He looked at the two again. A match Richard had been actively working on for months now. The Lofgrens were a swing vote on the council, and Richard had been trying, but failing, to gain Frans' loyalty. The hope was that a marriage between Birgitta and William would solidify an alliance.

Birgitta's eyes were lowered shyly, and she seemed uncomfortable with William's hand on her waist. They certainly lacked the chemistry that was impossible to miss with Richard and Phillipa.

"Shall we?" Hammond asked, not wanting to dwell on it at the moment.

Runa moved lightly, the fabric of her skirts swirling around her, while her red hair shone in the light. She was a far better dancer than Hammond himself, but she was a familiar partner. They had been instructed in dancing together as children.

"Don't look so scared," Runa said after a moment.

Hammond chuckled sheepishly. "I keep remembering how you used to scold me whenever I got the steps wrong."

Runa laughed. "I remember. Eydis giggling the whole time, of course."

"Of course."

Even two years younger than him, and when she had been much smaller, he had been embarrassed by her scoldings. Worse than that had been her persistent sass.

"I invited her to come tonight," he said.

Runa shook her head. "She wouldn't come."

"She enjoys her anonymity," he said. "I can't say I blame her."

"It's not that," Runa said. "Or rather, not just that."

Hammond almost missed a step as he tried to read her expression. But an all too familiar look from her made him recover quickly. While he might have enjoyed seeing how Rathdrum cowered from the intensity of her glare, he had no desire to be on the receiving end. "What do you mean?"

"You can hardly expect me to betray a confidence," she said, with a sly smile as she twirled.

"I wouldn't dream of it," he said, unsure how else to respond.

He had chosen her as the safe option, and now was reminded of just how safe that decision was. Runa had known him since childhood, so she knew things he preferred to keep quiet in society. But there was a comfort in talking to someone who knew him well, without any need to use it to her advantage.

"I still don't understand people," Hammond muttered. "Just when I think I do, they surprise me."

"You could always go home," Runa pointed out. "Live a quiet life at Wolf's Rest."

"That's tempting," he admitted, glancing toward the mural on the wall. Before quickly looking back, so he wouldn't ruin the dance.

"But then you wouldn't be one of the most powerful men in the republic." She gave him a knowing smile.

"I don't hold office anymore," he reminded her. "Stefan is the counselor now."

"I'm aware." Her distaste was evident in her voice as they both glanced over to where Stefan Marszalek was talking with a group of prefects.

"Him, at least, I understand," Hammond said.

"Because there's nothing to him beyond pride and ambition," Runa said, her tone scathing.

Hammond at least knew Runa well enough to know when it was time to change the subject.

"May I ask you a question?"

She gave him an encouraging, but still sassy look. Still the precocious child he remembered. "You may. But I reserve the right not to answer."

"Do you have any calculations?" he asked.

"That is a bold question," she said. "Especially on a dance floor."

"I'm sorry," he said. "It's just nice not to have to pretend with someone."

"No need to apologize," she said. "With anyone else, I might say that a lady can hardly be expected to reveal her intentions any more than her confidences. But, since it's you, I'll be honest. For the moment at least, I have none. I don't need them."

It was almost a relief.

As the song ended, the orchestra lingering on the last notes, Runa stepped back, and descended into an elegant curtsey that awed him a little. Only a half curtsey. She did outrank him, after all.

"We should find new partners before the gossips start to talk," she said. "I can't protect you from socializing anymore."

"And here I thought I was protecting you."

"A mutually beneficial alliance," she said.

Conrad Trevar appeared at her side, asking for the next dance. She accepted, giving Hammond a friendly smile before letting Conrad lead her away.

Beauty & The Wolf

CHAPTER 1

Ballrooms were far from Throthgar's natural habitat. Unlike Hammond, he hadn't grown up between Callatis and Wolf's Rest, learning how to navigate high society.

Instead, he had grown up in the woods and mountains around Wolf's Rest, running through the fields, and exploring the forests. He had taken lessons in etiquette and decorum at his uncle's insistence, so he knew how to behave. But he didn't take to it easily.

He had acquired the taste enough to live in the city for the last year or so. However, he spent more time in the market, and on the roofs of the city, than he did at social parties. When he did, it was usually in his work for the guild, taking advantage of his name to open doors other thieves couldn't.

And he did enjoy the amenities that came with it.

Still, as he made his way through the mingling guests, he paused a moment to look at the mural on the wall. At the familiar mountains and trees that Graham had captured with stunning detail.

Home.

But he refocused his thoughts, and looked around to find Carolyn Selelon.

He was surprised that he didn't see her on the dance floor. Instead, she stood alone, watching the dancers. Even Hammond was dancing with Runa. Yet it seemed no one had asked Carolyn, despite her longing look as she watched the dancers.

The light shimmered off her black hair, and his eyes followed the way it cascaded down her back, and the violet silk of her dress hugged her curves.

He wanted to go over, rest his hand on the small of her back, and lead her to the dance. No woman had ever caught his attention the way she did, and he felt drawn to her like the tide was pulled by the moon.

Throthgar looked around the ballroom again, reminding himself to focus on business before pleasure.

This time he found Byron Galloborne, who stood away from the dancers, talking to Conrad Trevar.

Conrad noticed his approach first, and murmured a warning.

To Byron's credit, he didn't hesitate. He turned, and met his gaze squarely. "Throthgar. I didn't expect to see you here."

"No one did, apparently," he said, coming to stand next to him. "But when I heard about Richard's announcement, I couldn't resist."

He was only an inch taller than Byron, but he was broader. And wilder.

Conrad looked at them for a moment, then made his excuses and slipped into the crowd.

"Is that why you're here?" Byron asked, refusing to be intimidated. "Or is that an excuse?"

"Signy didn't send me," Throthgar said. "She would string me up if she knew I was giving you a hard time."

"I doubt that would stop you." Byron sighed, turning towards him. "What do you want, Throthgar? I thought you approved."

Throthgar glared at him.

Signy Danielson had been his best friend since they were children. She was the daughter of one of the tenant farmers on the Thorinson estate, and they had spent their childhood climbing trees and exploring together, along with his cousin Ragnar, and their friend Katori.

When they had come of age, Throthgar had employed her as his steward. Signy had no desire to work on her family's farm, but did have the skill to keep his estate running smoothly.

Until a year ago. Throthgar had left for a ride one morning, and everything had been normal. When he returned, he found Byron and Signy sitting close on a sofa in his parlor, clearly touched by the Maiden.

He had been more taken aback than displeased. Last autumn, he had given his blessing when she moved south to live with Byron on his estate.

"I approve of you two as a couple," Throthgar corrected. "I don't approve of you hiding her at your distillery as if you're ashamed of her."

"I'm not hiding her," Byron said.

"Then why isn't she here?" Throthgar challenged, gesturing to the ballroom around them. The Summer Solstice, and a Galloborne ball, seemed like the perfect opportunity for Byron to introduce his lover, both to his family, and to society.

Byron waved toward his cousin, giving him a wordless look.

"Richard isn't a good enough excuse."

"No, he's not," Byron agreed. "But I didn't think now was the best time to introduce her to him. The social season is starting, and all eyes would be on her if I brought her here. Why would I do that to her?"

That was a valid argument. Throthgar didn't like it, but it was true.

"You're leaving out the part that she didn't want to come." Caitlyn Galloborne came to stand next to her brother, giving Throthgar a defiant look. Unlike her brother, she wouldn't be afraid to pull rank on him.

"I thought that would sound like an excuse," Byron said, glancing at his sister.

"That doesn't mean she likes being left alone," Throthgar countered.

"Which is why she's going to Ulfvard next week," Byron said. "I haven't locked her in the tower."

"I still don't like it."

Caitlyn rolled her pale blue eyes. "Much as I adore Signy, you must know she's not ready to face society. And she has no desire to."

While Throthgar wanted to argue, he knew he couldn't. Signy hadn't been raised with the lessons he had. Instead, she had teased him for them. In her letters, she said she regretted that, now that Caitlyn was trying to teach her. By her own admission, she was terrible at it. And Callatis high society could be merciless when someone slipped.

"I am glad she has a friend like you," Caitlyn said. "Though this probably isn't a conversation we should be having here."

"They can't hear," Byron said, absently spinning the gold and ruby ring he wore on his left thumb.

Throthgar hadn't even noticed him cast the spell to hide their conversation. But when he glanced at the ring, the jewel flashed, in a way he knew from spending time around Hammond.

Caitlyn nodded. "Are you satisfied, Throthgar?"

"As much as I can be," he admitted. She certainly had a point. He looked back at Byron.

"I'll introduce her to Richard once she's ready," Byron said. "All of this is her decision."

"As it should be," Throthgar said.

Byron nodded. "We'll see you at the arena tomorrow?"

"I wouldn't miss it," Throthgar said.

"We'll be in the Di Antonios' box if you'd like to join us," Byron said. And Throthgar recognized the gesture of goodwill. "I believe Hammond will be there as Richard's guest."

"I'll consider it."

Byron nodded, before Caitlyn tugged at his arm.

"If you'll excuse us, Throthgar."

He nodded.

Before, he might have put up a bit more resistance. But their points were valid. And he did have an unexpected distraction.

With his business taken care of, now he could turn his attention to pleasure.

He found Carolyn quickly this time. She had moved away from the dance floor, and now spoke with Corisien Arnon and his wife, Freyja.

An idea clicked, and he glanced over to where he had seen Corion Arnon a moment earlier.

Corisien's younger brother was a few inches shorter than Throthgar himself. Notoriously handsome and charismatic, with dark hair and green eyes that women seemed to find especially appealing. His manners were perfectly refined, while tales from his travels gave him a roguish charm that created fascination.

"It's been a while, Thorinson," Corion said, as Throthgar came over to him.

"I didn't know you were back in the city," Throthgar said. "Last I heard, you went south for the winter."

"I did."

Corion glanced to his right, and Throthgar followed his gaze to a tall, elegant high elf with honey-blonde hair, dressed in a gown the color of blackberries.

As if she sensed their gaze, Bronwyn Llewellyn glanced toward them. Her eyes swept over them both, but lingered on Corion, meeting his gaze. In a way that even Throthgar knew was decidedly inappropriate for a ballroom.

Not that Corion's gaze was innocent, either.

Their silent seduction lasted a moment, before she gracefully swept her hair over her pale shoulder and turned back to her conversation.

"You're just following her around the countryside now?" Throthgar smirked, realizing exactly why Corion had gone south for the winter.

"I would follow her to the ends of the world if she asked me to," Corion admitted, completely unashamed as his eyes lingered on his lover. But after a moment, he inhaled, turning back to Throthgar. "I'm glad to be back in the city, though."

"I'm glad you are," Throthgar said. "Do you remember that favor you owe me from White Falls?"

"Are you calling it in?" Corion asked, quirking an eyebrow.

"Yes," Throthgar said, without hesitation. "Do you know the woman your brother is talking to? The one with the raven hair."

He glanced over to where Throthgar gestured. "Carolyn? Of course."

"Would you introduce me? It might be better to be introduced by a mutual friend, rather than just going over."

Corion frowned, green eyes narrowing slightly.

"What?" Throthgar asked.

"This isn't for your work, is it?" Corion asked.

"I wouldn't be asking if it was," Throthgar said, almost offended that his friend had to ask.

"It's just that Carolyn is..." He frowned, trying to find the right words. "She's a romantic. She's not the type to be interested in casual flirtation."

"That's not my intention," Throthgar assured, looking over at her again, and the way she once more watched the dancers longingly. "I promise."

❧ CHAPTER 2 ☙

As a child, Carolyn had dreamed of the day she would finally be allowed to attend a ball. She had watched her mother, aunt, and older sister get dressed in beautiful gowns and glittering jewels. Always waiting for her turn.

She had read fairy tales of evenings filled with magic and romance, and played out elaborate fantasies of what might happen when her day finally came.

Fantasies of a ballroom like this one, and all eyes on her. Of a charming prince coming up, completely entranced by her beauty.

Phillipa had reminded her that Cardea didn't have princes. But Carolyn had been eight years old at the time, and didn't care. She had been too lost in the clouds, as a handsome nobleman swirled her around a dancefloor.

When she was nineteen, she had finally been fitted for her first ball gown. A beautiful blue silk dress, with a full skirt, and layers of frothy petticoats that had flared out when she twirled. And she had barely been able to stop dancing in front of the mirror when she had it on. When she hadn't been twirling, she had been admiring the way the bodice hugged her waist and showed her breasts off to advantage.

Surely people would notice her, she had thought, as she ran her hands over her waist.

But while the dress had lived up to her childhood dreams, the ball itself hadn't quite. It had been at the Bellerose estate, and the ballroom had been beautiful. She had felt as though she were floating on a cloud most of the evening. Even if it hadn't been as romantic as she had hoped. No one had appeared to sweep her into an epic love story worthy of the romance novels she spent so much time reading.

She had told herself there would be other balls. Other opportunities.

But each invitation had brought a little less excitement and anticipation. Until now, at twenty-six, she enjoyed the chance to dress up, but hardly dared to hope for more.

The idea of a Galloborne ball had caught her attention for the novelty of it, and as an excuse for a new gown. Occasionally she had caught herself slipping into daydreams. But she had told herself not to drift too far. Instead, she wanted to enjoy the ball itself.

Maybe that was why she had to hold back a wave of bitterness as she watched Phillipa dance with Richard.

Phillipa wasn't a romantic - she was ambitious, and practical. And yet she was the one being swirled across the floor, by the closest thing Cardea had to a charming prince. All while Carolyn watched from the edges of the dance floor, overlooked and unseen. Just as she usually was.

She decided not to torment herself, and turned away from the dancers. From experience, she knew the best way to enjoy these parties was to focus on anything else.

Instead, she took in the beauty of the scene.

The room seemed to glow in the enchanted lights, while the guests glittered and shone in their colorful silks. An eight-piece orchestra guided the dancers as they moved to the music. Four sets of tall double doors along the outside wall were thrown open to welcome the cool evening breeze, which carried in the sweet smell of the flowers.

It was all so lovely, she caught herself sighing wistfully. The Galloborne ball certainly didn't disappoint in its grandeur.

Freyja Arnon caught her eye, and waved her over to where she and Corisien were talking to Godric Sorensen. Carolyn returned her smile and approached them.

"It's so good to see you again," Freyja said, kissing her cheek.

"You as well," Carolyn said, returning the gesture. "Did you enjoy your stay in the mountains?"

"I did," Freyja said. "I enjoy the city, but I'll always prefer home."

Carolyn had grown up with the Arnon brothers, and knew them well. At various times, she had even found herself enamored with the younger brother, Corion.

Corisien had caused quite a stir by marrying a merchant's daughter from the north. But Freyja was as intelligent and business savvy as she was beautiful, and had charmed her way into society. She was so elegant and refined, it was easy to forget that she hadn't been born into the nobility. Her long, platinum blonde hair hung down her back in an intricate braid, and she wore a rich, rust-colored red silk gown that Carolyn couldn't help but admire.

"Your dress is so beautiful," she sighed, gently brushing her fingers over the gathers in the skirt.

"Isn't it?" Freyja asked, shifting a little to show off the movement of the silk, and the petticoats beneath. "I found the silk in the market up north, and I knew it would be perfect for tonight. Yours is beautiful as well. Purple truly is your color."

Carolyn blushed as she flared out the skirts to show them off. The outer layer had a scalloped hem, with embroidered flowers, that came a few inches below her knees, revealing the folds of a lighter purple underskirt. "Thank you."

"I think pretty clothes are the one thing Carolyn loves more than her romance novels," Corisien said, his tone lightly teasing.

Carolyn blushed sheepishly. "We all have our vices." Wanting to change the subject, she turned to Godric. "I suppose I should welcome you back as well."

Godric gave a strained smile. "Thank you."

"I don't think Godric wanted to come back," Corisien said, clearly amused.

"The city isn't so bad," Godric said. "It's society that I'm not fond of. It's a bit of a culture shock after living in the forts."

Carolyn was taken aback by his candor. It wasn't exactly common among the nobility.

"There's Corion," Corisien said, looking over Carolyn's shoulder.

"And Throthgar," Freyja said. "That's unexpected."

Carolyn made a questioning sound at Freyja's expression as she turned to look.

Her heart fluttered in her chest.

She recognized Corion, of course. But not the man next to him. Though she wished she did.

He was tall, with broad shoulders that filled out his dark blue doublet. Dark chestnut hair came to his shoulders, with a short, neatly trimmed beard. His sleeves were rolled up above his elbows, showing off the powerful muscles in his arms, and he moved with an animalistic grace. At that moment, he had her full attention. She didn't know him, but desperately wanted to.

His eyes were on her as they reached the small group, and she found herself light-headed, unable to look away from him.

"Are you done tormenting Byron?" Godric asked.

Carolyn blinked in surprise, trying to break herself out of the daze she had fallen into.

"I don't know what you mean," the man said. His eyes flashed with amusement... but something about his gaze still said he knew precisely what Godric meant. "I simply had business with him."

Carolyn didn't believe him.

But she also didn't care.

Especially when he turned his gaze back to her, and she felt her stomach somersault inside her.

The corner of his mouth curled, in a smile that was wolfish, but not cruel. And devastatingly handsome.

"We haven't met yet," he said.

"No, we haven't," she said, realizing her voice was weak and breathless.

She was vaguely aware of Corion's amused expression as he spoke. "Carolyn, may I introduce Throthgar Thorinson? Throthgar, Lady Carolyn Selelon."

A Thorinson. Her heart pounded in her chest.

She tried to calm herself, and stay grounded. But as Throthgar Thorinson kissed her hand, being grounded was impossible.

She didn't know how Phillipa managed it.

"It's a pleasure to meet you," he said, his voice deep and husky. He looked at her through long, thick lashes, with icy blue eyes that weakened her knees.

She blinked, trying to clear her thoughts. "The pleasure is all mine."

He gave her that wolfish smile again, not letting go of her hand.

She found herself desperately hoping he would ask her to dance.

But before he could, Phillipa swept over to them. Glowing with satisfaction, and beautiful in the light of the ballroom.

CHAPTER 3

Carolyn adored Phillipa. Her cousin was one of the few people she was close to in her family. One of the few that saw her. Who, despite their differences, didn't judge her for her daydreaming, or romanticism.

Still, there were times when she felt self-conscious next to her beautiful, golden cousin. It was impossible to compete with Phillipa's charisma, or the way her presence demanded attention wherever she went. Especially at that moment, when she radiated a satisfied glow.

"I'm glad I found you," she said, wrapping a hand around Carolyn's arm.

In contrast, Carolyn had never been so disappointed to see her.

"You're certainly enjoying the ball," she said, forcing herself to smile.

Phillipa glanced over to where Richard was talking to Frans Lofgren. "I am."

The others were too polite to comment on her momentary lapse in composure, and Phillipa took a deep breath to collect herself.

"Forgive me," she said, kissing Freyja's cheek. "It's been too long, Freyja."

The Selelon and Arnon territories were neighbors, leading to the friendship between the two families. While Phillipa wasn't as close with the Arnons, they were still familiar with each other.

As she greeted a distracted Corion, Phillipa's eyes finally landed on Throthgar. Sending a flutter of nerves through Carolyn.

"Phillipa, may I present Throthgar Thorinson," Freyja said. "Throthgar, this is Carolyn's cousin, Phillipa Bellerose."

Carolyn watched Throthgar as he inclined his head to Phillipa.

"A pleasure," he said. She thought his tone was different than when he had said it to her, but didn't trust herself not to imagine the difference.

Phillipa looked him over again, now curious. "I was just telling Hammond that I had never met a Thorinson. Now I've met two tonight."

He gave her a wolfish smile. This one a bit more mischievous. "We do tend to travel in packs."

"They're almost impossible to avoid in the north," Corion said. "You get tired of them quickly."

"I'll remember that the next time you want to stay in my house, and drink my mead," Throthgar said.

But Carolyn could tell it was good-natured teasing on both sides.

"I didn't realize there were so many wolves here in the city," Phillipa admitted.

"Do you know if Adrian is here tonight?" Corisien asked Throthgar. "I've been meaning to talk to him about some business."

Throthgar shook his head. "He's at the estate. He probably won't be back in the city for several weeks."

"Hammond mentioned his sister lives here as well," Phillipa said, clearly looking for more information.

It seemed to surprise to everyone else as well.

"I didn't even know he had a sister," Carolyn admitted, trying to remember if she had ever heard mention of her. But nothing came to mind.

"Eydis likes her privacy," was all Throthgar said.

Carolyn watched the way the corner of his mouth curled as he smiled. Then her heart skipped a beat in her chest as he looked at her, squeezing the hand he still held.

Most people tended to whisper about how the Thorinsons were wolves. They were wild, barely civilized, and just as ready to fight as their barbarian ancestors had been.

Despite their wealth, they still worked their own land, hunted game, and brewed their mead. They married wood elves, and forest witches from Molka. And they seemed to be the one family Geoffrey Randell liked even less than the Sorensens.

But Carolyn had always been more interested in the other side of their reputation. Where they were romantic heroes, with epic love stories that bards sang, and authors still told. Fierce Wulfgar, and how he had won over the wood elf Ogin, establishing the family line. Somber Baldur, and the beautiful Aina - the only one who could make him smile. Danr and Valentina, the tragedy that had ended an imperial dynasty. Those were the stories that came to her mind when she thought of the Thorinsons.

Throthgar perfectly fit her image of those Thorinson heroes. To have him in front of her, living and breathing, made her breath catch in her chest.

Bronwyn Lewellyn seemed to sense an opening, and swept over to them. Or rather, she swept over to Corion. Bringing the sweet, heady scent of her perfume. Blackberry and vanilla.

Corion's attention was immediately captivated by his lover, offering her his hand, and an adoring smile. Bronwyn accepted, while she leaned over to kiss Freyja's cheek. "It's so good to see you again. It's been too long."

"Far too long," Freyja agreed.

The high elf was a little taller than Carolyn, her honey-blonde hair elegantly twisted up and curled. Like most elves, she didn't wear the crinolines and petticoats that human women wore to create the full skirts of their ballgowns. But her skirts were made with enough rich fabric to sweep around her feet as she moved. Her gold and amethyst jewelry was intricate filigree so delicate it looked as if the slightest touch might crush it.

"You kept me waiting," she murmured to Corion, when she had finished greeting the others.

"I was trying," he said apologetically. "Throthgar called in a favor, and I couldn't get away."

"I'm here now," she said.

Corion smiled, wrapping an arm around her waist and kissing her temple, while Bronwyn hummed. She seemed aloof, but a soft smile tugged at the corner of her lips.

Carolyn caught herself sighing a little as she watched the interaction.

Despite Bronwyn's haughtiness, which far exceeded Phillipa's, there was a sweetness in the way they looked at each other.

"Would you like to dance?" Throthgar asked.

She started, eyes widening as she turned back to him and met his gaze. And this time she was sure: The smile he gave her differed significantly from when he had addressed Phillipa.

"If you would do me the honor," he added, a husky quality to his voice that set her heart aflutter.

"I- I would love to," she said breathlessly, knees suddenly weak.

He smiled again, his hold on her hand shifting so he could lead her onto the dance floor.

As he did, she was aware that Phillipa watched them. But she didn't care.

"It's been a while since I danced with someone," Throthgar said, as they stepped onto the floor.

"You don't attend parties often?" she guessed. "I've never seen you before." She was positive she would remember if she had.

"That," he said. "And I haven't met many people I cared to dance with."

"Am I the exception?" She looked up at him hopefully.

He chuckled, a hand coming to her waist and gently pulling her against his chest. She couldn't help but gasp, shivering at the touch. Even through her gown and corset, she could feel the heat of his hand.

"You are," he said, setting off the flutter again. As if his eyes released butterflies inside her rib cage.

Before she could recover, the orchestra began a new song, and she found herself swept away by it. If her feet touched the ground, she was barely aware of it. The ballroom itself floated on the swell of the music, carrying them up to the stars.

It seemed too beautiful to be real, and she wondered if it was a dream. But then she felt the heat of his hand on her waist, and his woodsy scent washed over her.

"Are you alright?" Throthgar asked.

"I am," she assured him. "I just keep worrying this is a dream."

"I do, too."

She blinked, and missed a step of the dance. But he lifted her off her feet so she wouldn't fall. It didn't help her stay grounded at all, in any sense.

He smiled, and she thought she might melt completely.

In the back of her mind, she heard Phillipa's voice reminding her that she should be careful, and on her guard. But she felt safe in his arms. Even more, when he looked at her, she felt seen. A feeling she had longed for as long as she could remember.

The song ended too soon, and she felt herself come back down to reality. But when Throthgar looked into her eyes, she was breathless all over again.

"You're so beautiful," he murmured, a hand coming up to brush his knuckles against her cheek.

She would have blushed, if her cheeks weren't already flushed and heated. "Thank you."

He glanced towards the refreshment table along one wall. "Should we dance again, or would you like a drink to help you cool down?"

"Dance with me again," she said, without hesitation.

Throthgar smiled, pulling her close as the music began again.

Blue & Red

☙ CHAPTER 1 ❧

While Runa claimed she had brought Godric to show off her war hero cousin, that wasn't the entire reason. She had hoped that he would intimidate every social-climbing bachelor with eyes on her position.

A plan that had been ruined almost immediately, when he had left her side to speak with some of his friends.

Runa had done her best to stay busy, and find safety in numbers. But there was only so much she could do.

She had managed to avoid Stefan Marszalek, who was focused on socializing with the nobles who had just returned to the city.

Hammond had saved her from the nuisance that was Brendan Rathdtum, thankfully.

Pierre Clement was a different matter entirely.

During the Cymbrian War, the siege on Callatis had left the republic with only 80 of the customary 200 prefects. A field day for every lesser noble, or even some commoners with high social standing, who sought to raise their positions.

Most of the current prefects were young. Too young, according to her father. And Runa was inclined to agree. She certainly agreed with Hammond's opinion that most lacked the intelligence for the position. If nothing else, they seemed to think their new standing exempted them from social rules.

Pierre Clement was from a merchant family. Charismatic enough that Roland Selelon had nominated him to the council. But lacking the self-awareness to notice how few people actually enjoyed his presence. His position gave him access to some of the most exclusive social circles, but Runa didn't know of anyone who wanted him there.

Clement was telling her a story about a recent meeting of the prefects - or at least, that was what she thought it was about. She wasn't actually paying attention.

Instead, Runa cast her eyes around for a way out of the situation.

She could have walked away, or just told him to leave her alone. But Richard would never forgive her if she caused a scene at his ball.

Her eyes landed on Richard then. He was about ten feet away, talking to a group of other nobles and prefects.

He looked over as if he sensed her gaze boring into the back of his head.

She cast a pointed look at Clement, who didn't even notice. He enjoyed the sound of voicing his own accomplishments too much to notice that she wasn't listening. Then she gave Richard an expectant look.

He considered for a moment, then gave a curt nod. A moment later, she felt a surge of relief as he excused himself, and came over to her.

"Runa," he said, as he approached her. "I just realized I haven't greeted you this evening. Please forgive the oversight."

"No need to apologize," she said, accepting the kiss he pressed to her cheek. "You've been distracted."

He gave her a scolding look at the light teasing. Reminding her that he had come to her rescue.

Even wearing heels, her eyes barely reached his jaw. Not that she had ever let that get in her way. She returned his gaze steadily, refusing to be intimidated.

"Would you care to dance with me?" He cast a dismissive look at Clement. "You don't mind if I steal her, do you?"

His tone made it clear it wasn't really a question, and Clement had no choice but to nod.

"I would be delighted." She ignored Pierre as Richard lead her onto the dance floor.

"Thank you," she said, as they fell into step with the music.

"That look is very hard to deny, and you know it," Richard said.

"So I've been told," she said, as she let him swirl her around the floor. "Has Phillipa abandoned you already?"

"Not abandoned," he said, almost too quickly. "Just making me wait."

And doing an excellent job of it.

"Are you alright with that?" Runa cocked her head curiously.

Richard glanced over at Phillipa, with something Runa had never expected to see in his expression. It was admiration, fascination, and even longing, with that characteristic determination.

"I understand the game," Richard said. "And I respect when it's played well."

"That sounds like the Richard Galloborne I know."

He chuckled.

A common belief held that Richard's determination and ambition were the result of becoming head of his family at such a young age. But Runa knew it had always been a part of him, even in childhood.

"You're enjoying it, aren't you?"

He looked over at Phillipa again, his pale blue eyes thoughtful. Then he met Runa's gaze. "I am."

"And what about when you catch her, and the game ends?" Runa asked.

It was one thing to have a goal and pursue it. That was Richard's specialty.

"That's what excites me," Richard admitted, as he spun her. "I want to see what she can do."

"What she can do for you," Runa corrected him.

"That's what matters."

That was the Richard Galloborne she knew indeed.

Something to her left caught his attention, and Runa glanced over curiously. Richard looked over as well, and she saw him frown as they watched Carolyn Selelon dancing with Throthgar Thorinson.

"That's unexpected," Richard muttered.

It surprised Runa as well, but only for a moment. The more she considered the couple, the more natural it seemed.

"I think it's a suitable match," she admitted.

Richard looked a little doubtful.

"Are you going to make your announcement soon?" Runa asked, changing the subject. Both for her own interest, and to distract him from his clear confusion at the sight of Throthgar and Carolyn.

Richard looked around the room, then nodded. "I think now would be a good time."

As the song came to the end, Richard angled them toward the dais where the orchestra played. He sketched a bow to Runa before stepping onto it.

"If I may have your attention," he said.

Everyone in the ballroom turned towards him, a few people moving closer to the dais, while Runa had an ideal position. She found Godric appearing at her side, and she couldn't help but give him an annoyed look.

"There you are."

Richard went on before Godric could do more than look sheepish.

"I want to thank all of you for coming," Richard said. "It's been far too long since the Gallobornes hosted a ball, and I'm pleased that drought is finally at an end. My sister, Elizabeth, has exceeded my expectations."

He gestured to where Elizabeth stood with Azalea Gartner, and several other friends. She blushed to have so many eyes on her, but smiled at her brother's praise.

"The Summer Solstice is a time for us to celebrate the change of seasons. Traditionally, we celebrated surviving the winter, and the abundance Aurora blesses us with to prepare for the next one. It's a time to enjoy the fruits of our labor. A time when we enjoy our accomplishments - and show off. Lord Randell will be hosting his tournament, where many of our finest will compete."

He gestured to Geoffrey Randell, who raised his wine glass a little as all eyes turned to him.

Runa couldn't help but roll her eyes at Geoffrey's smug expression.

The Randells had hosted a tournament for the Summer Solstice for generations. A fact he was needlessly proud of. Though it was one of the most anticipated events of the year.

Her friend Elaine Howell, a pretty redheaded woman two years older than Runa, came to stand beside her.

"I can't wait for that smirk to be wiped off his face," Elaine whispered.

Runa nodded in agreement.

"I wish Henry the best in the tournament." Richard raised his glass in a toast to Henry Gerrod, who looked sheepish as so many turned towards him. As if he hadn't been the champion for the past two years in a row. Vera gave him a proud smile, squeezing his arm.

Geoffrey gave his son-in-law a pleased look. But then Richard's words seemed to register, and his smile slipped a little. If he were anyone else, Runa might have felt a moment of pity for him.

"But we have a tradition that has stood for much longer than the Randell tournament," Richard went on, unapologetic for what he was about to do. "Tonight, we have the honor of hosting Lord Marcus Di Antonio. It is a source of personal pride that we were able to coax him out of the Aurellian District tonight." He paused to allow the polite applause. "Tomorrow, he will preside over the opening ceremony for the gladiatorial games in the arena."

Marcus stepped up beside Richard, Lucilla glittering on his arm.

"Since the days of the Empire, the games have represented strength and power," Marcus said, his voice a little deeper than Richard's. He was impossible to ignore, both a preening peacock and a commanding general.

Beside her, Runa felt Godric stand up a little straighter. No doubt a habit from several years spent serving under Marcus.

"It's a tradition that continues here in Cardea. And which it is my great honor to preside over," he went on.

There was a polite smattering of applause around the room. Heartier expressions came from those who enjoyed the arena, and the gladiators.

"And it's a point of personal pride to sponsor the two reigning champions of the arena." He gestured grandly to the curtain over a door next to the dais. "Aelia Orsini, Panther of the Arena! Hero of the Battle of Delorway Hill in the Cymbrian War, and a three-year champion among the female gladiators."

As he spoke, the red velvet curtain drew back, and Aelia Orsini strode into the ballroom, with a grace that suited her title. The red and gold show armor she wore flaunted her long, toned limbs, and bronze skin. Her long, dark hair was colored golden blonde at the ends, woven into braids tied up at the back of her head. Under one arm, she carried her helmet, which featured a prowling panther ornament, and a plume of black feathers.

This time, there was more applause. But a decided difference between the polite, and the enthusiastic.

As Aelia shifted her weight onto one leg, her lips didn't smirk, but her eyes did.

When the applause died away, Marcus gestured to the doorway again.

"Lucius Gaspari, the Lion of the Arena!"

Runa caught a flash of annoyance from Richard. She knew well how irritating he found it that Marcus's gladiator was represented by the animal the Galloбornes claimed as their sigil.

Lucius, meanwhile, seemed to relish that all eyes were on him as he stalked over to the dais. His dark hair was close-cropped, skin the same bronze tone as Aelia's. Also like Aelia, his armor was designed to show off his body, and powerful muscles. The helmet tucked under his arm featured a roaring lion's head, and a red feather plume.

A few of the illuminating glass orbs shifted closer to them, shining off the polished show armor the gladiators wore.

Runa glanced around, looking for Hammond. Sure enough, she found him standing in a corner, hands moving subtly as he manipulated the lights.

"I've said before that Aelia and Lucius may well be some of the finest gladiators ever to set foot in an arena, and I stand by that," Marcus said, with the tone of a proud father.

Runa swore she saw Lucius' chest swell in pride, his dark eyes flashing as the corner of his mouth twitched in a smile. Aelia wasn't as obvious, but she still looked smug, sweeping her long braids over her shoulder.

"Many of you know that I've long held a deep respect for the arena," Richard said, drawing attention back to him. "And tonight, I have an announcement."

⸙ CHAPTER 2 ⸙

Runa could see Richard savoring the moment. He looked over the ballroom, where everyone waited to hear his announcement. She knew what it would be, but still found herself caught up in the anticipation.

"For years now, I've been interested in sponsoring a gladiator. But I was determined to find one who could rival even the mighty Aelia and Lucius. Someone who deserved to stand in the arena, and represent this long tradition that has symbolized the power of Aurellia, and now Cardea."

Runa leaned towards Elaine. "I notice Marcus doesn't look insulted. He must have found someone truly impressive."

From the corner of her eye, she saw Geoffrey seething in the corner. He had never tolerated anyone trying to take attention away from his tournament. The arena's opening ceremonies had always offended him, never mind that it was a tradition dating back further than Cardea. But Richard making such a show of it would draw even more nobles into the arena.

"On a visit to Breakwater Landing last year, I visited one of the arenas there, and I found what I've been searching for."

A shiver raced down Runa's spine, and she found herself squeezing Elaine's hand.

"May I present at last: My gladiator." Richard's voice rose, resounding through the room. He waved a hand, and the velvet curtain over a doorway beside the dais was pulled back one more time. "Lagan Stiggson, Master of the Seas!"

The gladiator stepped through the doorway, striding across the dais, as the lights came to focus on him, just as they had on Aelia and Lucius a moment earlier.

Richard had spared no expense on his gladiator's show armor. Dark blue lacquered pauldrons detailed in gold were held in place with polished black leather straps. Like most gladiators, his legs were bare, save for a skirt that came to just above his knees, teasing at the powerful muscles in his thighs, with bracers on his shins. He was shirtless save for those leather straps across his chest.

"Runa, breathe." Elaine giggled, squeezing her arm.

Runa inhaled shakily, realizing she had been so distracted by the sculpted muscles of his chest and stomach that she had forgotten to do just that.

Like Aelia and Lucius, he carried his helmet under one arm, though Runa couldn't quite make out the crest, only the blue feather plume. His hair was dark, falling past his shoulders, though the front was pulled back so his handsome, clean-shaven face was shown off to advantage. When he came to stand near the others, she saw he was taller than Lucius, and just as broad. They sized each other up, but there didn't seem to be any animosity.

"Impressive," Godric murmured.

"Leave it to Richard to find someone who could rival Lucius," Runa said, unable to take her eyes off the gladiator.

Lagan's gaze swept over the crowd, clearly undaunted at being the center of attention. If anything, he seemed to enjoy it.

His eyes met hers, and Runa became suddenly aware of her heart pounding in her chest. She squeezed Elaine's hand, needing an anchor before that look swept her away like an undertow.

Richard was speaking again, and Lagan turned his gaze back to his sponsor.

"I've never seen you react to a man like that," Elaine whispered, brow arched in amusement.

"I never have!" Runa whispered back. She wasn't sure what to do. This sensation was utterly new, and she had no idea how to respond.

He wasn't from Cardea, she was sure of that. If she had to guess, he was from the tribes that lived on the northern islands, or the tundra. He had the bearing of someone who had grown up in a rugged land. But he had left before the cold winds could wear away his good looks.

She realized she had been so lost in her thoughts that she had failed to pay attention to what Richard was saying.

Lagan was watching her again. The corner of his mouth twisted in a smug, but very dashing smile.

Runa wanted to be annoyed at the arrogance, but found she was flattered at being singled out.

Again, she realized she had tuned Richard out. And her attention was only drawn back when Marcus spoke.

"To be clear," the Aurellian prefect said. "Tomorrow will be the first time these two will face each other. They've never fought in the arena, or the training yard."

That got the attention of several people in the crowd. Runa had never paid enough attention to the arena to know if that mattered to most people.

Lagan and Lucius exchanged looks, making a show of sizing each other up. Runa was sure that it was staged, even as they both squared their shoulders, puffing out their chests. Aelia smirked as she watched, shifting her weight, hip cocked, and adjusting her braids again.

Runa was far from the only person in the room thinking about anything but their prowess in the arena.

"They certainly play off each other perfectly," Elaine murmured.

Typical for Richard, that the pieces would all land so perfectly for him.

"What's his weapon?" someone asked.

Lagan gave a cocky smile. "You'll have to find out tomorrow."

Richard gave a satisfied smile of approval.

"A trident." Runa hadn't realized she was speaking until the words were out of her mouth.

But the way Lagan paused, as if momentarily thrown off, confirmed her guess.

"How do you know?" someone asked.

Rathdrum, she realized.

She looked at Richard, who was giving her an annoyed look. "You called him the Master of the Seas. What else could it be?"

When she looked back at Lagan, his mouth was curled in a smile again as he watched her. She was used to that flash of respect when she took people by surprise. In this case, she returned the smile. But only a little.

"You'll see tomorrow," Richard said. "If you decide to grace us with your presence, Lady Sorensen."

Runa met his gaze, making sure he knew his condescending tone didn't amuse her. Neither was she intimidated by that infamous lion glare. She never had been, and certainly wasn't about to start now.

Next to her, Elaine giggled. And she noticed

Hammond hiding a chuckle as he stood off to the side.

She thought Lagan's gaze was still on her, but she avoided looking in his direction. Until she couldn't resist.

He was. And their eyes locked again.

Richard had recovered, once more in control as he spoke.

Marcus waved, and Lucius missed it, but Aelia smacked Lucius' shoulder to get him to move. She jerked her head to the door beside the dais. The three of them saluted the crowd with a fist pressed to their chests.

Lagan was behind the others, and he glanced over his shoulder. Giving Runa one last look before he returned to the antechamber.

The red velvet curtain fell closed behind them, but an air of anticipation hung over the ballroom.

"Until tomorrow," Marcus said.

Richard nodded. "Until tomorrow."

The two men clasped wrists, their friendly rivalry visible in every inch of their body language.

Richard turned back to the crowd, with a more genuine smile than Runa had seen on him in years. "As I said, this has been a goal of mine for years now. I'm looking forward to tomorrow. Until then, however." He held up his glass of wine in a toast to the crowd. "Enjoy the ball." With a slight bow to his guests, he stepped down from the dais.

"Are we going?" Elaine asked.

Runa hesitated. She had only been to the arena a few times. It wasn't her preferred entertainment. And she had planned to attend Azalea Gartner's birthday party.

"I think so," she said, her thoughts still filled with the memory of the gladiator's intense, warm brown eyes.

≈⊰ CHAPTER 3 ⊱≈

The antechamber off the ballroom was twice the size of the hut Lagan had grown up in. By the time he had been fifteen, he had been forced to duck through the doorways, and under the beams. But the antechamber's ceiling was high enough that his fingers didn't even brush it if he jumped up. It was luxuriously decorated, with two armchairs and a settee upholstered in red velvet, with gold gilt on the dark wood. A scarlet carpet with a gold design worked into it was set before the fireplace, though there was no fire lit at the moment.

On one wall was an ornately carved sideboard. The remnants of their dinner had been cleared away, but there was still a glass pitcher rimmed with gold, filled with water, and a set of matching glasses.

"That couldn't have gone better," Lucius said, his voice deep and boisterous.

Lagan couldn't help but grin as he went over to the sideboard and poured himself a glass of cold water. He raised the tumbler to Lucius in a mock toast before taking a drink. "Well, I had a good mentor."

Lucius' chest puffed out, and he started to respond.

"Aelia," Lagan said, before Lucius could say anything. "Your instruction has been invaluable."

Lucius deflated, shooting Lagan a glare.

"You're welcome." Aelia resumed her seat, lounging in one of the armchairs with her long legs stretched out and crossed at the ankles. Her glass still sat on the dark wood side table. "You can pay me back by wiping the arena with Lucius' arrogant ass tomorrow."

"I think I can manage that," Lagan said, taking a seat in one of the other armchairs.

Lucius huffed. "Traitors. Both of you."

Aelia smirked, giving Lucius a mock salute with her glass before taking a sip. "You call yourself a champion, but you've never actually had a real challenge in the arena. I'm looking forward to tomorrow."

Despite his indignation, Lucius recovered quickly, and turned to Lagan. "Was it as easy as you expected?"

Lagan rubbed his jaw as he took a moment to reflect.

He hadn't seen a reason to be nervous beforehand. In Breakwater Landing, he had earned plenty of attention for his exploits in the arena there. He had been sponsored by a merchant named Colum Doherty, and in the thriving port city, he had enjoyed the lavish parties the merchants threw. But when Richard had offered him Callatis, he hadn't been able to resist.

At the time, he had thought the city couldn't surprise him. He had thought he had seen grandeur and opulence. And he saw no reason to be intimidated by people simply because of their wealth, or titles that meant nothing to him. Underneath it all, they still breathed and bled like any other person. He had told Aelia and Lucius as much, and they had exchanged amused looks.

When they had rehearsed the presentation earlier that day, the ballroom had seemed impossibly large. He hadn't realized a single room could be so massive.

But it had been one thing to see in the daylight, with sunlight coming through the massive windows, empty save for the servants taking care of last-minute preparations.

Seeing it filled with the nobles as they glittered, with the heady scent of flowers and perfumes, had been another thing entirely.

"Not quite," he admitted.

Lucius chuckled sympathetically. "I can appreciate that you're not intimidated by wealth. But their wealth isn't their weapon - it's their attitude."

"I see what you mean," Lagan admitted.

He was used to being sized up, and having all eyes on him. As a sailor, he had faced mercenaries, pirates, and even monsters. He enjoyed non-hostile attention. But he had never experienced that kind of intense judgment. Even wild animals that wanted to eat him hadn't made him feel so much like a piece of meat.

Lucius sat down on the settee, leaning back against the armrest while he stretched his legs along the length. "Most of them wouldn't last five minutes in the arena. But no one judges us more intensely."

"We're entertainment," Aelia reminded. "They're deciding if we're worth the price of admission."

And Lagan understood that.

But despite all the eyes on him, and their unflinching scrutiny, only one pair stood out in his memory.

"Who was the woman with red hair?" he asked. "In the blue dress."

They didn't ask who he meant.

"Runa Sorensen." Lucius grinned. "You do like a challenge, don't you?"

Runa Sorensen. He repeated the name silently, feeling a shiver dance up his spine. "The Sorensens are a ruling family?"

Lagan had been given some education on the social hierarchy of Cardea, particularly the city. Richard thought it essential that he knew the important families, whether they were ruling class,powerful, or wealthy. He had studied the names, but they had all blended together with so little context.

Aelia nodded. "Yes."

Lagan's thoughts fixated on her. Those clever green eyes, and soft, dark red curls around her fair face. The way the dark blue silk had hugged the curves of her body—the curve of her red-painted lips when she had given him that confident, self-assured smile.

"The Sorensens and Gallobornes are allies," Aelia said helpfully. "Runa and Richard grew up together, and they're close friends. So to speak."

"Does she come to the arena?"

"Careful," Lucius warned. "Her father is notoriously protective."

"I just asked if she comes to the arena," Lagan said, trying to keep his tone light.

"Rarely," Aelia said.

"Seemed like you caught her attention, though," Lucius said. "And Godric seemed interested as well. He'll probably come."

Aelia looked up from taking a drink. "Did you know Godric was back in the city?"

Lucius shook his head. "I thought he was still stationed at Sun Pass."

Lagan looked between them questioningly.

"Stark business," Aelia said. "Godric is Runa's cousin. The man who was standing next to her."

He nodded, vaguely aware that she had once whispered to a man next to her.

The heavy velvet curtain over the doorway was pulled back, and all three gladiators looked over as Richard and Marcus entered the antechamber.

"Well done," Richard said, looking at Lagan in approval. "We certainly got them talking."

"Now you two just need to give them a fight worth that talk," Marcus said.

"That should be easy enough." It would be easier than facing that crowd again, Lagan thought.

"Good," Richard said. "I would hate to disappoint them."

"For now, head home and get some rest," Marcus said, looking at all three of them for a moment. "Tomorrow we'll really give them a show."

Beauty & The Wolf (reprise)

◌◌ CHAPTER 4 ◌◌

The ballroom descended into excited chatter as soon as the curtain fell behind the gladiators. People asked their friends where they would be the next day - at the Randell tournament in the fields outside the city, or in the stands of the arena. And once that was settled, the debate began as to which gladiator would be the victor.

Carolyn felt a pang of sympathy for Azalea Gartner, whose birthday was on the Solstice. Her birthday celebration seemed to be forgotten as they all discussed the gladiator.

But when she looked over to where Azalea was speaking with Elizabeth Galloborne, she didn't seem at all upset by it. So perhaps it didn't bother her.

Carolyn herself had no idea where she would be. Her father was friends and allies with Geoffrey Randell, so he would undoubtedly attend the tournament. Her brother Quinten also planned to compete, while the other two disliked Marcus and Richard.

She had no doubt Phillipa would be at the arena. Though her attention would be on Richard, far more than on the gladiators.

Her thoughts were interrupted when Throthgar took her hand, and he leaned in to whisper in her ear. His hot breath on her neck sent a shiver down her spine. "Will you walk in the garden with me?"

He looked into her eyes as he waited for her answer.

"I would love to," she admitted. As much as she enjoyed dancing, the ballroom had begun to feel overly warm, and close.

Throthgar smiled as he offered her his arm, leading her to the closest set of double doors, which opened onto the terrace. The table from dinner had already been cleared away as if it had never been.

Others had the same idea, coming out to linger in the fresh, floral-scented air.

They descended the short steps down to the stone path that led into the garden, where enchanted glass orbs hovered along the path, making it easy to follow.

Overhead, the two moons, Callista and Larissa, provided more than enough light on their own. The months of Aurorstra and Selentra were the only times the moons entered the same cycle, while the summer and winter solstices were the only nights when they were both full. They were bright in the black velvet sky, surrounded by twinkling stars, shining down on them with soft, silver light.

Realizing she had come to a stop, Throthgar stood beside her.

"Isn't it beautiful?" She sighed as she looked up at the sky, and the constellations in their endless dance.

"It is," he said. "Almost as beautiful as you."

Carolyn blushed, lowering her eyes to meet his. "Do you mean that?"

"I do," he said. "I almost didn't come tonight, but now I'm glad I did."

"Why did you come?"

She spent most of her time in the city, and attended parties regularly. While her family's circle wasn't particularly fond of the Thorinsons, that wasn't enough to explain how she had never met him before.

He nodded back towards the manor as they continued into the garden. "I wanted to see Richard's gladiator, but could have waited until tomorrow."

"How did you know what the announcement was? Phillipa said he was trying to keep it a secret."

"Lucius and I have a mutual friend. I think he let it slip to her."

Carolyn giggled, imagining the tall, intimidating gladiator gossiping with a friend. "Will you be attending the games tomorrow, then?"

"Definitely." He turned to look at her. "Will you?"

"I don't think Phillipa will give me much choice," she said. That would be her excuse if her parents tried to insist she should attend the tournament.

"Then I'll—" Throthgar stopped, looking to his right as if he had heard something.

A moment later, Carolyn heard a soft, breathy gasp. Throthgar quirked an eyebrow in amusement, while she suppressed a giggle. They both peeked around the tall, wrought iron frame that created a tunnel of wisteria flowers.

Just as she had thought, they saw a couple tangled in an embrace under the flowers. Moonlight through the branches revealed the shape of them as they kissed. Carolyn blushed, biting back another giggle. Not that she could stop watching, finding herself entranced by the scene.

As they shifted, the man ran his fingers through long, honey-blonde curls that fell down the woman's back.

Grabbing the cuff of Throthgar's sleeve, she tugged him away.

"It's Corion and Bronwyn," she whispered, a giggle finally escaping her.

Throthgar smirked. "That's what I thought."

He took her hand, pulling her deeper into the garden to give Corion and Bronwyn privacy.

"I'm surprised they're still here," he said.

"Not for much longer, I imagine," Carolyn said. She hoped a twinge of envy didn't sneak into her voice.

While Corion and Bronwyn rarely ever arrived at parties together, they always seemed to leave at the same time.

"They're not very subtle, are they?"

"I think it's romantic," she admitted.

"Romantic, but not subtle," he grinned, making her giggle again.

"This will loop back around to the house," he said, leading her along the path. "But I'm not quite ready to go back inside yet."

"Neither am I," she agreed. She hesitated a moment, debating if she should say the next words. "I'm glad you came tonight."

"I am too." He squeezed her hand.

Carolyn's heart fluttered in her chest, and for a moment she was light-headed, swooning at his gentle voice.

"I shouldn't let you charm me so easily," she murmured, the practical side of her winning against her romanticism. At least for a moment.

"Why not?" He stopped, turning to face her. And the light of the two moons was enough for her to see his expression, which seemed earnest.

It was hard to remember. Even more so when he reached to brush her hair off her forehead. She very nearly swooned again.

"Phillipa says I'm far too romantic," she admitted. Her cousin was far from the only one. "I read too many novels with happy endings, and get carried away with daydreams."

As soon as the words were out of her mouth, she wondered if perhaps she was being too honest. Maybe she shouldn't admit such a weakness to a man she didn't know.

"I understand," he said. His knuckles brushed lightly against her cheek. "But my world changed the moment I saw you. Now all I want is to make you smile."

Her cheeks warmed as she blushed, and she looked down to hide her smile.

Throthgar chuckled, lifting her chin. "There you are."

For a moment, she wondered if he would kiss her. Wondered if she wanted him to. Part of her certainly did... but not yet. She turned her head slightly, eyes drifting down to the stones beneath her feet.

"I'm in no hurry." His thumb stroked her cheek.

"Does that mean you're going to court me properly?" she asked, gaze returning to his. She didn't quite believe it. But she wanted to.

She desperately wanted to.

The corner of his mouth curled at a slightly different angle, creating a roguish grin. And the expression made her knees weak.

"I should warn you, I'm not entirely proper," he said. "But I'll do my best."

Another giggle escaped her, and he squeezed her hand.

"In which case, we should probably go back inside," he said. "Before anyone thinks we're following Corion and Bronwyn's example. I wouldn't want to make a poor impression."

"I doubt anyone noticed I'm gone." She sighed, looking toward the light that emanated from the open doors of the ballroom.

Her parents hardly noticed her at any time. Certainly not when they were surrounded by the distractions of a ball. They would be too busy avoiding each other as they spoke with friends. If it went well, they might even be able to stand each other for the next fortnight. Her brothers and their wives would all be similarly occupied.

"Hammond noticed," he said, without a hint of doubt. "Phillipa probably did, too. And she seems to have Richard's ear."

Carolyn found herself drifting closer to him as they continued up the path.

"Are you afraid of the Galloborne lion?" she asked.

"I'm afraid of how my cousin might curse me if I make Richard angry," Throthgar admitted.

"I never thought of Hammond as particularly frightening," she said. "I doubt he could threaten you."

She couldn't stop her gaze from sweeping over him, and the way his broad shoulders filled out his shirt. She had felt his solid muscles when they danced.

Hammond had gained some level of fame for his accomplishments during the war, but they were easy to forget. His reputation was as a politician, and a scholar.

Throthgar gave her a toothy smile. "In a fair fight, no."

She gave him a quizzical look, but he just smiled as he led her up the steps, back onto the terrace.

"Family secret," he said.

The warm lights, and the music, welcomed them back into the ballroom. And Carolyn sighed as she was once more awed by the majesty of the room.

"Shall we dance?" he asked, a hand coming to rest lightly on her lower back, the warmth from the touch spreading across her skin.

"Yes." As if she could give any other answer.

Throthgar smiled, sweeping her back onto the floor.

Wolf's Lullaby

⊰ CHAPTER 1 ⊱

Hammond rarely lingered at balls, or any party for that matter. Usually, he would put in the required appearance, then make an exit as soon as he wouldn't be missed. He preferred to be gone long before midnight, returning to the comfortable quiet of his study.

But tonight, he had known there would be no chance to slip away. Richard would expect him to be there no matter how late the other guests stayed.

A few guests made their excuses after Richard's announcement. But most were perfectly content to stay, so he knew it would be a while. Thankfully, the next day's events meant no one would want to stay until dawn. Hammond clung to that knowledge.

He avoided the dance floor, choosing instead to make the rounds among the guests.

One of his first stops was with Byron. It wasn't surprising that Throthgar had confronted him about Signy. Thankfully, Caitlyn seemed more miffed than her brother. But both of them assured him they understood.

An hour or so before midnight, the Starks took their leave. They were the first ruling family to leave, and left the door open for others to follow.

Hammond was talking to Stefan Marszalek when he saw them leave.

While he did his best to hide his envy, across the room he saw that Godric didn't bother. His eyes followed the Starks out, clearly wishing he could go with them. But they all knew Runa wouldn't dream of leaving early, and she wouldn't let her cousin leave without her. She was currently deep in conversation with Elizabeth, Azalea Gartner, and several other girls. Hammond couldn't tell if it was a serious conversation or simple gossip.

While Runa was fending off half the bachelors in the room, more than a few young women had attempted to get close to Godric throughout the evening. He was second in line for the Sorensen family's seat on the ruling council. And while no one thought he would ascend to that position, he was still a member of a ruling family, with land in the Sorensen territory, and a considerable fortune—more than enough to mark him as a prize.

None had succeeded, though. The only people Hammond had seen him dancing with that evening were Runa, Elizabeth, and Elaine. All of whom he was safe from.

Finally, Hammond finished making small talk, and made his way towards the satee Godric had claimed in a small alcove.

"Has the great Hammond Thorinson finally deigned to greet his childhood friend?" Godric asked as he approached.

Hammond chuckled sheepishly. Godric and Runa shared many things, not the least of which was their dry sense of humor. And the ability to make you feel self-conscious with a single look.

But while Runa was adept at the subtlety of society, Godric was a soldier.

"I saved the best for last," Hammond said.

Godric scoffed, but lowered his arm from the back of the satee and moved to the side to make room. "You're certainly at home here."

"Am I?" Hammond glanced around the ballroom as he sank onto the settee. "I don't feel it."

There were still quite a few people in the ballroom, but a few more were leaving, including Geoffrey Randall and his wife. Henry caught Hammond's eye and inclined his head in a silent good night as he and Vera trailed after her parents.

"I'm surprised they didn't leave right after the announcement," Godric muttered.

"He wouldn't dare," Hammond said. "That would mean admitting Richard got to him."

"We all know he did. What's the point?"

"The principle of the issue."

Godric chuckled. "And you say you don't fit in."

He did have a point.

Hammond's eyes drifted to the mural on the far wall again—the familiar mountains and trees.

"Graham's work?" Godric asked.

Hammond nodded. "A little too well done. It's making me miss the Rest."

The days spent running through the fields with Godric, Graham, and their friend Alex, had been so much simpler. And at this moment, he longed for those golden summer days.

"I'm going north as soon as I can," Godric said.

"As soon as Runa lets you?" Hammond couldn't resist turning the tables after being called out.

Godric rolled his eyes. But they both knew his cousin was one of his few weaknesses. "I'm surprised you're here. Isn't tomorrow your father's birthday?"

"Yes." It was probably why he found himself homesick tonight.

Right now, his family would be holding a bonfire behind the main house. Singing and dancing around the fire, feasting on the first fruits of the summer, and the meat of an elk from the woods. Aunt Düsana would be telling legends of the gods, and the family's history.

"But Richard asked me to be here tomorrow."

"The arena?"

Hammond nodded. "I've never seen him so excited about anything." He glanced at Richard, who looked no different than usual as he spoke with Stefan. "In his way."

He was looking forward to the arena as well. It was why he had stayed. And his father had agreed it would be best.

Godric looked toward the antechamber the gladiators had disappeared into. "Is he as impressive as he acts?"

"You'll have to see tomorrow," Hammond said, giving him a sly look.

"Bastard," Godric muttered. But he did look amused. "Well, the arena certainly sounds better than the Randell tournament."

"The other option is Azalea Gartner's birthday," Hammond said. "She's a Child of Aurora, too."

They both looked to where Azalea was still talking to Runa and Elizabeth. She was a lovely young woman, from one of the three original ruling families. Her long, golden blonde hair was woven into complex braids, her smile visible from across the ballroom.

"I'll send my regards," Godric said. "But the gladiator caught Runa's eye, and I think she'll be going to the arena."

"Really?" Hammond blinked in surprise, and looked to where Runa was giggling with the other girls. He knew she had guessed Lagan's weapon. But he hadn't been paying attention to her during the presentation.

"That was my thought," Godric said. "I can't miss that."

"Don't tell your uncle."

"I wouldn't dare."

Hammond hadn't seen Godric in a couple of years. But he was glad that they had fallen back into easy familiarity. It felt like ages since he had spent time with a friend, without business being involved. And there wasn't that lack of trust he sometimes felt with Graham.

A ballroom was hardly the best place to catch up, though.

"I'm going to the Rest for my birthday next week," Hammond said. "But we should find a night we're both free. I'll invite Kat, and a few others, and we can catch up properly."

"I'd like that," Godric said. "I haven't seen Kat yet."

"Don't wait too long," Hammond said. "She'll take it as an insult."

"I'll go the day after tomorrow," Godric said. "I still have a hard time imagining her as a business owner."

"She's taken to it," Hammond said. Though he felt himself blush a little as he thought about Katherine's shop.

Godric didn't miss it, and quirked an eyebrow... but took pity on him. "I'll let you know what nights I have free."

Hammond nodded. "I'll see who else is in the city."

Across the room, Runa drew away from the other girls, looking around the room until her eyes landed on them. Hammond saw hope glimmer in Godric's green eyes as she came over to them, Elaine at her side.

"Do you think she'll have mercy on me?" he asked.

Hammond chuckled, and they rose as Runa reached them.

"Are you ready to go home?"

Godric hugged her.

Runa laughed softly, returning the hug for a moment. "Let's say good night to Richard, then we can go."

Hammond followed them over to where Richard was talking to Marcus, and a few of the more sensible prefects.

"Are you leaving?" Richard asked.

"We are," Runa said, allowing Richard to kiss her cheek politely. "I said good night to Elizabeth, but I wanted to thank you for the evening. It didn't disappoint."

"Will you be at the arena tomorrow?" Richard asked, his tone a little challenging. He respected Runa, but could still hold a grudge.

"I think so," Runa said. And if she realized how much she was surprising the others, she showed no sign.

"Come to our home afterward," Lucilla said. "We'll have a room where you can rest, and change for the party. You can send your maid with a dress ahead of time. I'm afraid our box is full, or I would offer you a seat."

"I'm sure we can find seats," Runa said. "Thank you, Lucilla."

Marcus kissed her hand politely. "It would be a delight to offer our hospitality. I expect to see you as well, Godric."

"I'll be there," Godric said.

Marcus clapped a hand on Godric's shoulder. "Good man."

As Godric and Runa left, Elaine went over to her family, who left soon after.

Over the next hour or so, the rest of the guests drifted out. Until finally, Hammond followed Richard out of the ballroom, into the entryway, with the last handful of guests.

Among them were Phillipa, and the Selelons.

Throthgar and Carolyn stood away from the others in a small alcove. They spoke in hushed voices, while their gazes and fingers lingered on each other.

That was something Hammond would have to dwell on later, after he had rested.

Instead, he watched as Richard approached Phillipa.

He had observed their game all evening - the way Richard stepped towards her, and Phillipa sometimes let him, and sometimes slipped into the crowd.

This time, she turned toward him with a sweet smile. After leading him along all evening, it seemed she would reward him with a proper good night.

As Hammond didn't have anything else to do, curiosity got the better of him, and he drifted closer to see if he could eavesdrop on the conversation.

"I'm glad we have a moment," Richard said, without any sign of accusation.

"So am I," she said. "I had a wonderful evening."

"That was my sole aim," Richard said.

Hammond glanced over to see Phillipa's satisfied smile. But he was behind Richard, so he couldn't see his friend's expression.

"Will you be my guest at the arena tomorrow?" He asked.

"I would be honored," she said.

Hammond wondered if she was considering the fact that the Selelons would no doubt choose to attend Randell's tournament. But he suspected it wouldn't matter to her.

"I'll see you tomorrow, then," Richard said.

"I look forward to it."

Hammond shook his head. He understood Phillipa's game. In theory, at least. But he didn't understand the way Richard played along.

Phillipa kissed Richard's cheek, and gave him one last smile.

As she stepped away, she noticed Hammond, and gave him a knowing look. "It was a pleasure to meet you, Lord

Thorinson. I enjoyed our conversation at dinner."

Richard turned back, and Hammond had no doubt that his friend knew he had been listening.

"It was a pleasure to finally meet you, Lady Phillipa." He stepped closer, and accepted her hand to kiss it. "I enjoyed our conversation as well."

Finally, the Selelons left. Phillipa gave Richard a last look over her shoulder as she followed them out.

The last guest in the hall was Carolyn, who looked after her family, but seemed reluctant to leave Throthgar. Even when she tried to, Throthgar didn't let go of her hands. And she certainly didn't seem to resist as he pulled her back to him. If anything, Hammond thought he saw her sigh as she smiled.

They exchanged a few more words, and Hammond thought Carolyn might melt as his cousin spoke. Throthgar raised her hands, kissing her knuckles, before finally letting her go. Her steps faltered a little.

Hammond shook his head, going over to Throthgar. "I guess you enjoyed the party."

"I did," Throthgar said, with his wolfish grin. He stepped outside, into the light of the moons, and the glass orbs that still glowed cheerfully.

Hammond followed him onto the step.

Together they watched as a footman helped Carolyn into her family's carriage. And Throthgar only looked away once the carriage was out of sight.

"Carolyn Selelon?" Hammond asked, looking over at his cousin.

Throthgar shrugged. "I'm just as surprised as you."

Hammond gave a bemused smile, looking up at the two moons, which appeared almost full. Not quite, he knew.

"I'll see you tomorrow?" Throthgar asked.

"You'll be at the arena?"

"I wouldn't miss it," Throthgar said.

"Then yes, I'll see you tomorrow," Hammond said. "Have a good night."

When Throthgar had passed through the gate, turning toward the city, Hammond returned to the manor.

With the last of the guests gone, Richard was shedding his black and gold vest as Hammond approached him.

Before either of them could speak, they heard footsteps on the stairs.

"Good. All the fools are gone."

❦ CHAPTER 2 ❧

Like a mournful ghost haunting the halls of the manor, Matilda Galloborne stepped out of the shadows on the stairs. Her black silk dressing gown trailed behind her, in stark contrast with her pale skin.

This was the first time in years Hammond had seen her without jewelry, or the dark makeup she always wore. Without it, she looked even more like a wraith wandering the halls. There was almost nothing left of the girl Hammond had known as a child—only a woman filled with malice and disdain.

She had been beautiful, in a sharp, statuesque way. But it had faded in the last few years of wine and self-neglect.

The golden glow that lingered from the ball dissipated, snuffed out by her very presence.

"I didn't think you would be awake," Richard said.

Matilda's lips pursed, her eyes haunted. "I wasn't. Then I woke up, and discovered I was out of wine."

"Isn't it a little late for wine?" Hammond asked.

As soon as the words had left his mouth, he wished he hadn't said anything. Even before Matilda glared at him, her upper lip curling in disgust.

"Early, you mean." Richard gestured to the grandfather clock nearby.

The intricate clock face told them it was nearly half past two.

"I don't care," Matilda said, surprising neither of them. She looked at Richard. "Well? How was your ball?"

"It went well," Richard said, not bothering to give details they all knew she had no interest in.

"Miss Bellerose was impressed?" She didn't hide the disapproval in her voice. But then, it seemed as though everything she said was tinged with disapproval.

"I think so," Richard said.

"And your announcement?"

"It went well," Richard said, chest swelling in pride at the success.

Matilda sighed. "Is this necessary, Richard? It just seems like such a waste of time and money."

"So you've said." Richard gave his sister an annoyed look.

When they were side-by-side, it was easier to see their resemblance. Even without the Galloborne coloring, they had the same eyes, the same body language, and many of the same expressions. Both of them had their lips pressed together in a thin line, holding each other's gaze. Two immovable forces at odds with each other.

"I don't know which is worse," Matilda said. "Your pursuit of this Bellerose girl, or wasting time in the arena. Honestly, Richard, I thought you were smarter than most of these idiots."

Richard glared at her. "Go get your wine, Matilda. I'm going to bed."

She started, looking at her brother in surprise.

Hammond suspected that much of her attitude was to keep people at a distance, but Richard was the one who ignored that. He didn't seem to notice how difficult she was. So it always took Matilda by surprise when she pushed him to a breaking point.

"Hammond, are you staying here tonight?" Richard asked, turning away from his sister.

Hammond blinked, taking a moment to catch up with the sudden turn in the conversation. "Yes. I have everything I need for tomorrow here."

Richard nodded. "Good. You'll stay for breakfast, of course."

"Of course," Hammond said.

"Then I'll see you in the morning," Richard said. He looked back to his sister, who stood stubbornly beside him, looking offended. "Good night, Matilda." He turned towards the stairs, heading towards his room.

Matilda huffed. "Honestly."

Hammond knew not to walk into that trap. "Have a good night, Matilda."

He followed Richard up the stairs, turning down the hall to the guest room he used when staying at the Galloborne manor.

It was about the same size as the bedroom above his shop, though less personal. Like the rest of the house, the furniture was black polished wood, with gold gilt work. There was a four-poster bed, and a sideboard against the wall to the right of the door. A pair of double doors led out onto a balcony, and the sight through the glass called to him.

Hammond went over to the sideboard, where a water pitcher waited, next to a set of tumblers and mugs. Along with a tin of tea leaves he had brought from home. He murmured an incantation to boil the water as he poured it over the tea infuser, then left it to steep as he changed into a pair of sleep pants.

He took the tea out onto the balcony, taking a deep breath of the cool, fresh air. Letting his breath out slowly, he leaned back against the balcony railing.

Now it was quiet enough to hear the river murmur as it tripped over the stones. The light breeze that moved through the garden beneath the balcony carried the sweet scent of flowers.

As he took several slow, deep breaths, he finally began to calm down.

Long periods of time around large groups of people wore him down the way few things did. But they were an essential part of his position.

He sighed again. How was it possible that all his cousins were so difficult? And how had it become his responsibility to keep them in line?

It occurred to him that this interest in Carolyn Selelon might be a good influence on Throthgar. Perhaps she could tame the Wild Wolf a bit.

But for now, he brushed those thoughts aside. There was nothing to be done about it tonight, or even tomorrow.

Taking a sip of his tea, he looked up at the two moons.

Callista and Larissa. The eyes of Selene, the Titan of Dusk.

Only during the months of the Solstices did they come into sync, becoming full on the solstice itself.

He remembered the first time he had heard his aunt Düsana tell the story of Selene's handmaidens.

They had been mortal elves once - priestesses in Selene's temple. Until the First War of Ruin, when Seneca the Fallen God had attacked the temple. Callista and Larissa had stood against him in a desperate stand to guard the temple. They, and the temple, had fallen before the Titan sisters arrived to force Seneca back. But their loyalty had been rewarded with immortality, and a position of honor as Selene's handmaidens. They were charged with watching over the mortal world, and reporting back to their mistress.

The story had haunted Hammond ever since. He sometimes caught himself thinking about the kind of faith it took to stand against a god, even when you stood no chance of defeating him.

He turned his gaze to the city. At least from here, everything seemed quiet. Most people were probably asleep by now, resting before the busyness of the next day. And as Hammond finished his tea, he decided he was ready to do the same.

For a moment he lingered on the balcony, though. And found himself wondering where Heather was. A thought that had crossed his mind several times in the last few days. As much as he was looking forward to the arena the next day, he was looking forward to a few days after that even more, when he would see her again.

He looked up at Callista and Larissa one last time, and he felt as if they looked back at him.

A shiver ran up his spine, but he told himself it was just his exhaustion making him imagine things.

Taking a deep breath, he turned back inside.

The Evening Air

It was only a few minutes carriage ride between the Galloborne house and Sorensens'. But as they pulled through the gate with the gold-plated orchid sigil, Runa was ready to climb into bed. As pleasant as the evening had been, it had been a long one.

When the carriage pulled up to the steps of the house, a footman in the dark blue Sorensen livery opened the door for them.

As soon as he helped Runa step down onto the gravel walk, she was greeted by the sweetness of the fresh air, and the scent of flowers blooming in the gardens around the house, while the fountain behind her splashed cheerfully.

Godric sighed in relief as he stepped out of the carriage.

"Was that so bad?" Runa asked. Despite how tired she was, she wanted to linger in the fresh air for a moment.

"Yes," Godric said decidedly. "Never do that to me again."

"I make no promises."

He glared at her, but she refused to be intimidated by it.

"We have the victory party tomorrow, remember?"

Godric followed her up the steps of the house. "You're serious about going to the arena, then?"

The footman held the door open for them, and Runa nodded her thanks, but didn't pause on her way to the staircase. Godric was close behind her. He had already taken off his formal vest, which he had slung over his shoulder. No doubt he would toss it in a corner as soon as he reached his room.

Unlike the blacks and reds of the Galloborne's decor, the Sorensen house was made up in peacock blues and greens. With gold gilt work on the relief detailing, and the swirls of the banister. The curtains on the tall windows were pulled back, flooding the room with moonlight.

"Well, I certainly don't plan to attend Randell's tournament," she said.

"You usually attend Azalea's birthday party, don't you?"

"Usually," she admitted.

It was far more appealing than the Randell tournament. Most years, it was also more appealing than the Di Antonio arena. A quiet day at the Gartner home was far more enjoyable than the heat and noise of the arena.

Azalea had told her to go to the arena tomorrow, however. "I wouldn't keep you from that."

Runa had blushed... but she did want to see Lagan fight.

"Richard has wanted this for so long, it seems right to support him," she added.

"Him, or his gladiator?"

Runa paused on the first landing, looking back at him. "I don't know what you're talking about."

"I'm sure you don't." He didn't believe her.

Not that she had expected him to. But that didn't mean she had to acknowledge it.

"Your father is planning to go," Godric reminded her.

"I know," she said.

Her father attended the arena regularly during the summer, and rarely missed the Summer Solstice games. Runa herself had gone a handful of times, but this was the first time she had the desire to go for her own reasons.

"I would tease you about Lagan, but I'm too tired to think of something clever right now," Godric said.

"Get some rest, then. I'm sure you'll have plenty of opportunities tomorrow."

"I'm still not forgiving you for tonight," he said, poking her waist playfully.

Runa didn't have the energy to swat his hand away, so she settled for giving him an unamused look.

"Good night, Godric," was all she said as she turned down the hallway to her rooms.

"Good night, Runa."

Her room was in a corner at the back of the house, with windows along two walls that looked out over the gardens. When she stepped inside, the double doors to her balcony were open, allowing the breeze to carry in the evening air.

The thin, light blue summer blankets on her four-poster bed were already turned down, the enchanted orbs dimmed to a soft, welcoming glow. It was peaceful and quiet, making Runa sigh as she closed the door behind her.

As much as she had enjoyed the ball, it was still a relief to escape to her own space, away from the crowds.

Her maid, Gianna De Leone, was laying her nightgown out on the bed. She was a few inches taller than Runa, her dark brown hair braided down her back. "Welcome back, m'lady."

"Thank you, Gianna." Runa returned her smile.

"I have a bath waiting for you, so you can relax before bed." Gianna came over, and began unlacing the back of Runa's bodice. "How was the ball?"

"Better than I expected. I don't think there was anything scandalous. And Elizabeth put together a beautiful ball."

As Gianna helped remove her skirt, petticoats, and crinoline cage, Runa thought back over the evening.

Throthgar and Carolyn dancing was the most shocking thing she could think of, as she looked back. And that was enough to make people talk, but not to cause a scandal. It might have caused more of a stir if people knew who Throthgar was. But he would just have been a handsome stranger to most of them. At the start of the social season, when nobles who lived outside the city flocked in for the parties and social opportunities, there were plenty of introductions to be made.

As if in response to that thought, she remembered Lagan, and she felt her heart flutter.

"Are you alright?" Gianna asked.

Runa realized she had stopped breathing again, at the same time Gianna removed her corset. Just as she had when she first saw him.

"I'm fine," she said, feeling her cheeks flush. "We're planning to attend the arena tomorrow, and the party at the Di Antonio house afterward. I'll have you meet me at the house to prepare for the party."

If Gianna was surprised, she didn't show it. "Have you decided what you're going to wear?"

"Probably something cool for the arena," she said, as her camisole was pulled over her head. "Then a gown for the party."

Once her stockings were off, she sighed and curled her toes in the carpet. Gianna wrapped her in her silk robe, before she made her way into her washroom.

Her porcelain tub was filled with warm water, scented with rose oil and witch hazel. She sighed as she sank into the water.

Left with her thoughts, while she washed herself off with a cloth, she found those thoughts filled with Lagan.

Wondering which of her dresses Lagan would like. Or how she should style her hair.

It wasn't the kind of thoughts she was used to having. But they continued to unspool from there. What was his favorite color? His likes and dislikes?

"You seem distracted."

"A little," she admitted, running the cloth over her lower leg.

When she got out of the water, Gianna helped her dry off, then she put on her nightgown. The lightweight blue silk whispered against her skin as she pulled it on, enjoying the cool fabric against her skin.

Back in the bedroom, Runa sat down at her vanity, going through her evening beauty regimen from memory.

"What time would you like me to wake you up tomorrow?" Gianna asked, while brushing her hair.

"Do you know what time my parents are planning to have breakfast?"

"Half-past eight."

"Wake me at eight."

Earlier than she wanted to wake up, since it would give her only six hours of sleep. The games started at noon, and there wouldn't be time to get ready if she slept any later.

Gianna nodded, and tied off Runa's braid. "Will there be anything else, m'lady?"

Runa shook her head. "Not tonight. I should get some sleep while I can."

"I'll see you in the morning, then." Gianna curtsied before leaving Runa alone.

She stepped over to the doors of her balcony, lingering in the fresh air. The flowering bushes in the garden swayed in the breeze, and she could hear the small waterfall in the garden. After a moment, she closed the doors before climbing into bed.

Love & Division

⚜ CHAPTER 1 ⚜

Henry inhaled deeply, letting go of the tension in his shoulders as he savored the cool night air. He sat on the railing of the balcony outside his and Vera's bedroom, back pressed against the cool stone of the wall.

Below him, the gardens were bathed in moonlight, the leaves edged in silver. Like the Galloborne house, the back of the property was bordered by the river, which babbled cheerfully over the stones.

Through the open doors, he could hear Vera and her maid at her vanity, while the maid brushed her hair. He couldn't make out the individual words, but he knew Vera's voice from the sound and the cadence.

She wasn't entirely pleased with how the ball had gone, and he could hear a note of dissatisfaction in her tone as it drifted out to him. But he couldn't quite feel the same way.

Richard had talked about hosting a ball for several years. He considered it part of his responsibility as the head of a ruling family, and a member of society. Though it had been clear Matilda, despite being mistress of the house, had no interest in hosting a family dinner, let alone a ball. Caitlyn had been considered. No doubt she could have been persuaded to come stay for a few months to do so. But that would be temporary, and wasn't the image Richard wanted to present.

Conveniently, Elizabeth had come of age, and quickly taken up the slack her older sister left when it came to running the household. Before long, Matilda no longer pretended to care, and Elizabeth had taken it all in stride. Richard had cautiously begun hosting larger parties, becoming more ambitious as his sister proved more than capable of each challenge he set before her.

Henry couldn't deny that he was pleased. The youngest Galloborne had always been a quiet, sweet girl, so he was glad to see her come into her own. Running the house seemed to make her happy, and he had observed her becoming less shy as she settled into the position.

More than that, he liked to see the Galloborne house brought back to life. It had been so quiet since Annabelle Galloborne had died.

Henry might not be the most social creature, but he agreed it was only right for each ruling family to host their share of parties. That was Vera's opinion, as she had made clear when she had taken control of the Gerrod house on their marriage. And who was he to argue? So he let her host whatever parties she saw fit, and he had encouraged Richard's desire to do the same.

He rubbed his jaw as he looked out over the garden, and reflected on the evening.

As far as he was concerned, the ball had gone flawlessly. Aside from the discussion about Wulfgar Thorinson at dinner, he hadn't noticed any conflict among the guests. Though conflict seemed inevitable anytime the Thorinsons were mentioned.

He heard the tone of the voices in the bedroom shift, indicating that Vera was bidding her maid a good night.

He stepped in just as the door closed behind the maid and looked over at Vera, who was rubbing a last bit of ointment onto her arms.

She gave him an amused smile in the mirror. "Yes, Henry, it's safe."

She wore a soft gray nightgown, her dark brown hair braided down her back.

"I don't think your maid is dangerous," he insisted.

She scoffed lightly. "Of course not. Just female gossip."

He looked away, sheepish at being called out. "I just thought you'd prefer some privacy while you two talked. And it's a beautiful night out."

Vera hummed as she rose from her vanity stool, smoothing her nightgown over her belly and hips. It drew his attention back to her, eyes sweeping appreciatively over the soft curves of her body. But his eyes returned to her face.

"Did you enjoy the ball?" he asked. He decided it was best to bring the subject up, and have her voice her frustrations, rather than letting them stew.

"It was one of the finest balls I've attended in years," she admitted. "I have to commend Elizabeth for her work."

Henry nodded in agreement. "I'm glad she's taken to running the household the way she has."

Vera nodded. "Matilda was positively negligent." She considered for a moment, before choosing her words carefully. "Did you know about the gladiator?"

"I didn't," he admitted. "I knew it was something he wanted to do, and I encouraged it. But I think he's learned the value of a dramatic reveal from Lord Di Antonio."

"I'm sure he has." Her lips pursed slightly as she went to close the double doors that opened onto the balcony. She pulled the lavender-gray curtains closed, blocking out the bright light of the sister moons. "I just wish he hadn't made such a show of it. My family's tournament has been a tradition for generations, and coming in like that was quite rude."

The Solstice tournament was a point of pride for the Randell family. Until recently, it had usually hosted all fourteen ruling families in attendance, as well as most of the prefects and noble families. It was only in the last twenty years or so that some had chosen to attend the arena, or host their own parties. Such as the Gartners, who hosted their daughter Azalea's birthday celebration. While they hadn't voiced their displeasure, Henry had still seen that Geoffrey and his children took the announcement as a personal offense.

Henry was convinced Geoffrey counted how many people came to the tournament, and he deemed it a success or failure based on how attendance compared to the previous year.

"The arena has been a tradition as far back as the empire," he reminded.

"He didn't have to debut his gladiator tomorrow," she insisted. "It's not as if they need more spectacle in the arena."

Henry doubted Richard, or Marcus, would agree. To delay his gladiator's debut would no doubt have been torture. But he knew Vera didn't understand the ways of the arena—or Richard, and his constant drive to excel at everything he did.

"He didn't mean any offense," Henry insisted. "If he's competing with anyone, it's Marcus, not your father." Even as he said the words, he knew it wasn't true.

"I'm not quite so sure," Vera said. "I know you love him like a brother, Henry. But between Marcus, and the Thorinsons, the company he keeps is questionable."

He didn't respond. This was a conversation they'd had many times.

After a moment, she sighed, and came over to take his hands. Her brown eyes softened as she looked up at him. "I'm sorry. I got carried away."

Henry smiled softly as he looked at his wife. "I understand."

Five years earlier, when he had been the Magistrate of Callatis, more than a few noble families had pushed their daughters his way. Geoffrey had been one of the most determined, and hadn't given Henry an excuse to escape the meeting. He had been a little overwhelmed by the onslaught of attention, but Vera had caught his attention. And had held it ever since.

"Don't worry about Richard," he said, brushing his knuckles over her soft cheek. "He's still young."

Vera sighed. "He's twenty-seven. And the head of a ruling family. There's a level of responsibility in that. You know that as well as anyone."

"He handles it better than most young men," he said. Even when Richard had taken his seat on the council, Henry hadn't doubted he could handle the position. But he was still impressed.

"He's creating division among the council to serve his own means."

"There's always division among the council," Henry countered. "If there's more now than usual, it's not entirely his doing. We all have our own agendas."

He had spent hours in the council rooms, listening to the various family heads argue their agendas. He knew how often they all refused to concede any point, or battered each other into submission. It was an atmosphere that bred hostility and resentment.

Vera didn't argue, but gave him a doubtful look.

"Lady Bellerose, and his gladiator, maybe just the distraction he needs," he offered.

"I think Lady Bellerose will only make things worse," Vera scowled.

"There's no point discussing it tonight," he said, lightly running his hands over her shoulders. "Let's get some sleep. Tomorrow's going to be a busy day."

Vera sighed. "You're right. You should get some rest." She smiled genuinely. "I expect you to be named champion in the tournament tomorrow."

Henry chuckled, returning the smile. "I fully intend to."

He leaned in to kiss her lips, and felt her relax as she returned the gesture.

Love Is Blindness

≈§ CHAPTER 1 §≈

Bronwyn had never expected to love a human.

She was a high elf—a proud daughter of house Lewellyn. Among humans, they were a ruling family of Cardea. Even among other high elves, they were a noble family with a long history. They had been nobility in Callatis since it had been a city of the Aurellian Empire. And they had been part of the rebuilding when Cardea had established itself as a republic. Her grandfather currently held their seat on the council, as he had for nearly a century.

While her older sister, Meiriona, was their father's heir, her preferences left it extremely unlikely she would produce an heir. So either Bronwyn, or her children, would eventually inherit the family. In the meantime, she had her own estate, which provided her with more than enough to live on, even with her penchant for luxury.

She was free to love and marry as she chose. Unlike her sister, she had never favored male or female lovers. So there was the unspoken understanding that it would be best if she produced a child. But either way, she had always expected to love another high elf. Perhaps a wood elf, if she met one with a proper pedigree. A tall, lithe, refined elf.

Corion Arnon - broad-shouldered, muscled, vibrant Corion - was not what she expected.

When they had been introduced at a winter ball a year and a half ago, he had looked at her in awe, and apparent interest. An expression that had certainly stroked her ego. But she hadn't thought much of it, even as she had accepted his invitation to dance.

Like her, he was the second child of a ruling family. The Arnons weren't a founding family but were old and respectable. He was a social creature who enjoyed his position, but was also restless, and adventurous. He had been twenty-four at the time - less than half her age. Though, by the standards of high elves, they were considered roughly equivalent.

Over several weeks, she had found herself fascinated by his stories of traveling the continent. Of fighting monsters, and finding lost treasures. Something about him had enchanted her, until the unexpectedness of the connection no longer bothered her. A part of her even enjoyed the shock her friends expressed when she appeared on his arm.

The first time she had taken him to her bed, she had found herself distracted by the scars on his body.

"Why don't you have a mage get rid of them?" she had asked, as she traced a jagged line of scar tissue that curved around his side.

"They're souvenirs." He shrugged. "I got that one from a minotaur in the Baltain Mountains."

And she had come to love those scars, because they were a part of him. A testament to all he had seen and done. And he could tell the story of each one. She knew them well now, having traced them with her fingers and lips. Just as she loved and knew him.

She also loved the silk scarf tied over her eyes, and the other one that tied her wrists to the headboard. Creating a world made entirely of Corion's touch, his voice, and their shared passion. So his calloused hands on her skin, and the sound of their intermingled breath, filled her attention.

Both their bodies were coated in a sheen of sweat from their lovemaking.

After a few minutes, Corion lifted his head from her chest and kissed over her heart. "Stars, Bronwyn. I missed you."

She hummed, still not quite ready to form words as she enjoyed the lingering glow of pleasure.

He stroked her cheek gently, and she turned her head into the touch to kiss his palm.

Then his lips were on hers, gentle and sweet.

When he pulled back, the bed shifted as he moved away from her and got up.

"Where are you going?" Her voice was weak, and she suddenly became aware of just how thirsty she was.

"I'm just opening the door." Sure enough, a moment later she heard the click of the double doors as he pulled them open.

Bronwyn sighed as a cool breeze came in, whispering against her skin.

Corion's townhouse was smaller than her own, but it did have a garden that surrounded the house. She could hear the leaves rustling outside the small balcony, and smell the flowers that lined the walk up to the front door.

While she couldn't see him, she could picture him framed in the doorway. The way the moonlight would illuminate the contours of his muscles.

She knew he only kept the house for her sake. He had been content to live in his family house. But his parents and brother were there often, and she preferred more privacy. So he had taken the house for her. She appreciated the offering, as well as the fact he hadn't simply suggested he move into hers.

She had already decided that she would suggest he skip the formality next season, and they would stay in her home. But she hadn't proposed the idea to him. Not yet. She would bring it up once they had made their plans for the winter.

"Are you ready for me to untie you?" he asked. She heard him fill a glass of water at the sideboard.

Bronwyn inhaled, gathering her thoughts. The fresh air helped to clear her head. "Just my wrists. Don't take the blindfold off yet."

He chuckled, and set the glass on the nightstand before leaning in to kiss her lips. When he pulled back, he untied the scarf that bound her wrists to the headboard.

He caught her hands as she lowered her arms, rubbing the marks on her wrists.

Bronwyn hummed at the attention. "Thank you."

"You're welcome." He kissed her wrists, before reaching for the water glass, and pressing it into her hands.

Bronwyn sat up, and drank deeply from the cool water. When she was done, she handed it back so he could take a drink as well.

It had been less than a fortnight since they were last together. He had spent most of the winter in the south with her. And while she had spent the spring visiting friends as she made her way back up north, he had still shown up regularly.

Ten days earlier, they had been together in Green Crest, but she had arrived in Callatis just a few days later, while Corion had wandered off on some adventure or other. She was sure she would hear about it, when they had time to relax after the Solstice.

But tonight, their physical reunion had been more pressing.

Now, she relaxed among the pillows, savoring his presence.

He reached over to brush a lock of hair off her forehead. "You look beautiful."

"I'm sure I look a mess," she sighed.

Despite the hours her maid had spent curling and sculpting her hair that afternoon, she was sure the curls were gone now. Even if they had survived the ball, their love making would have been too much. Elven hair didn't take well to curling, and hers was particularly stubborn.

He brushed his knuckles over her cheek. "My beautiful, proud Bronwyn."

She hummed, turning her head into his hand.

After a moment, Corion stood up again. She didn't bother to ask this time, instead just resting. As her heartbeat slowed, and the thrill of his body on hers subsided, she became aware of how tired she was.

Corion returned, and began to wipe her skin with a damp cloth. "It's a bit late to run a bath. Will this do for now?"

"It's acceptable," she said, lifting one of her arms for him to wipe away the lingering sweat.

He kissed the inside of her wrist before focusing on his task.

When she was clean, she heard him turn the cloth on himself.

"Are you still planning to compete in the tournament tomorrow?" she asked.

"Mhmm. It's expected."

She hummed, stretching from head to toe. "You humans are so crude and violent. You celebrate a sacred day by overpowering and beating each other, or cheering as you watch. Your lives are so short, and yet you insist on putting yourselves in harm's way for a thrill."

"It's fun," Corion said, his tone playful.

Bronwyn rolled her eyes behind the blindfold. "You're as bad as any of them."

He lay down next to her, and she shifted closer so she was pressed against him.

"I'm sorry I'm such a simple human, my lady."

"At least you're handsome," she said, turning her head. "And a very good lover." She nuzzled her nose against his, searching for his lips.

He cupped her cheek, closing the distance to kiss her gently.

"I still expect you at my dinner tomorrow night," she said. "Fight if you must. But I want you at my side when I enter the drawing room."

"You have my word," he said, his forehead pressing against hers. "You won't come to see me in the tournament?"

"No." She scoffed at the very thought.

She had attended a tournament for Corion once. As much as she loved the man, she had no intention of doing so again. It had been so loud, insufferably crowded, and overwhelming to every one of her senses. Never mind the stress of watching him fight, and worrying he would get hurt.

"I'll give you a token," she said. "But that's the most you can ask of me."

"That's more than enough," Corion murmured. "And what are your plans?"

"I'll attend the temples in the morning, before it's too crowded."

"Rhonwen Nerys is performing, isn't she?"

"You remembered."

Nerys was a high elf bard, known for her romantic and erotic poems.

"You should invite her to dinner tomorrow, so I can let her know how grateful I am for her work, and the amorous mood it puts you in."

Bronwyn rolled her eyes again. But the idea did strike a chord in her. "I may. But that doesn't mean you should say anything that might embarrass her."

"I wouldn't dare," he said. And his voice was sincere. "I promise to be on my best behavior."

He had attended more than a few elven parties with her. And while she knew they made him feel out of place and uneasy, he had learned to navigate them. For her sake, at least. Enough so that her friends were no longer shocked by her choice of a lover, and several had even complimented him. He never let his discomfort show, and she loved him all the more for it.

"The dinner won't go late," she said. "And afterward, you may benefit again from the soft voice, and passionate sonnets of

Rhonwen Nerys again. So don't wear yourself out at the tournament."

"With that incentive, I almost don't want to compete," he said. "Maybe I should escort you to the reading instead."

"No," she said. "I want to enjoy the reading, not be distracted by you, and your depraved thoughts. You'll have my attention when the evening is done."

"Depraved thoughts?" She could practically hear the arch of his brow. "This from the woman who asks me to blindfold her, and tie her to the bed."

Bronwyn sighed in mock irritation. But she pulled her blindfold off, blinking in the bright moonlight as she adjusted.

"There are those beautiful eyes," Corion whispered, touching her cheek to turn her towards him.

Her eyes fluttered again as she met his gaze. His expression was adoring as he stroked her hair.

"My Bronwyn," he whispered, all teasing gone from his voice as he leaned in to kiss her forehead.

She snuggled closer to him, her head resting on his shoulder. His arms wrapped around her, holding her close. As much as they loved to tease each other, and the difference between their people, these were her favorite moments. Laying in his strong arms, with the steady beat of his heart, and letting herself melt into the moment.

Almost without meaning to, she fell asleep like that. Wanting nothing else at that moment.

Roses In Moonlight

⋘ CHAPTER 1 ⋙

Phillipa couldn't sleep.

She rolled over, sighing in frustration. In only a few hours her maid would come in to help her prepare to attend the games in the arena. But before that, she needed to get what sleep she could.

Thoughts of the ball, and the day ahead, refused to calm down and let her sleep.

She debated if she should take advantage of her sleeplessness and turn the lights back on to write a letter to her mother. While she had planned to write one after the solstice celebrations, it couldn't hurt to recount the ball now.

Before she could decide, there was a soft knock on the door. Then it opened just enough for Carolyn to look in.

"Are you still awake?"

"I can't sleep," Phillipa admitted, sitting up.

"Neither can I." Carolyn came in, closing the door behind her. "Do you mind if I join you?"

"Not at all." Phillipa smiled, and pulled back the light blanket on the far side of the bed. Talking to Carolyn was even more appealing than writing a letter. As girls, they had spent many nights whispering and giggling into the small hours of the morning.

Carolyn came around the bed, slipping under the blanket and snuggling into the pillow.

Phillipa had been given one of the nicest guest rooms in the Selelon house for her visit, just a few doors down from Carolyn's room. It was spacious, with simple but tasteful decor.

"I can't stop thinking about the ball," Carolyn said, shifting her head to get comfortable on the pillow.

"I didn't expect it to go so well," Phillipa admitted. "I hoped it would, but I didn't expect it to."

"I certainly didn't." Carolyn giggled, and Phillipa could see her feet wriggling excitedly under the blanket.

No wonder she couldn't sleep. Phillipa smiled in amusement.

She didn't understand her cousin's romanticism. Not really. She enjoyed some of the same poems and novels that Carolyn did. But she didn't devour them, pouring over romantic or erotic texts in every spare moment.

But they had also had very different upbringings, as she was well aware.

"You really like him, don't you?" Phillipa asked.

The moonlight was enough to see Carolyn's smile, and the blush that practically made her cheeks glow. "I do."

When Phillipa realized just how focused Carolyn and her suitor were on each other, she had been in the middle of avoiding Richard. Making him pursue her across the ballroom.

But she had broken the game for a moment, to get information about the Thorinson she had never heard of before tonight.

"Would it change your mind if you knew he was a thief?" Phillipa asked.

She was glad that Carolyn paused, rolling onto her back as she seriously considered it. "Where did you hear that?"

"Richard."

Freyja and Corisien had answered a few questions for her, but she wasn't close enough to them to expect complete candor.

She did expect it from Richard, however.

Carolyn thought for another moment. "I don't care."

"I just want you to be aware," Phillipa said.

"Don't you support the guilds?"

"I do," Phillipa said. "I don't have a problem with him being a thief, so long as he's sincere with you. I just want you to be safe."

Carolyn reached over to take her hand. "Thank you. I appreciate it."

She squeezed her cousin's hand. "He is handsome."

That lovestruck smile returned. "He is. And so different from most men I've met."

"He has land on the Wolf's Rest estate, too," Phillipa said. "With a more than decent income."

Carolyn lifted her head. "How much did Richard tell you?"

"Enough." Phillipa couldn't help giggling a little. "You can't blame me for wanting to know."

She considered for a moment, clearly debating internally. "What else did he tell you?"

Carolyn might not be ambitious like her cousin. But they both loved to gossip.

Phillipa smiled as she lay back down, rolling onto her side to face her cousin. "He's Hammond's first cousin, the only child of Kristoffer's brother, Magnus. There's only one other direct cousin, but Richard doesn't know much about him. He came into the city about a year ago, and started working for the Thieves Guild. Richard wouldn't say what his alias is, just that he's one of the best."

"I'm not surprised," Carolyn said. "He's so strong! I could feel it when we danced, and he lifted me so easily."

"I saw Throthgar talking to Byron, and it seemed serious, but Richard didn't know what it was about."

"Godric teased him about tormenting Byron," Carolyn recalled. "I didn't see it, though."

"I wish I knew," Phillipa admitted, frowning. "Do you know when you're going to see him again?"

Carolyn smiled again. "Tomorrow, at the arena."

Phillipa could hardly say she was surprised. The way they had been looking into each other's eyes when they said goodnight, of course, they had agreed to see each other again.

"I'm glad you're coming to the arena. I don't want to go alone."

"I've only been a couple of times," Carolyn admitted. Her eyes widened as she gasped. "I have no idea what to wear!"

For a moment, Phillipa thought she might jump out of bed and run to her closet.

She reached over to touch Carolyn's hand.

"We can decide tomorrow. You'll need something for the arena, and a dress for the party at the Di Antonios. Lucilla offered us a room where we can clean up and change." Phillipa couldn't help her smile at that.

"You must be thrilled," Carolyn giggled.

"I am."

Of all the people in the ballroom, Lucilla was one of those she had most wanted to impress. While they hadn't had a chance to speak much, Lucilla's tone and expression when they did indicated she had made a good impression. So she looked forward to getting to know the social queen of the Aurellian District.

She looked over at her cousin, squeezing her hand again.

"What about Richard?" Carolyn asked. "Do you still think he's worth all this effort?"

"Even more so now that I've seen that house," Phillipa admitted. She looked up at the canopy, but her imagination showed her the ballroom again. "I just wish I had met Matilda."

"You don't," Carolyn insisted.

"She can't be as bad as you say." Ever since she had arrived a fortnight earlier, she had hoped to meet Matilda. But every time she mentioned it, Carolyn insisted it wasn't a meeting to wish for.

Carolyn shook her head. "I told you, ever since her husband died, she's been... terrifying."

"I doubt that."

"Terrifying" seemed excessive.

Carolyn shook her head. "You'll see."

A small part of Phillipa wondered if perhaps Carolyn wasn't exaggerating. Or not as much as she thought, at least.

Matilda Galloborne had been married for less than a year before her husband died under mysterious circumstances. She now held her husband's lands in stewardship for her son, but had retreated to the Galloborne house. By all accounts, she lived in the city rather than the estate, but had practically disappeared from the social scene.

Phillipa did feel a bit nervous at the thought of the meeting, but she refused to dread the idea. She was fairly confident she had made a good impression on the rest of the Gallobornes. She just had to win over Richard's twin sister.

Carolyn sighed happily, snuggling into the pillow again. And Phillipa followed suit, her mind finally quieting enough to sleep.

The Summer Solstice

∽≼ CHAPTER 1 ≽∽

The 20th Day of Aurostra, 1544

Dawn arrived with a peacock plume of dusty violets, silvery greys, and fiery oranges. Aurora guided her chariot over the mountains in the east, melting away the dark blanket of her sister's night. The Summer Solstice was her day, and she put on a show to remind them.

Her priestesses were there to greet her as the first glimmer of her presence appeared on the horizon. Clad in bright-colored silks, they laid garlands of flowers, and bowls of fruit, on her altars. While the devout came with the sunrise, giving thanks for the gifts she brought: long summer days, light, fertility, and harvest.

Children gathered around, listening with rapt attention as the priestesses told them stories. Of how Aurora and Selene had created the world tree, then the gods, and the many creatures. They told of the heroic exploits performed by those claimed and blessed by the sisters.

A few of the children tried to look up at the sun, wanting to catch a glimpse of the Titan as she rode across the sky. But they were forced to look away, blinking away the spots in their vision.

The priestesses laughed, distributing handfuls of fruit before sending them off to play.

The celebration began to spill into the waiting streets as the sun ascended above the mountains. Where merchants and entertainers were eager to do their part. Nearly every street corner had a dancer, juggler, bard, or mage to entertain the crowd. Stages had been erected for plays and performances.

The air was a cacophony of scents and sounds, filling the air with merriments.

By contrast, the houses of the upper class remained closed up, as their inhabitants slept. It was almost midmorning when the servants began to open the curtains and let in Aurora's light.

In the Sorensen house, Gianna awoke Runa as the clock in the hall chimed eight o'clock. She blinked groggily, wanting to stay in bed and fall back asleep. But she accepted the cup of tea she was offered. It was prepared just as she liked: sweetened with honey and cream. Sipping it gave her a few minutes to return to her body and collect her thoughts.

"Breakfast is served, and your parents are already downstairs." Gianna said as she finished the tea, bringing over her sky-blue silk dressing gown.

As tired as she was, Runa reminded herself that she would be able to rest the next day. She had arranged her schedule to be sure she would have a chance to recover from the celebrations.

When she had risen from bed, and pulled on the robe, Gianna rebraided her hair before she went downstairs.

A set of double doors opened into the breakfast room at the back of the house, with a second set leading onto a balcony. Both were open, so she could feel the morning breeze as she approached. Through the large windows, she could see garden beds of roses in blush pink, and dark red.

A white linen tablecloth draped the oval breakfast table, with a dark blue runner. Vases of flowers, and delicate potted orchids, stood among the gold-washed salvers.

Tor Sorensen sat at the head of the table, talking with Godric, who sat to his right. Despite his age, and position, he was still a tall, broad northerner. His hair was the same red as Runa's, save for a few flecks of white appearing at his temples, and in his well-groomed beard. He smiled at Runa as she came in. "Good morning, Darling."

"Good morning, Papa." She went over to kiss his cheek.

Her mother, Pia Sorensen, sat at the other end of the table, in a lavender dressing gown, similar to the one Runa wore. She was slender, her brown hair pulled back in a braid. She squeezed Runa's hand as they exchanged kisses on the cheek.

"You're just in time," Tor said. "Your mother has been interrogating Godric about last night."

"His answers are less than satisfactory," Pia said. "All he can tell me about Phillipa's dress is that it was wine-colored, and that Richard was a perfect host."

"That's not good enough, apparently," Godric said.

"Hardly." Runa smiled as she took her usual seat, between her parents and across from Godric. "At least he didn't spend half the evening sulking."

A footman brought over a plate of fruit, and eggs on toast, setting it before her.

"Just the last hour or so," Godric admitted. "Once I got through all the introductions. And all the young women who are suddenly very interested in what life is like in the forts."

"In your inheritance, more like," Runa frowned, taking a bite of egg and toast. She had done her best to rescue her cousin from the social climbers that had circled him much of the night. As if any of them were good enough for his time, let alone attention.

"That's to be expected," Tor said, giving Godric a sympathetic look as he sipped his coffee.

As Runa ate, she answered her mother's questions. Telling her of the acquaintances she had spoken with, and the gossip she had learned, as well as all the details of the gowns, and the fashion trends that were emerging for the season. Tor and Godric watched them in amusement.

"Don't forget Throthgar and Carolyn," Godric said, during a lull in the gossip.

Pia looked up from taking a drink. "What's this?"

"Oh, that's right," Runa said, remembering that part of the evening. "Throthgar arrived as we were going through to the ball, and the way he looked at Carolyn, it was as if the Maiden turned his head. They spent the entire evening together, and she seemed completely enchanted."

Pia hummed as she took a sip of juice. "That poor girl. If Aline had bothered to do her job as a mother, Carolyn wouldn't be so easily swept off her feet."

"She could do worse than Throthgar." Runa considered the match as she looked at the crumbs and streaks of egg yolk left on her plate.

Her mother nodded. "True. I had worried she would be charmed by some scoundrel. But if anyone can give her the love story she dreams of, it would be a Thorinson."

Carolyn's romanticism was well known - as was her parents' neglect. They were too busy with their own arguments, and their four other children, to pay attention to their youngest daughter. The gossips often whispered that Carolyn seemed doomed to be a tragic tale for the bards to sing. A cautionary tale for young women who became too lost in daydreams.

But Runa had always found that she hoped for something better. It might be some romanticism of her own, but she wanted to believe that Carolyn could find the love story she dreamed of.

The hope may have been selfish. She had thought that, if Carolyn could find that love, perhaps there was someone who could catch her attention as well. Though the more disappointing the men who flocked around her were, the less likely it seemed.

"What of Richard and Phillipa?" Pia asked after a moment, stirring Runa from her thoughts. "I would have loved to watch her work."

"It was quite impressive," Runa said. "Richard spent most of the evening chasing Phillipa around the ballroom. When they weren't both socializing, of course."

"I expect nothing less from Marguerite Bellerose's daughter." Pia had an amused smile as she took a drink of water.

"I'm still surprised he played right into her hands like that," Godric said. "I didn't expect Richard, of all people, to fall for such a simple trick."

Tor laughed, raising his cup a little to his nephew. "You've never had a girl make you chase her." He gave Pia a pointed look. "I assure you, Godric. The fact it's simple is exactly why it works."

"We wouldn't be here if it didn't work." Pia met her husband's gaze, with an equally pointed smile.

"Was there any trouble with Randell?" Tor asked, after a moment.

Runa shook her head, swallowing a bite of melon. "Not really. At dinner, Phillipa and Hammond were discussing Wulfgar Thorinson. It sparked a debate between Randell and Lucilla, but it didn't seem to get far. I was too far down the table to hear it, but Phillipa told me about it later."

"That's Thorinson history for you," Tor shrugged, taking another sip of coffee.

"It seems it all came down to a matter of opinion. Was Wulfgar a traitor, or a liberator?" Runa shrugged. "It's one of those things where you can never hope to change someone's mind."

Tor nodded.

"And of course, Richard announced his gladiator," Godric said. The one part of the evening that had been of interest to a soldier like him. "I was telling your father about it before Aunt Pia came in."

Runa felt herself pause at his words.

Almost like a prophecy, Carolyn has been swept off her feet by Throthgar, and Runa's head had been turned. Her heart fluttered in her chest as she remembered the sight of Lagan in the ballroom.

She lifted her eyes to meet her cousin's, searching for signs of betrayal. The quirk of his eyebrow reminded her of his promise to get back at her for the night before. But she saw no indication that he had mentioned it. Yet.

"He mentioned you wanted to join us at the arena," Tor said, looking at Runa.

"After how Richard has been so enthusiastic about his gladiator, I am curious." That wasn't quite true. She still had no real interest in watching the gladiators fight.

But she did want to see Lagan.

"Is he handsome?" Pia asked, with a mischievous smile.

"Aren't they all?" Runa asked, keeping her tone light. "I thought that was a requirement."

"Runa doesn't want to say that yes, he is," Godric said. He gave her a smug look. "Extremely."

She saw an opening, and gave her cousin a sweet, mocking smile. "How would you know, Godric?"

Godric hardly batted an eye. "I served more than a year with Kat. Spend enough time with her, and you learn a few things about what catches a woman's eye."

Tor chuckled. "I would imagine."

"He is handsome," Runa admitted. "From the far north, I believe."

"Richard said he's from the Hvall Archipelago." Godric took another bite of his breakfast.

That had been Runa's guess.

The Hvall Archipelago was a small series of islands north of Cardea. It was home to tribes of fishermen, reindeer herders, and traders who would sometimes sail south to barter. They rarely made it as far south as Callatis, though Runa had seen a few in the markets of Sapphire Bay. None had been as handsome as Lagan, though.

"If he came down to Cardea, he's probably a sailor," Tor said thoughtfully. "Or used to be, at least."

"They don't usually come this far south, do they?" Runa asked.

"Rarely," Tor said. "A few of the more adventurous ones do. The younger ones, usually. I get the impression they think cities are dens of corruption."

"Are they wrong?" Godric asked.

"You're a bit young to be so jaded, Godric," Pia chided.

"I've earned it," Godric muttered, taking another drink of water.

"What's his weapon?" Tor asked, and Runa suspected he was drawing attention away from Godric.

"Richard wouldn't say, but I suspect it's the trident," Runa said. "With a title like Master of the Seas, could it be anything else?"

"I'm even more interested now," Tor admitted.

In his youth, her father had captained a ship for the Smuggler's Guild. Until marrying Pia De Fuentes had brought him up in society, later putting him at the head of a ruling family. Runa knew he still had a fondness for all things associated with the sea, and was always eager to speak with another seaman.

"I am as well," Pia said, looking up from her coffee.

"Does that mean you'll join us, Love?" Tor asked.

"Well, if Runa's going, I might as well." Finished with her breakfast, Pia set her silverware on her plate.

"And we've been invited to the Di Antonio's party afterward," Runa said. "With a room to rest in after the fights."

"Excellent." Pia set her napkin on her plate. "In that case, I should go upstairs and decide what to wear. The dress I planned to wear isn't appropriate for the arena."

"I still haven't decided what to wear," Runa admitted.

"I can help you once I'm dressed," Pia said, rising from her seat. "Take your time, and I'll meet you in your room." She reached out to Runa, who squeezed her mother's hand.

"Thank you." When she turned back to her food, she noticed Godric watching her, looking amused again. "What?" She demanded.

He shook his head, but didn't wipe away his smile.

✎§ CHAPTER 2 ᚠ᪥

Callista and Larissa had long since left the sky by the time Hammond awoke. Their cool light had been replaced with Aurora's golden glow, filling the Galloborne guest room.

He lay in bed, watching the rays of light through the windows.

As he looked out at the wisps of white clouds drifting across the sky, he became aware of a weight on the bed next to him. One that was familiar, so he hadn't realized at first that it was out of place this morning. He only noticed when the weight shifted.

Looking over, he found Vetr curled up next to him. Hammond stared at him for a moment. But his surprise soon faded.

As he sat up, Vetr opened his bright blue eyes, and looked at Hammond in annoyance. The white wolf was as comfortable in the Galloborne manor as he was in the shop.

"How did you even get in here?" Hammond asked, glancing around the room to ensure all the doors were still closed.

Vetr yawned, bored by the question. Instead, he rolled over, exposing his belly. And Hammond knew better than to argue with that request.

Hammond had already planned his move to the city when he met the wolf pup. Taking a wolf to Callatis had hardly seemed like a wise idea. But Vetr had been persistent, refusing to leave him. While his cousin, Hannah, had told him he needed a companion after the war. And the wolf's beautiful blue eyes had been hard to resist.

"You always find a way," Hammond murmured, scratching Vetr's ears.

The wolf yipped in agreement.

A knock on the door made them both look up. "Come in."

A footman entered, carrying a covered breakfast tray.

"Good morning, my lord." He nodded his head as he brought the tray over to the sideboard. "The family are all eating breakfast in their rooms this morning, and Lord Galloborne has asked that you meet him in his office once you're ready."

"Thank you," Hammond said.

"I also brought food for your wolf, sir. The cook remembered that you usually ask for raw meat and lightly cooked vegetables for him."

Vetr's ears perked up, aware they were talking about him. Jumping off the bed, he trotted to the sideboard, looking up at the footman expectantly.

"He certainly approves," Hammond said, amused at the wolf's demanding look.

The footman set the bowl down, and it barely touched the floor before Vetr buried his nose in it.

"Do you have any idea how he got in here?" Hammond asked, getting up from the bed as well.

"He showed up at the servant's entrance a couple of hours after dawn, sir," the footman said. "We recognized him, of course, so we let him in. A maid mentioned she saw him waiting outside your room when she came down the hall, so she opened the door for him. She thought you would rather he be with you than left in the hallway, since Lady

Matilda has..." He stopped, unsure whether it would be rude to say what he had been thinking.

"I understand," Hammond said. "Give the maid my thanks. I would rather he be with me."

The footman bowed. "Will you be needing anything else, my lord?"

"That will be all, thank you."

Once the footman was gone, Hammond turned his attention to the tray on the sideboard. The breakfast was simple. A couple of hard-boiled eggs, a soft roll, a bowl of fresh fruit, and a piece of soft cheese. All on matching plates and bowls decorated with red and gold roses.

Vetr had finished his breakfast by the time Hammond took his first bite of the roll. Licking his lips, he looked up at Hammond.

"Well maybe if you took your time, you wouldn't be done so quickly," Hammond said.

Vetr cocked his head at such a foreign concept.

Hammond sighed, but picked up the piece of cheese and tossed it to the wolf. "That's all you get. I need my strength for today."

Once he had eaten, Hammond dressed for the day. Nice enough for a festival, but comfortable enough for the day ahead.

"Are you ready?" Hammond asked, as he rolled his sleeves up above his elbows.

Vetr had laid back down on the bed, but lifted his head at the question. He rose slowly, stretched, yawned, and then jumped from bed.

"I don't have all day," Hammond told him. "Richard is waiting."

The wolf just shook his head, before trotting through the door Hammond held open for him. Human schedules were of no concern to him. And of that, Hammond couldn't help but be a little jealous.

Regardless, they made their way down the hall from the guest room to the main staircase.

Most of the decorations from the night before were still up, though it all looked different in Aurora's light. The almost dreamy, romantic glow he remembered was gone. But the sunlight had a different kind of joy and promise in its place. It was almost homey and welcoming. As much as the grandeur of a ruling family's house could be.

As they reached the main floor, Elizabeth came into the foyer from the garden, handing her sunhat to her maid as she did. "Good morning, Hammond," she said cheerfully, her voice light and musical. "And Vetr. What an honor."

Without hesitation, Vetr trotted over, pressing against her legs through her skirt, insisting on attention.

"Are you enjoying yourself?" Hammond asked dryly.

The wolf's tail wagged in answer.

"Wild indeed," he muttered, shaking his head.

Elizabeth giggled. "He's a sweetheart."

He most decidedly was not. But Hammond didn't have the heart to tell Elizabeth that.

"Are you going to visit my brother?" she asked, looking up at him.

He nodded. "We'll probably leave for the arena soon."

"I just stopped in his office to wish him luck," she said. "I'm sure I'll hear all about it tomorrow, one way or another."

"You're not joining us?" Hammond had thought Richard would demand all his siblings be there, as a show of support.

"No, I'm attending Azalea's birthday celebration," she said, then cooing to Vetr as he continued to press against her.

Richard could be reasonable after all, Hammond thought. Elizabeth wasn't suited to the arena, and Azalea Gartner was her best friend. So it only made sense to let her attend the celebration.

"I doubt he needs it at this point," Hammond admitted. "I don't think he or Marcus cares who wins, so long as they get people to talk."

"An easy victory, then," Elizabeth said. "I'm glad he won't be disappointed."

"Aren't we all," Hammond murmured.

Elizabeth gave him a sympathetic smile. "Well, I should go get ready. Happy Solstice, Hammond."

"You as well, Elizabeth."

"And you too, Vetr," she said, giving the wolf one last scratch on his haunches.

Vetr whined as Elizabeth straightened, and headed towards the stairs.

"Com'on," Hammond said. "You got all that attention, now we have work to do."

Vetr didn't like that idea, and he whined to make sure that was clear. But when Hammond started to walk away, he quickly fell into step once more.

They found the door to Richard's office open, and Richard himself sat at the large, carved wooden desk. Sunlight came through the windows behind him, leaving him shadowed in his black leather, wingback chair.

He looked up at the sound of their approach. "Hammond, there you are. And Vetr." He looked at the wolf admiringly as they entered the office.

Unlike a few minutes earlier with Elizabeth, Vetr looked noble and dignified. There would be no whining, or demands for attention now. But at a gesture from Hammond, he did sit down.

"I do wish I could get a lion to do that," Richard murmured, eyeing the wolf.

"That might be beyond even you," Hammond chuckled, sitting in one of the chairs before the desk. It was black leather, and wingbacked, like Richard's. But noticeably smaller, so as to leave no question about who was in control.

Richard shrugged. "Still. It is impressive how you can command him."

Vetr made a noise in his throat. Not a whine, or a growl, but something in-between.

"Command might be too strong a word," Richard corrected himself.

"He behaves when you're around," Hammond said. "He usually does what he wants."

Richard met Vetr's gaze, quirking an eyebrow.

The wolf just yawned.

The corner of Richard's mouth tugged in amusement, and he finished signing the paper on his desk. "Just don't let Matilda see him. He scared her last time she saw him, and she threatened to skin him for a new winter coat."

Vetr growled, and Hammond was close to doing the same, feeling the hair on the back of his neck rise.

"If she did, there would be one less Galloborne," Hammond said, his voice low and dangerous.

Richard looked up at him, startled. But only for a moment, before it was replaced with a smile. "Hammond, sometimes I forget you're a wolf in sheep's clothing."

Hammond looked over at Vetr, petting the top of his head, and scratching behind his ears.

"We'll leave for the arena soon," Richard said, dipping his black glass and gold-accented quill back into the ink pot. "I've already ordered the grooms to prepare our horses. Byron and Caitlyn should be almost ready, and I told Graham that we're leaving without him if he isn't ready in time."

Hammond chuckled.

The corner of Richard's mouth curled in a smile, glad his joke had been appreciated. "I just want to take care of a few things, so it doesn't pile up tomorrow."

"Anything important?"

Richard shook his head. "Mundane things. One of the farms on the estate needs a new tenant, and the house needs some routine repairs."

"I'm impressed you have the patience for it today," Hammond admitted, leaning back in his chair.

"I needed some way to distract myself," Richard scowled. "I've been waiting for all of you to be ready, haven't I?"

"I'm sorry to keep you waiting," Hammond said dryly.

Richard waved it off. "Henry sent a note wishing me luck for today." He held out the single sheet of paper in question.

It was Henry's usual style. Brief and to the point, barely taking up half a page. He wished Richard and his family a happy Solstice, and good fortune in the arena.

"I wished him luck with the tournament," Richard added. "I included you as well, since I felt you wouldn't mind."

Hammond nodded that it was fine, then quirked a brow. "Do you think Vera knows?"

Richard scoffed. "Don't make me laugh." He sighed, leaning back in his chair. "Even when they first met, I asked why it had to be Vera. Out of all the women he could have married."

"It could have been worse," Hammond reminded him, wishing he hadn't mentioned Vera in the first place. "There's nothing to be done about it now, though. So we should focus on today. And Lagan's debut."

That succeeded in diverting Richard's attention, and he quickly finished up the papers in front of him. Once they were handed off to his steward to dispatch, they headed out of the office.

The mansion's front door was open once more, and Vetr ran ahead of them. Yipping in excitement to be out in the sunlight once more. Though Hammond could hear nervous whinnies from the horses, and the grooms doing their best to soothe them.

When he and Richard descended the stairs to the path, it all seemed well controlled.

Eight liveried and mounted guards were nearby. One of whom held the Galloborne banner, with the roaring gold lion, which swayed in the slight breeze.

William and Caitlyn were already in the saddle, prancing around and laughing as they talked. Graham was there as well, talking to Byron while they stroked their horses' foreheads.

"You made it," Hammond said.

"Apparently," Graham said, with a sheepish smile. "I don't know if I slept at all last night."

"That's what tomorrow is for," Byron reminded, before swinging up into the saddle.

Hammond was looking forward to that. He would have one day to rest, before his father would arrive for their meeting with Heather. The thought was like a spark. An unfamiliar rush of excitement that had nothing to do with the Solstice filled him, though he couldn't have explained why.

One of the grooms brought forward Richard's horse: a sleek black stallion he had named Stornborne. Closely followed by Hammond's dark brown fjord horse, Fjornir.

Vetr trotted over to the horse, sniffing at its white forelock in a familiar greeting that Fjornir bent his head to return. Unlike the Galloborne horses, Fjornir had been bred on the Thorinson estate, so wolves hardly phased him. But he turned his head to Hammond as he approached.

"It's good to see you," Hammond murmured, rubbing the horse's forehead. Fjornir lived in the Galloborne stables, since Hammond's house had no place to keep him. While he trusted the stable hands to take good care of the horse, he still took any opportunity to ride.

When he was in the saddle, Hammond guided Fjornir to Richard's side. Vetr trotted beside him, knowing how far to keep from the horse's hooves.

"Let's go already," William said, cheerful but impatient.

"I think he's more excited than you are," Hammond said.

"That's William for you." Richard gave a signal to the guards, who began to form up.

Four of them, including the bannerman, rode in front, before Richard and Hammond. Behind them, Caitlyn fell in alongside William. She continued the story she had been telling him, about a recent ride with some acquaintances on Byron's estate. Byron rode next to Graham, in a much quieter conversation that Hammond couldn't catch. The four remaining guards brought up the rear.

Because Richard didn't do anything without fanfare.

CHAPTER 3

Before the Aurellian Empire, Callatis had been a small port city. A center of trade for the small kingdoms and tribes along the coast. A position that had made it a key point when the Aurellian empire had expanded.

In 680 of the Third Era, during his campaign to reunite the empire, Marcus Di'Antonius had chosen it for his main seat. After the wars, he had made the city his home. Building it into a center of power and culture. Exposing the once barbaric tribes to the best aspects of the empire, and its civilization.

By the end of the war against Ganzorig the Orc and his horde, in 1014, Callatis had been in ruins. Less than a thousand people had been left among the rubble, with a burned-out harbor that put a stop to trade.

Abandoned by the empire, those who remained had chosen to rebuild. Some lower-ranking Aurellian citizens had stayed, choosing to take their chances. Including a marble merchant who had maintained control of their quarry, making them invaluable in rebuilding.

While the remaining Aurellians had agreed to submit to the ruling families, they had asked to make their home on the north side of the Silver River, which they had shamelessly named the Aurellian District. With a bust of Emperor Aurelian as their sigil.

Two bridges connected the district to the main city. The Golden Bridge connected the marketplace in the main city with the one in the Aurellian District. While the Antoine Bridge, near the homes of the ruling families, let out into a grassy park, between the marketplace on the eastern side, and affluent homes on the west.

The Antonine Bridge, and the path through the park, were cleared for the Galloborne party to ride across. And beyond it, the Aurellian District was like a different world.

Outside the park was a fountain featuring four marble naiads who danced, or poured water from conch and cockle shells. Regarded as one of the most beautiful sculptures in the city, if not the republic.

Hammond looked around in fascination. While he had been across the river many times, he had never been there on the solstice.

Just as in the city, the main avenue was decorated with brightly colored garlands. He saw the priestesses of Aurora distribute fruit to children, who laughed as they ran around the plaza.

There was a temple circle in the central part of the city. But the ones here were grander, and more ostentatious.

A respectful distance from the temples, merchant stalls were set up along the street. Dancers and mummers performed on street corners, their brightly colored costumes almost fading into the background of the decorations. Their music intermixed with the buzz of excitement in the crowd around them.

The smell of fresh-baked pastries and roasting meat reached his nose.

Vetr paused, head turned towards a grilling pit, where a haunch of pork was being roasted on a spit. Hammond could see the wolf debating if he could get away with going over to see what he could find for himself.

"Vetr," Hammond called, his voice firm.

The wolf pretended to ignore him for a moment. But then shook his head and whined, before trotting back to Hammond as if it had been his own idea.

Caitlyn's mare whinnied nervously as Vetr passed her, but she expertly kept the horse in line.

Ahead of them rose the arena—a work of art in limestone and gold.

The Di Antonios had requested to be a ruling family during the establishment of the republic, reminding the council that they were the (admittedly indirect) descendants of Emperor Marcus Di'Antonius. But having just rid themselves of the empire, the founding families had no interest in letting Aurellians rule at all— especially not the descendent of an emperor, who regarded the city as his right.

Not that it had stopped them from ruling the Aurellian District. A position Marcus' grandfather had solidified by rebuilding the arena.

The games had never stopped. But the arena, which had once rivaled the royal arena in the imperial city itself, had fallen into disrepair over time.

But Tallus Octavius Di Antonio had not only rebuilt it. He had made it a work of art. Commissioning artisans to craft new statues, and paint murals throughout it. Even the gladiator barracks near the arena were filled with art, whether the gladiators appreciated it or not.

Tallus had also re-established the system of gladiator sponsorship. He had focused on finding the most impressive gladiators. Attractive, powerful men and women who knew how to put on a show when they fought, and who were charismatic enough to mingle at parties. He had then convinced (occasionally coerced) other nobles to sponsor them.

Through his efforts, gladiators became public figures, until they were practically worshiped in the streets. They were socially sought after, their sweat distilled into a perfume that women, and men, paid ridiculous sums for.

"What do you think of Solstice in the Aurellian District?" Richard asked, as they neared the high walls of the arena.

"If it's this crowded here, I'm glad I'm not in the city," Hammond admitted. He glanced toward the sound of music and applause from across the street.

Richard chuckled.

The ball the night before had been one thing. It had been a familiar social setting, with people he knew. Even if he didn't necessarily like them, that had been nothing compared to the chaos of a festival, where so many colors, sounds, and smells bled together like a fever dream.

He looked at Vetr, whose white coat was like a snowbank. Simple, and easy to focus on. He took a deep breath, before looking straight ahead again.

The massive, gold-plated gates of the arena were thrown open, already bustling with a stream of people entering for the games.

A pavilion with a purple canopy had been raised on a patch of grass off to the side. The Di Antonio banner, a gold griffin on a violet field, was planted in front of it. To leave no doubt as to who held court there, and was responsible for the festival.

Marcus and Lucilla sat under the statues of Consus the Father, and Galatea the Mother, each on a carved, gilded wooden throne. Both wore purple, with hammered gold circlets in the shape of laurel wreaths.

During the empire, the purple dye had been the rarest and most prized, making it a sign of wealth and power. While magic could replicate and make it more easily accessible now, it still gave the impression of power. And Marcus used only natural purple dye to drape himself and his household.

Hammond didn't miss Richard's expression as he took in the sight. Impressed, motivated, and a little covetous.

In his youth, Marcus had traded the fashions of the republic for classic imperial styles. He had told Hammond it had been a way to express pride in his heritage, when he had been fifteen or so. But he found them more comfortable than the trousers or jackets, and so he had continued to wear it. Hammond found he had a level of respect for that, even if he didn't necessarily understand it. It certainly made the man look like a statue of Marcus Di'Antonius come to life.

Marcus was shameless when it came to flaunting his position as ruler of the district.

CALLATIS CHRONICLES VOL. 1

"Has anyone told him we don't have kings in Cardea?" Caitlyn asked in amusement.

William chuckled. "I don't think he cares."

Armored guards flanked the dais, in the Di Antonio livery. No doubt they were perfectly capable, but it was strange to see Marcus without either Aelia or Lucius by his side. Hammond wondered how acutely Marcus felt their absence.

His aide was nearby, while Lucilla's two handmaids stood by her chair.

"Richard!" Marcus grinned as he saw them, rising from his seat. Making his excuses to the people standing near the dais, he strode over to them.

All sign of longing was gone from Richard's expression as he dismounted, and went to greet their host.

"Now I can return your hospitality," Marcus said, clasping Richard's wrist. "Last night was grand, to be sure. But this is how you celebrate the Solstice." He gestured to the arena.

The Callatis banner, fourteen gold crowns on a green background, hung on the right side of the gate. While the bust of Aurelian, gold on white, hung on the left.

Between them, directly above the gate, was the Di Antonio's griffin. Popular gladiators, like Lucius and Aelia, had their own banners that hung along the top of the arena, declaring that they would be taking part in the games.

"Don't I know it," Richard grinned. "I almost can't believe it's finally happening."

"It will be a good day for it," Marcus said. "I already saw them getting ready. Lucius and Lagan are both in top form. Speaking of which, I have a gift for you."

Next to Lucius' red banner, with his gold star insignia, hung a teal banner that Hammond had never seen before—a gold kelpie rearing up from the waves on a teal background.

"Lagan wanted an owl - he said it was the symbol of his tribe," Marcus said. "But I told him a kelpie would be more appropriate for the Master of the Seas."

"It's perfect," Richard said. And Hammond noticed that he seemed touched by the gift. "Thank you, Marcus."

"You're most welcome, my friend," Marcus said. "I'm glad you finally have your gladiator. I've looked forward to this."

"As have I," Richard said. "And there's quite a turnout."

Marcus looked towards the stream of people passing through the gate. Most of whom paused to stare in awe at the glittering regalia.

"As it should be." Marcus clapped Richard's shoulder. "Come to the pavilion. We have refreshments before we go up to the box."

Marcus took a moment to greet the rest of the party as they passed him on their way to the pavilion.

Lucilla was already gesturing to a servant, who brought over chilled wine, and a bowl of water for Vetr.

"Thank you." Hammond nodded to the footman who had brought the water.

"We can hardly have you upstaging our hospitality," Lucilla said. Like Marcus, she dressed in purple. Her gown was lavender, embroidered with gold. But the sheer violet drape over her shoulders matched her husband's mantle.

"I thought that's what the party tonight is for," Hammond said.

Lucilla smiled, a little condescending. "If we weren't hospitable now, then it would be hollow tonight."

Her tone was so decided, that it was difficult to argue. "I'll trust your expertise."

"A good answer," she said. "Your mother raised you well."

"We're just waiting for a few more people to arrive," Marcus said. "Then we'll go up."

As if on cue, a carriage drawn by four white horses arrived. On the dark blue door was the gold orchid of the Sorensen house.

Tor stepped out of the carriage first, turning back to help Pia, then Runa down. Godric was close behind, offering Runa his arm.

Lucilla waved for a servant with a tray of cooled drinks to follow as they went to greet the Sorensens.

After marrying Pia, and leaving the Smuggler's Guild, Tor and his ship had served in the Stark forces. While he had retired, he still had the respect of those he had served with. Not the least of which was Marcus. There was rare respect in his voice as he greeted the older man.

"We're honored to have you here, my friend," Marcus said, clasping Tor's wrist.

Tor and Pia had been a part of Hammond's life for as long as he could remember. It wasn't until he was four or five that his father explained that Tor was a distant cousin, rather than a direct uncle. But it hadn't changed that he saw them as family, just as he thought of Runa as another sister.

"I don't see you for years, now here you are again," Hammond said, clasping Godric's wrist.

Godric smiled as he returned Hammond's grip. "We're making up for lost time, I suppose."

"We are glad to have you back," Richard said.

"I'm not staying," Godric said. "Not for long anyway."

Runa sighed. "So you keep saying."

"It's too early to look so disappointed, Runa," Lucilla said, as she came over to kiss Runa's cheek in greeting.

"Godric provoked her," Hammond said, earning himself a mock glare from Godric. He simply shrugged. While he was close to both of them, Runa was the one he preferred not to offend.

She was the vindictive one.

"It's typical for soldiers to forget how to behave in society when they first come back," Lucilla said. "We'll have to re-educate him."

"It's not so bad," Marcus said, wrapping an arm around Godric's shoulder. "We just need to remind you of the advantages of the city. The food is much better, and the beds are far more comfortable."

"He's certainly not complaining about those," Runa said, accepting Richard's arm now she had been abandoned by her cousin.

"I never claimed to," Godric said, glancing back at her. "I want to return to the estate, not the forts. It's society that I don't like."

Hammond chuckled as he followed the group.

Only when they reached the pavilion did he remember that Vetr was with him. Or was supposed to be.

Realizing that he had taken his eyes off the wolf made him freeze momentarily. Then he cursed as he looked around. But there was no flash of white to indicate the wolf was nearby.

"Is something wrong, Domine?" a footman asked, referring to him with a traditional Aurellian term of respect.

"Did you see where Vetr went?" he asked.

"I'm sorry, I did not."

Hammond sighed, kicking himself for not keeping a closer eye on the wolf. He should have known better.

"Are you alright?" Godric asked, coming over to him.

"Vetr is missing," Hammond said, frowning.

"He probably went to find something more to eat," Richard said. "You know how he is with food."

"I'm sure he'll be fine," Marcus said. "No one's screaming."

Lucilla gave her husband an appalled look, as if the concept of screaming at her festival was the worst possible thing that could happen. Though, with Vetr, it was only a matter of time.

In response to that look, Marcus waved two guards over, and instructed them to search for the wolf. "Don't try to capture him; just keep an eye on him."

"Thank you," Hammond said. Though he still debated going off to look as well. Before he could, Richard caught his upper arm.

"He'll be fine," Richard muttered in his ear. "I want you here."

Hammond sighed, but nodded.

CHAPTER 4

The Starks were the next to arrive.

Like the Galloborrnes, they came on horseback, rather than by carriage. But there were no bannermen. No ostentatious show, save for the liveried horses. They were a party of six people, most in light armor. Save for Maria, who wore a red dress.

Jonathan helped her down, pausing to kiss her briefly. A rare show of emotion from the somber head of the family. Maria smiled at him, before they turned to greet Marcus and Lucilla.

Hammond recognized Aksel Stark next to them, one of Jonathan's cousins. Like Godric, he had recently returned from serving in the border forts for several years. But unlike Godric, he made no secret of his love for the city.

A few steps behind them was General Reinhardt Steinmann. Even out of his armor, the man was a mountain. A head taller than even Jonathan, and impossible to miss. He was an older general, who had served in the Stark forces for more than twenty years, becoming Jonathan's most trusted advisor. Marcus, Godric, and even Richard, greeted him with respect. As did Hammond, who had served under him for a time during the Cymbrian War.

Tor greeted him as an old friend.

Runa smiled as she greeted the grizzled old soldier. "It's good to see you, Reinhardt. Are Johanna and Lily here?"

"No, Johanna doesn't like the arena much," he said, giving Runa a fatherly smile. "They're enjoying the festival."

Lucilla had taken Maria by the arm, chatting as they made the rounds through the guests.

But Hammond found mingling hard when he couldn't stop thinking about Vetr. He stood by Richard's side, but kept looking beyond the pavilion in hopes the wolf would appear.

To his surprise, Vetr did appear. Trotting around the statue of Numitor and Faolan, a chunk of meat in his jaws. His tail held high in victory.

But then Hammond noticed who walked beside him.

Eydis. One of the few people that Vetr listened to. Her friend Ella walked with her... as did Katherine.

"Godric!" From anyone else, the tone would have sounded flirtatious. But from Katherine, it was just a friendly greeting. She broke into a run, throwing her arms around Godric's neck as she hugged him. "It's been too long!"

Godric returned the hug, grinning as he did. "It's good to see you, Kat."

She pulled back, resting her hands on his shoulders as she looked him over. "I'm glad to see you still in one piece." She traced a faint scar on his forehead. "A close call, but not enough to ruin that handsome face of yours." Her finger flicked down his cheek.

Godric looked her over, but didn't linger on her exposed skin. It was the same friendly concern she showed for him. "You look good, too. I'm glad."

"How long would I have had to wait if we hadn't bumped into each other?" she asked, bracing her hands on her hips as she met Godric's eyes.

"I was going to come to see you tomorrow," Godric said quickly. "I told Hammond so last night."

"He did," Hammond confirmed.

Katherine smiled. "You should still come and see the shop. I'm quite proud of it."

"We were talking about having a welcome dinner in my home," Hammond told her. "Just you, and a few others. Later this week, before I leave."

"I think that's a fantastic idea," Katherine said. "Just tell me when."

"City life seems to agree with you," Godric said. He seemed a little surprised.

And Hammond couldn't blame him.

"It does," Katherine said. "I'm much better now. I promise."

"Good. I was worried after the war."

"For good reason," Katherine said, though Hammond thought the edges of her smile were a bit frayed. She didn't mention that she was better, but not entirely.

But it wasn't a discussion to have at the Solstice celebration. And Katherine herself preferred not to discuss such things at all.

Before either man could respond, the other women reached the pavilion.

Vetr glanced over at Hammond, completely unapologetic. Then trotted over to the refreshment table, and a suitable patch of grass beneath it.

"I'll talk to you more later," Katherine said. "For now, I should pay my respects." She kissed them both on the cheek, before going over to Marcus, Jonathan, and Reinhardt.

Hammond, in turn, headed towards his sister.

She and Ella had stopped outside the pavilion, Eydis leaning against one of the poles that supported it.

"I woke up in the Galloborne house, with Vetr next to me," he said as he approached. "Why did I pay you for last night exactly?"

"You paid me to spend the night in your house, and I did," she said, with a smug grin. "Your hall boy was the one who let him out before I woke up."

"And you just decided to leave anyway?"

"I had to get to the temple," she insisted. "Does that make it better?"

"Far be it from me to claim searching for Vetr is more important than appeasing Aurora," he said dryly, looking over to where Vetr was gnawing on his bone.

"He's a Thorinson wolf," she said, following his gaze. "They always find their way home."

"That saying is about our family, not the wolves," Hammond reminded.

Eydis laughed. "Don't tell Hannah there's a difference."

She had a point. Hannah Thorinson made no secret that she preferred her wolves to most people. Even her cousins, in some cases.

"I didn't expect to see you here," he admitted.

"What, you thought I would miss this?" She grinned. "Hardly. I want to see this gladiator Richard is so proud of. And Ella likes..." she glanced at her friend, who stood nearby, giving her an annoyed look. "Watching the fights," she finished.

But she gave Hammond a look, and a mischievous smile, as if to say there was more to it. Though he could hardly begin to guess what.

Hammond had met Ella several times, but didn't know her beyond being his sister's friend.

"You shouldn't be in the city," he said. "It's father's birthday."

"You're here," she countered, without missing a beat.

"I'm working," Hammond said. "And he told me to be here."

"Well, I sent him a letter with all my love, wishing him a happy birthday. But I told him Ella wanted me here today. Besides, you said that he would be in the city the day after tomorrow. So I'll see him then."

There was no winning with Eydis. Even as children, Hammond couldn't remember ever besting her in an argument. If he ever got close, she tended to fight dirty.

He was trying to think of a response when he noticed that Eydis was watching something over his shoulder, and she seemed to have turned pink. Hammond glanced back, but all he saw was Lucilla speaking with Runa, William, and Graham.

"What's wrong?" He asked.

"Nothing!" But she was a little too quick to say it. Her gaze shifted to Katherine, who was chatting comfortably with some of the others. "How is she so good at that?"

"Practice," Hammond said. "It does make a difference."

Eydis wasn't amused.

"This is your sister, Hammond?" Richard asked, as he approached. There didn't appear to be any recognition.

While Richard hadn't spent as much time around them as William, Graham, and Elizabeth, they had been around each other often as children. And he didn't think Eydis had changed that much. But he had admitted to Hammond that he had no memory of her.

"Eydis Thorinson," Hammond confirmed. "And her friend, Ella Spencer. Eydis, you've met Richard."

"A long time ago," Eydis said, inclining her head awkwardly. "Lord Galloborne."

"Miss Thorinson," he greeted. "Miss Spencer." There was more recognition in Richard's expression when he looked at Ella.

But Ella attended more social events than Eydis, so Richard would have seen her at various dinner parties and ballrooms in the city.

"Join us," Richard said, gesturing for them to enter the pavilion. "I'm sure Marcus won't mind."

"Not at all," Marcus said, coming over. "It's an honor to have Hammond's sister with us. Please, come in."

As the girls entered, a servant came over with a tray of refreshments. Lucilla's hospitality on full display once again.

Ella seemed more at ease than Eydis. While Hammond didn't know Ella well, he did know she was a thief. One specifically trained to slip into the upper levels of society, which was no doubt why she handled it so effortlessly. While Eydis, a noblewoman who did her best to avoid the trappings of her position, was the one who seemed out of place.

"Eydis!" Runa smiled as she came over. "I didn't expect to see you here."

Eydis blinked in surprise, but then her face lit up. "Didn't expect to see me? This was the last place I expected to see you!"She eagerly took Runa's hand, as if clinging to the familiarity. "What are you doing here?"

"Well, Richard is so enthused about his gladiator, I decided to come."

"You're blushing," Eydis noted, perceptive as always.

"I don't know what you're talking about," Runa said primly. "It's just the heat." And before Eydis could tease her further, she turned to Lucilla, who was nearby. "Lucilla, have you met Hammond's sister, Eydis?"

Lucilla looked Eydis over. But if she was surprised to learn that Hammond had a sister, it didn't show in her face. "It's a pleasure to meet you. Will you be joining us in our box this afternoon?"

"Oh, no," Eydis said, laughing casually. "Ella prefers to sit in the front, so she can see the fights."

"Ella is enamored with Lucius," Katherine said, coming to stand next to Lucilla.

Ella turned bright pink. "Katherine!"

Katherine just laughed. "What? You're hardly the only girl in the audience who is."

"Don't tell her that," Eydis said. "She'll get jealous."

Ella gave a small whine as she looked away in embarrassment, crossing her arms over his chest.

Hammond felt a pang of sympathy. Being subjected to Eydis and Katherine simultaneously sounded like a nightmare. He wanted to help, but couldn't think how.

"Is that why you asked for canopy seats?" Lucilla asked Katherine.

"I thought it might be nice for her to watch comfortably," Katherine nodded.

Lucilla looked at the girls for a moment, considering, then gestured to a servant. "Reserve three of the canopy seats for Miss Fischer and her party. In the front row, if possible."

Outside of the boxes, the canopy was the most coveted seating in the arena. It was part of the first few rows, covered by a purple canopy. On festival days, there were servants with refreshments. Much like in the boxes, but closer to the action. The seats were a sign of favor from the Di Antonios.

Ella's eyes widened as she looked between Katherine and Lucilla in shock.

Katherine smiled, leaning over to kiss Lucilla's cheek. "Thank you, m'lady."

"Behave, Katherine." She looked at Ella. "In the empire, women weren't allowed to sit in the front rows, since too many of them would try to throw themselves at the gladiators. Or they would swoon and faint." She gave a sly smile. "Fortunately, that rule no longer applies."

Eydis giggled. "That sounds like Ella."

"They still can't have orcs or dwarves in the front rows," Hammond said. "But instead of lusting after the gladiators, they try to jump in and join the fights."

"Sounds chaotic." Eydis grinned at the prospect.

"Don't look so excited," Hammond said.

Eydis huffed, but otherwise ignored him.

Marcus called for Lucilla, and she smiled politely before returning to her husband's arm.

Needing a break from the back and forth, Hammond went over to the refreshment table. Vetr still lay underneath, gnawing on his prize.

"Did Eydis buy that for you, or did one of you steal it?" Hammond asked, crouching down in front of him.

Vetr lifted his head, panting happily.

"Right. I don't want to know." Still, he smiled as he scratched the wolf behind the ears. "You scared me, Vetr."

There was still no sign of apology on the wolf's face. He had gotten what he wanted, and shame was a foreign concept to him.

Hammond shook his head.

Eydis called his name, and he looked over to see her grinning as she pointed toward the path.

He stood up, and his heart sank as he saw Throthgar approaching them.

Eydis ran over to their cousin, and Throthgar lifted her off her feet as he hugged her.

"Hey, Little Wolf."

Hammond caught a look from Richard - a glare, and a wordless command to keep the situation under control.

Hammond waved acknowledgment, before going over to where the two were talking animatedly.

"We used to be close, Hammond," Throthgar said as he approached. "Now, every time I show up, you look so suspicious."

"That's just city Hammond," Eydis said. "He's far less fun here."

"You never thought I was fun, even at the Rest," Hammond countered. It was why the words barely phased him.

"It's still true." Eydis shrugged.

"Be nice," Throthgar told her. "I'm not here to cause trouble. I was planning to come for the games, but plans changed."

Eydis looked at him in confusion. "Huh?"

"Then why are you here?" Hammond asked.

Throthgar grinned, looking towards a carriage that had just arrived. "Her."

"Her who?" Eydis asked.

But Hammond could already see Carolyn Selelon being helped down from the Bellerose carriage

By The Green Grass

Carolyn smoothed her skirts over her knees, trying to calm her nerves as the Bellerose carriage drove through the Aurellian District. Despite the fact she had been trying to do that from the moment she had woken up that morning.

She had spent more than an hour agonizing over what to wear today. Both to the arena, and for the party afterward. So much so that she had nearly run out of time to do her hair.

For the day, she settled on a fairly simple purple silk skirt, with a brocade bodice in a similar shade. It was one of her favorite outfits, the bodice cut perfectly to show off her curves.

Across from her, Phillipa looked out the window in fascination.

Unlike Carolyn, she had planned this visit to the Aurellian District, and come prepared. As soon as she had arrived in the city, she had ordered a wine-colored gown in the Aurellian style. The fitted bodice, and the intricately draped skirt, were tailored to perfection. While her honey-blonde hair was swept up to be off her neck in the heat, showing off the gold and ruby necklace she wore. Though less grand than the night before, she looked stunning.

As fashionable as Carolyn liked to consider herself, she had been horrified to realize she had nothing in the Aurellian style. She had never had reason to have one made. And her maid, Enora, had been unprepared to do her hair in a new style.

"I can't remember the last time I was here," Phillipa said. Her eyes lingered on a fountain in the plaza they were driving past.

"I haven't been here in years," Carolyn admitted.

With the Aurellian District firmly in Marcus Di Antonio's control, the Selelons had few connections here.

The main city of Callatis was beautiful. But this was something else entirely. Every building was a work of art in its own right. Accented with intricately carved columns and reliefs, surrounded by fountains and statues. It was so romantic, she found herself regretting that she hadn't spent more time there.

That was something she might have to change in the future.

Her eyes fell on the arena ahead of them. A massive elliptical structure, surrounded by a grassy lawn, with statues of heroes and gods looking down on the crowds.

The carriage stopped to let them out near the pavilion set up under the statues of Consus and Galatea.

The Galloborne banner was posted next to the Di Antonios', indicating they had already arrived. Hammond would be with Richard, no doubt. But would Throthgar?

Her heart fluttered in her chest at the thought, even as she tried to suppress it.

"You're thinking about him again."

Carolyn started. She was so unused to anyone paying attention to her. Having someone around who noticed her was a new situation. Not always a comfortable one, either.

It made her realize she was blushing.

Phillipa gave her a knowing smile as the footman opened the door.

From her seat, Carolyn couldn't see if Richard was watching the footman help Phillipa from the carriage.

A moment later, Carolyn was helped down as well.

She spotted Richard coming towards them, his gaze fixed on Phillipa. Carolyn had seen his expression before - determined ambition.

Hardly romantic.

But she didn't get to watch their reunion. And didn't particularly care.

Throthgar was coming towards her across the lawn.

She smiled, but fought the impulse to move toward him. While she might not be as ambitious as Phillipa, that didn't mean she couldn't make a man come to her. She knew the same principles of flirting that her cousin did, even if she was less keen to use them.

Throthgar returned her smile, and his step quickened as he drew closer. When he reached her, he caught her waist, lifted her off her feet, and spun her around.

"There you are," he said. "I missed you."

"I missed you, too," she admitted. Since he had said it first, she didn't hesitate to return the sentiment.

He was just as handsome as the night before, even without the dreamy air of the ballroom. He wore a blue linen shirt that brought out both the color of his hair, and his blue eyes. And his voice was just as appealing. Rich, a little rough, like strong, dark liquor.

He set her back on her feet, and touched her cheek lightly. "I hoped you would come."

"I couldn't stay away," she admitted, catching the hand on her cheek and squeezing it.

"I know I promised to court you properly," he said. "But I wondered if you wanted to go for a ride outside the city."

"Now?" She blinked in surprise.

"Now." He grinned.

"But..." She looked towards the arena. "I thought you wanted to watch the fights."

"I want to see Lucius and Lagan fight," he said. "But they'll be the last fight of the day, and that won't be for hours."

She looked towards Phillipa, who was watching them. And she thought she saw a cautioning look in her cousin's expression. But she had never been the type to be cautious.

She certainly wasn't going to start now.

"Will you come?" Throthgar asked.

"Yes." She squeezed his hands. "Let's go."

He smiled, lifting their hands to kiss her knuckles. "Tell Phillipa, so she doesn't think I'm spiriting you away. I'll get my horse."

She felt herself blush. "Alright."

She turned towards Phillipa, ignoring the disapproval already apparent in her cousin's look.

"What are you doing?" Phillipa hissed, coming to meet her.

"I'm not asking for your approval," Carolyn said, squaring her shoulders. "I just wanted to let you know that I'm going."

Phillipa sighed. "Honestly, Carolyn."

"Phillipa." Her attempt at strength failed, and her expression turned pleading. "Please."

"I just want you to be safe," Phillipa said. "We only met him last night. And what will your parents say? You know people will talk!"

"It would be the first time they cared about anything I've done," Carolyn insisted. "And I don't care what the gossips say."

"Where are you going?" Phillipa asked. "At least tell me that."

"Outside the city."

"You can't be serious." Phillipa balked. "Carolyn!"

She hesitated for a moment. But only for a moment. "I'll be fine. Phillipa, I trust him."

"I'm not sure I trust your judgment," Phillipa admitted. "I know you *want* to trust him."

That may be true.

"I do trust him," she insisted. "And that's why I'm going."

Phillipa sighed, shaking her head.

Carolyn smiled, and leaned in to kiss Phillipa's cheek. "We'll be back before the last fight."

"If you aren't, I'll send out search parties." There was a genuine threat in her voice.

"I'll bring her back safely," Throthgar said, approaching them. "You have my word."

"I swear, I will make your life miserable if you don't," Phillipa said, her voice threatening.

Carolyn was distracted by the horse Throthgar was leading—a black fjord horse, whose shoulders were higher than the top of her head.

Throthgar smiled. "I promise, Njall is harmless."

"It's not the horse I'm worried about," Phillipa muttered.

"I've only ever ridden mares," Carolyn said, ignoring her cousin as she stared in awe at the powerful stallion.

"Well, now you're riding with me," he said. "I won't let anything happen to you."

Phillipa huffed.

Carolyn shot her a glare, but Throthgar didn't seem to notice.

He swung up into the saddle, then reached down to her. A footman came over to help her, but she brushed him aside, and accepted Throthgar's hand.

He lifted her with ease, helping her swing up behind him.

"Hold onto me," he said, adjusting his hold on the reins.

It was all the prompting it took for her to wrap her arms around his waist. His hand rested over hers momentarily, sending a happy shiver down her spine. It was a small gesture, but there was a sweetness to it.

Then he guided the horse away from the arena.

Rather than take one of the bridges back to Callatis proper, he turned to the east.

Njall fidgeted, tossing his head and snorting.

"We'll be out of the city soon," Throthgar said, patting the horse's neck. "Njall is from the country, so he doesn't like the city. He prefers being able to run free."

The horse whined in agreement.

"Like you?" Carolyn asked, tilting her head so she could see his expression.

Throthgar laughed. "Am I that obvious?"

"A lucky guess." She squeezed his waist.

As they approached Aurelian's Gate, Carolyn realized she had never seen the gate in person, let alone passed through it.

She rested her chin on Throthgar's shoulder, looking up at the intricate columns. Statues of a gladiator and a priestess flanked the gold-washed steel bars.

"The Aurellian District really is a work of art," she said, looking at the marble folds of the priestess's draped skirt.

"Do you like the city?" Throthgar asked.

"I can never really decide," she admitted. "When I'm in town, I find I miss the country.

But when I'm in the country, I miss the bustle of the city, and all there is to do."

"So you haven't made up your mind yet."

"I suppose not."

People were entering through the gate, coming from the nearby towns and villages for the festival. But she and Throthgar seemed to be the only ones leaving.

Carolyn blushed as people looked up at them, and she pressed her face against Throthgar's shoulder.

A guard waved for them to pass through the gate, and Njall huffed as they passed under the high stone archway. Past the golden gates, and into the open countryside.

"Not yet," Throthgar said. "Soon."

The horse tossed his head.

Carolyn's heart pounded in her chest, and she found herself almost as eager as the horse to be away from the city walls.

"Do you know where we're going?" she asked.

"I do," Throthgar assured her. "I have something I want to show you."

He guided Njall off the main road, turning to the right.

"Hold on," Throthgar said.

Carolyn gasped, clinging to Throthgar's waist as Njall broke into a gallop.

ᕦ CHAPTER 2 ᕤ

Carolyn couldn't suppress her giddy smile as Njall galloped past the rolling green hills around Callatis, adorned with bright-colored wildflowers.

With her cheek pressed against Throthgar's back, she could feel the powerful throb of his heart. It pounded against his ribs, though she couldn't be sure if it was from the thrill of the ride, or her arms around his waist. Hers pounded for both reasons, so perhaps his did as well.

The thought made her hug him tighter.

While she often rode outside the city, these hills were unfamiliar to her. And she rarely let her mare, Beauty, gallop so freely. Even when she did, Beauty wasn't this fast, or strong.

She had never ridden like this, with her arms wrapped around a man. She could feel hard muscles even more clearly than when they danced the night before. She wasn't sure if it was that, or the speed, that made her light-headed.

Throthgar turned off the road, onto a narrower one that led up one of the hills, to a copse of trees at the top.

"I promised we wouldn't go too far," Throthgar grinned, as he reigned Njall to a stop. "You can even see the city from here."

He pointed to the west, and Carolyn followed with her gaze.

Beyond the fields they had ridden past, Callatis sat like a shining beacon on the coast, with the blue sea beyond it. From this distance, it looked almost like a child's toy, but still close enough that they could see the layout of the city.

Throthgar dismounted, then lifted her by the waist to help her down. She could feel the heat from his hands through the layers of her bodice as he lifted her easily.

He kept his hands there as he set her down, ensuring she was steady before easing them back.

"I like to see the city from here," he said. "It reminds me it's not as big as it seems."

She stepped closer, looking down at the city.

There was the middle city, with the bustling market, filled with businesses, apartments, and townhouses. Several of the main streets lead to the ports on the coast, where merchant and pleasure vessels were docked.

The Rat District on the southern side, markedly less colorful, separated by one of the larger canals.

The Noble District, where houses became larger, and farther apart as you went north. The houses of the ruling families were closest to the Silver River, across from the Aurellian District, with its own ports on the shore.

On the southern coast, between the Middle City and the Rat District, was the Lotus District. Situated on an island that had once been marshland, it was connected to the city by two bridges, but clearly distinct.

She could see boats, barely half the length of her little finger at this distance, moving up and down the canals.

"It's so big," Carolyn giggled, looking at the city again.

To see it at scale - to see the Selelon House, with its property - gave her a new appreciation for how far the city extended along the coast.

"Not compared to everything else," Throthgar said. "Look at the ocean. Or the woods to the north."

Sure enough, both the woods and the sea dwarfed Callatis completely.

"I never thought of it that way," she admitted, looking out again.

She saw white foam on the waves as they formed, crested, and rolled onto the shore. But she couldn't see how the ships bobbed on the water from this distance.

"We only rode for about half an hour," Throthgar said. "Look to the north. See that range of mountains?"

"Numitor's Peak," she said. It was the mountain in the mural in the Galloborne ballroom.

Throthgar grinned. "That's right. It's about a day and a half ride there, but we can still see it from here. And even if you climb the mountain, you can't see Callatis from there."

"That's where Ulfvard is, isn't it?" She couldn't remember precisely where the Thorinson estate was, and hadn't yet been able to check on a map.

"They do call us northerners for a reason," Throthgar said.

She blushed sheepishly.

He gave her a kind smile that made warmth spread through her.

"Yes," he said, pointing again. "North, slightly west of the tallest mountain in the range, is Wolf's Rest, our family seat. My land is further north than the main house.

"The Gallobornes are west of us, in Northvale," Throthgar went on. "Their estate goes to the coast, with the Sorensens in Marine, north of them."

She nodded. The names she knew, though she hadn't paid enough attention in her lessons to know how they all fit together.

"Summerwoods is northeast from here," Carolyn said, gesturing in the general direction of her family's seat. Though she wasn't as decided as Throthgar.

"You're northeast of the Arnons, right?"

"Yes." That much she was sure of.

"That's a couple of days from the Rest," Throthgar said. "Maybe three. You could take the Northern Road, pass between the Arnon and Llewelyn territories, and most of the journey would be through Thorinson land."

Carolyn's eyes followed the Northern Road, from the western gates of the city, up to the north. It disappeared and reappeared among the hills, before finally winding out of sight. It was the road she and her family traveled to and from their estate.

"I'd like to see Wolf's Rest," she admitted, looking towards the point Throthgar had pointed out.

He chuckled. "Now which of us is being forward?"

She felt herself blush.

"I'd like to show it to you," he said.

"Why are you in Callatis, when you prefer the country?" She asked. "I'm guessing you aren't here for society. And I doubt a landed Thorinson needs to work as a thief to survive."

"Aren't you well informed?" Throthgar quirked an eyebrow. "Were you asking about me?"

"Phillipa was," she corrected.

He nodded. "Does it bother you?"

"No." She shook her head. "I don't care. I only care that you're sincere."

"I am that," he said, turning to face her. He brushed her hair off her face, looking into her eyes. "You have my word on that, Carolyn."

She shivered as she returned his gaze.

"To answer your question." His voice was soft, rumbling in his chest. "I had a friend who was my steward, who helped me run the house and land. But Byron decided to take her south, and it wasn't the same without her around."

Carolyn's mind raced as she processed what he said. First, a twinge of jealousy as he mentioned another woman. But then realization hit her when he mentioned Byron.

"Byron Galloborne's mystery lover is your steward?"

"Something like that," he said dryly. "I think being so mysterious about it is ridiculous. But Signy never was fond of attention."

"I had wondered," she said. "The Gallobornes aren't really the type to fall in love with commoners. But a woman connected to a powerful family makes more sense."

It inspired that much more curiosity in her, though. It was one thing to wonder what kind of woman could catch Byron Galloborne's attention. Even more to discover that the same woman was Throthgar's friend.

"They met when Byron came to visit me last fall. I admit, I haven't been as friendly to him since then."

"I think it's romantic," she said. "Byron always seems so proper and formal. He must really love her to whisk her away like that."

Throthgar looked back at her, and she recognized the bemusement in his eyes. It was a look Phillipa often gave her, whenever she accepted romance as an explanation for anything.

She started to feel embarrassed. But his expression softened, and she thought she recognized affection there.

"I hadn't thought of it that way," he said. "But I think you're right."

Well, that certainly wasn't something she heard often.

"Really?" She tilted her head to the side. "You don't think I'm being a silly romantic?"

"A romantic, definitely." His knuckles brushed against her cheek as he stepped closer to her. "But not silly."

She blushed. "Most people don't think there's much of a difference."

"Most people are idiots," he said bluntly, making her giggle.

He smiled, lifting her chin.

Her breath caught as he looked into her eyes, the intensity of his gaze making her knees weak.

He touched her cheek, which certainly didn't help.

"Are you going to kiss me?" she asked, trying to make her voice coy. But she heard it waver, ruining the attempt.

His smile was wolfish and playful at the same time, and she knew he hadn't missed the tremor in her voice. "Do you want me to?"

"Yes." The word came out almost before she could think. Even so, she meant it completely. "I do."

She expected him to lean in, but he didn't.

Instead, his hands cupped her face. She could feel rough calluses on his hands, but the touch was gentle. Paired with his eyes, she felt as if she were melting.

He pressed a gentle kiss against her forehead. Then the tip of her nose.

Then, only then, as she held her breath, and her heart pounded in anticipation, did his lips touch hers. All the breath seemed to disappear from her lungs as they did. And every thought vanished.

The kiss was soft and sweet, sending a thrill through her body. Like the magical light show she had once seen performed by a mage. But pure feeling rather than sight.

Created entirely by the man wrapping an arm around her waist.

She had dreamed of what her first kiss would be. It was why she had never let anyone kiss her, even when a few men had expressed interest in her. She hadn't wanted something halfhearted. Instead, she had wanted something so intense she could drown in it.

She had wanted this.

Too soon, Throthgar eased back. And while she didn't want it to stop, she found herself gasping for air.

Throthgar rested his forehead against hers, and she saw that his eyes were still closed. From this close, she could see that his eyelashes weren't quite black. They were dark chestnut, like his hair.

When he opened his eyes, meeting her gaze, her knees became weak again.

"I thought I might be falling in love with you," he said. "Now I know that I am."

Her heart leaped in her chest. "Do you mean that, Throthgar?"

He kissed her again. A little less gentle, but even more thrilling. "With all my heart."

She almost said the words in return. There was little doubt in her mind that she was falling in love with him.

But instead, she decided to play coy, and just smiled at him. He had only said he was falling, not that he loved her. She could keep her own feelings to herself a little longer.

In The Arena

Hammond hadn't entirely believed Marcus when he said that the arena on the solstice was a different experience. He had been here plenty of times before, including other feast days. The atmosphere was almost always charged with energy, like a celebration or festival of its own. The temples were happy to send priests or priestesses to bless the games, or present garlands to the victors. How could it be more intense or exciting than when he had attended the Feast of Numitor?

And yet, somehow, it was.

It might have been the fresh energy of a new summer. The days had just become brighter and longer, so everything felt like a new beginning. Rather than in the late summer, with heat and tension, when Numitor was celebrated.

Perhaps the opening ceremony had pleased Aurora, and she had blessed the games with pleasant weather.

Or it was simply that Richard and Marcus were so pleased as to be infectious.

The arena was a large, oblong space filled with sand, broken up with stone columns, and two statues of armored gladiators on plinths shrouded by vines. At the far ends, to the east and west, two laurel trees grew, their beds set apart by polished sandstone. There were also two lengths of waist-high lattice fence. All the obstacles were carefully arranged, so they didn't look haphazard or cluttered. More than a few times, Hammond caught himself analyzing the space, and ways to use the obstacles to his advantage in a fight. However, he had no interest in stepping into the ring the way some nobles did.

Around the perimeter, beneath the stands, were four sets of massive double doors that led into the underground chambers where the gladiators waited.

The Di Antonios' box was the largest in the arena, with cushioned seats for their guests, shaded with a gold embroidered, purple canopy. The Di Antonio and Galloborne banners were stationed on each side of the box, while Lucius, Aelia, and Lagan's banners hung over the edge of the stone balcony.

Their party consisted of Marcus and Lucilla, the Gallobornes, and Phillipa, with open seats left for Throthgar and Carolyn.

Two servants went between the guests, and the refreshment table in the back. They kept everyone supplied with cool drinks and ices to ward off the heat, as well as fruits and cold meats.

Vetr had chosen to haunt the refreshment table, waiting to see if a scrap of meat would fall to the floor. Or if the footmen would turn their backs long enough for him to steal something.

Richard was seated between Marcus and Phillipa in the front row, dividing his attention between them as they watched the fights. Unlike the night before, Phillipa didn't seem to be playing. She alternated between talking to Richard, and the others in the box.

Occasionally she glanced around, and Hammond could guess that she was wondering where Carolyn was. When she did, her eyes would land on Hammond, and he could feel a sense of guilt by association.

The thought he had any control over his cousin was laughable. A few of his cousins might respect him as the future head of the family. But he had never even bothered trying with Throthgar. He was two years younger than his cousin, and they had grown up together. It was impossible to hope that Throthgar would ever see him as an authority figure.

"Aelia's next," Marcus said, as the gladiators from the previous fight left the arena, and a trumpet sounded. His expression reminded Hammond of a father boasting about his child's achievements.

"Who is she fighting?" Richard asked.

"A new gladiator," Marcus said. "He goes by The Ghost."

Hammond did his best to hide his frown.

The Ghost was an old legend from the north. A vigilante sometimes mistaken for a vengeful spirit who appeared when Cardea was in great need. Though the last sighting had been more than half a century ago.

He looked over at the sound of motion at the back of the box. Throthgar pushed aside the curtain draped over the entry, holding it open for Carolyn to enter. Hammomd sighed, not missing the way Throthgar's hand brushed against her back as she walked past him. A subtle but intimate touch.

Carolyn beamed at Throthgar, taking his hand as they approached the empty seats behind Hammond.

"What did we miss?" Throthgar asked, leaning forward towards Hammond's seat.

Vetr appeared at Throthgar's side, looking up at him expectantly.

"Hey, Vetr," Throthgar murmured, reaching over to scratch the wolf's ears.

"Almost everything," Hammond said. "There's only two fights left."

"The ones that matter," Throthgar grinned, making Carolyn giggle.

The trumpets called again, and one of the gates opened.

A chorus of cheers greeted Aelia's appearance, so loud Hammond thought he felt the arena tremble at the force of the sound.

Aelia played to the crowd, raising her spear in response to the cheers. Which just excited them more. She moved around the column near her, to be sure no one's view was obscured.

Her armor was similar to the show armor she had worn at the ball, though less polished. A red skirt with gold embroidery and trim came just past her mid-thigh, her lower legs protected by bronze grieves. Like the men, her toned belly was exposed, with a layered bronze breastplate over her chest. Her wide belt had metal plates at the hips, embossed with a panther, to match the crest of her helmet. Her face was covered, but her braids could be seen beneath the peacock feathers trailing from the helmet crest. Another panther circled the buckler she carried on her left forearm.

"I didn't realize Aelia was so popular," Carolyn said, looking out over the arena, and the crowds, with wide, deep blue eyes.

"I think she's more popular than Lucius," Throthgar said. They still held hands, and he stroked his thumb over the back of her hand while he spoke. "Lucius might have plenty of girls fawning over him. But I think half the arena, men and women, would bow at Aelia's feet if she asked."

Carolyn giggled again.

"Oh, more than half," Lucilla said, with a knowing smile. "If Marcus's surveys are any indication."

Hammond snickered, looking out to where Aelia still reveled in the adoration of the crowd.

Another gate in the arena opened as the cheers started to die away. There was a smattering of cheers around the arena, but nothing compared to what Aelia had received.

"He can't be pleased with that response." By contrast, Marcus sounded thoroughly pleased.

"A little resentment makes things more interesting," Throthgar agreed. "What's his name?"

"The Ghost," Richard said. "I suppose he wants to cause a stir."

Hammond felt Throthgar tense.

"Don't," Hammond breathed.

"Disrespectful bastards," he muttered. But he leaned back in his chair. Vetr whined in agreement, resting his muzzle on Throthgar's thigh.

Hammond glared over his shoulder, before returning his attention to the arena.

The so-called Ghost was about Aelia's height, and a little broader. Nowhere near as broad or powerful as Lucius, or Lagan, he guessed. His armor appeared well-made, but not as grand as what Marcus and Richard had provided for their gladiators. His sponsor was either less prosperous, or less invested. It was a dull silver, trying to look like a ghostly apparition, though it was a bit silly in the bright midday. He carried a short sword and dagger, fingers flexing around the handles.

His swagger suggested arrogance, though. As did the way he attempted to play to the crowd the way Aelia had. And he did get some cheers.

"He's been fighting for the last few weeks, since the arena reopened. Sponsored by Casus Murena," Marcus said. "Not bad. But I doubt he'll give Aelia much trouble."

"Short-range weapons, against a spear?" William shook his head. "He doesn't stand a chance."

"Don't underestimate it," Marcus said. "Katherine uses a short sword and dagger. I wouldn't challenge her no matter what weapon I had."

Hammond looked across the arena to the canopy, where he could see Katherine lounging in her seat beside his sister. He had no doubt at least one blade was hidden on her body somewhere. She didn't look ready for a fight, but he knew from experience that that was an illusion.

Once more, he returned his attention to the arena as the two gladiators circled each other.

Aelia dragged the tip of her spear in the sand. Her movements were predatory, but flashy. Like any good gladiator, she knew how to put on a show. It was why the crowd loved her.

The Ghost spun his sword over the back of his hand, the hilt landing back in his palm. A flashy move in an attempt to appear casual and at ease.

Aelia swung her spear in a wide, flashy arc. Then stepped closer to her opponent. Testing him.

He didn't waver, or step back. Instead, he stepped closer, swinging his short sword at Aelia's armored left shoulder. But she flicked her wrist, swatting the blade away with her buckler.

He tried to take the opening. Lunging forward, he stabbed his dagger at her bare stomach. But her spear swung around, and he stopped inches before running into the blade.

The gladiators' weapons were dulled to avoid damaging their opponents. But a stab like that would still hurt.

The crowd cheered as the Ghost took a step back to regroup.

Aelia stepped back as well, giving him space.

Playing with him.

Marcus had found both his gladiators in the arena. They were shining examples of the opportunity the arena presented. Commoners with next to no options, who had stepped into the fights to take their chances. Only to catch the eye of the sponsor every gladiator wanted. Now they lived in luxury private apartments on the Di Antonio property.

But like Marcus, they were also soldiers. Hammond had seen both in action during the Cimbrian War. They had been terrifying on the battlefield. Aelia had once ripped through a line of archers with a barbaric ferocity that had left him stunned.

But here in the arena, in lighter armor that showed off her muscles, and curves... she was having fun. He could see a difference in the way she moved. He could still see traces of the soldier in the gladiator. But this was a game for her. And she knew how to play to the crowd.

Her spear arced through the air, almost lazily, getting a pleased murmur from the crowd. Throthgar hadn't been wrong. There were people in the crowd who would grovel at the ground she walked on if it would get her attention.

She let the Ghost come to her.

He squared his shoulders, stepping forward. And Aelia swayed, but didn't move.

The Ghost pretended to lunge. Trying to put on a show. And it might have worked against any other opponent.

She didn't flinch. Which only seemed to aggravate the Ghost. He surged forward again, feinting with his sword from above.

When Aelia's spear knocked it aside, his dagger drove toward her stomach. But Aelia spun out of the way in an effortless pirouette.

While he was adjusting his balance, Aelia closed the space between them.

The sole of her boot collided with his chest.

As the Ghost stumbled back, Hammond could see him try to maintain his balance.

But after a moment, he fell hard, landing on his back.

The crowd cheered, mixed with a few laughs.

"If you're going to appropriate a legend, at least do it justice," Throthgar muttered.

Marcus chuckled. "Half the fun of the arena is seeing people get carried away by their egos."

Aelia closed in.

"Not so soon, Aelia," Marcus murmured. "Draw it out longer."

To the Ghost's credit, he wasn't about to be taken down so easily. He rolled over, pushing his upper body off the sands of the arena.

Hammond's brow quirked, impressed despite himself.

Vetr left where he had been sitting next to Throthgar, and went over to prop his paws on the balcony's edge. He cocked his white head to the side as he watched the gladiators.

The Ghost realized he couldn't get back on his feet before Aelia reached him. Thinking fast, he shifted his body and made a sweeping kick toward Aelia's ankles.

She had just enough time to jump up and miss the kick.

The time it took her to recover was just enough for the Ghost to gauge where his weapons had fallen. And he dove for the dagger, which was the closest one.

Aelia stalked toward her opponent, and Hammond saw more of the soldier in her movements now. That kick had come close to colliding. And she didn't like close calls.

The energy in the arena tightened, waiting to see what she would do.

The Ghost rolled onto one knee as he stabbed at her again. But his aim was skewed, and the blade glanced off the polished metal plate on her hip.

Before he could regroup, the tip of Aelia's spear was at his throat. She stepped closer, and forced him onto his back again.

Aelia accepted surrender only when her foot was planted squarely on his chest. Her arm moved ever so slightly. Just enough to look as though she would thrust the spear into his throat.

Hammond felt his heart jolt. Forgetting for a moment that killing your opponent was strictly forbidden.

It looked as though Aelia said something to the Ghost. Before his head fell back on the sand, and he held up his hands in surrender.

The crowd exploded with cheers.

"Now that's how you put on a show!" Marcus said, as Aelia stepped back from the Ghost to bask in the adulation from the crowd.

⚜ CHAPTER 2 ⚜

The cheers from the crowd continued as two priestesses of Aurora came into the arena. One set a crown of flowers on Aelia's head, kissing her cheek as she did, while the other handed her a basket of fruit. A symbol of Aurora's blessing.

With her helmet off, Aelia's grin was visible as she spoke to the priestesses for a moment before turning back to the stands. Raising her spear again, to start another wave of cheers.

"She's worse than Lucius," Katherine said, rolling her eyes. But she smiled as she took a sip of chilled wine.

"I think she earned it," Eydis said. "How can someone call themselves the Ghost, and then be so weak? Have some respect for tradition!"

Ella giggled, but didn't comment. Instead, she bit into a fruit tart filled with sweet custard, and enjoyed the taste on her tongue as she listened to her companions.

The canopy, made of white linen, had space for sixteen people, and a small refreshment table manned by two of the Di Antonio footmen. She had dreamed of sitting here, right on the balcony looking down into the arena.

It hadn't disappointed so far.

The other seats were occupied by various Aurellian District nobles she didn't recognize. They had been friendly, and a few of the women had greeted Katherine. But the three had mostly kept to themselves, chatting as they watched the fights.

"You're getting a bit heated over a legend," Katherine pointed out.

Eydis looked as if she had been caught out, but quickly tried to hide it. "I just think it's disrespectful."

Katherine hummed. "At least it's not someone going into the arena calling themselves Wulfgar, or Brynnja. That would be disrespectful."

Eydis grumbled as she leaned back in her seat.

As Aelia finally left the arena, Ella shivered.

As much as she enjoyed watching the fights, and seeing the skills of the gladiators, the ending was her favorite part. It meant she was that much closer to seeing Lucius.

With Aelia and the Ghost gone from the arena, people in the stands stood to stretch their legs and chat amongst themselves. They had a quarter of an hour until the final fight, giving people time to mingle.

Katherine straightened from where she had been lounging in her seat. "I'll be back. I just saw a friend I want to say hello to." She smoothed her skirt as she stood up, then stretched her arms over her head before stepping out from the canopy.

Eydis turned to Ella, a teasing grin firmly in place as she propped her chin on her hand.

"What?" Ella could already feel her cheeks grow warm, but she had nothing to hide behind.

"Are you excited?"

"You're acting like a child," Ella said, doing her best to look prim and proper. She may have come from the lower end of the city, but her school teachers had ensured she didn't act like it.

"That doesn't answer my question." Eydis had a victorious smirk.

"Because your question is childish!" Ella insisted.

One of the footmen approached. "Would you like a strawberry ice, ma'am? You look a bit flushed."

"Yes, please," Ella said, a little too quickly.

"I'll have one as well," Eydis said, still grinning.

As the footman went to fetch the treats, Eydis stood up to stretch. "I'm looking forward to it. If I had known Richard was going to announce his gladiator last night, I would have gone to the ball."

"No, you wouldn't," Ella insisted, seizing on a foothold.

"How are you so sure?" Eydis challenged.

The footman returned, and they both murmured thanks as they accepted small glass cups with strawberry ice, decorated with a twisted slice of sugar-coated lemon.

Ella took a small bite of the ice, appreciating how cool it was in the heat. And when the footman had gone, she looked back at Eydis. "You went pale when you saw Graham in the pavilion. I don't believe for a moment that you would have gone to that ball."

Eydis shrugged, but Ella could tell she had won for the moment.

After taking a few bites of her ice, Eydis stood up. "I'll be right back. I want to take a look around."

Ella nodded. She was used to Eydis disappearing to scout out their surroundings. She was like a puppy who wanted to sniff at everything, and find out exactly what was happening.

With Eydis gone, Ella could relax, free of teasing. And she could let herself feel just how excited she was for the last fight.

"Ella." Eydis beckoned her out from under the canopy.

With a sigh she stood up, frowning as she stepped into the bright sunlight. "What?"

Eydis pointed to the right, to another landing of seats further up.

She saw Katherine leaning against the balcony, talking to a red-haired woman.

"Do you know her?" Eydis asked.

"I've seen her." Ella cocked her head to the side as she tried to remember. "Mostly just in passing around the city. But I think I've seen her in Katherine's shop a couple of times. Why?"

"Because they're acting casual, but I don't buy it."

Ella rolled her eyes, and turned back into the canopy. "Now you're just looking for conspiracies."

"I am not," Eydis insisted, following her. "I just think it's suspicious."

"Why are you suddenly suspicious of Kat?" Ella asked, lowering her voice now that they were around more people in the canopy. "I thought you liked her."

Eydis shrugged. "She's friends with Hammond, but all I really know is that they served together in the war. I'm not even sure if they were lovers, or just friends."

Ella rolled her eyes, but then paused. She had seen Hammond and Katherine together a few times. And while Katherine was flirtatious, and physically affectionate with all her friends, she supposed there was something pronounced about the way she was with Hammond.

"Does it really matter?" Ella asked.

"I'm his sister. Don't I have a right to know who he takes to bed?"

"Most siblings wouldn't want to know," Ella countered.

"You're an only child," Eydis said dismissively. "Besides, we're Thorinsons. We're involved in each other's lives."

"Does that mean you knew Throthgar was infatuated with Carolyn Selelon before he whisked her away today?"

"They met last night!" Eydis said defensively.

"Do you mean Throthgar and Carolyn?" Katherine asked, as she returned.

"Yes," Ella said. "Eydis was telling me how Thorinsons are supposed to be involved in each other's lives, so I asked how much she knows about her cousin's new love."

Eydis huffed.

"Oh, Carolyn is a sweetheart," Katherine said. "She's the youngest of five siblings, and she reads romance novels to deal with her family ignoring her. Poor thing."

Eydis blinked. "How do you know that?"

Katherine gave Eydis a mysterious, cat-like smile. "I know everything, Little Wolf."

"That's what my Aunt Düsana says." Eydis rolled her eyes in annoyance.

Katherine laughed lightly, smoothing her skirt over her long legs. "Carolyn is one of my customers. One of my best, actually."

"I've seen her at parties, but I don't think I've ever spoken to her," Ella said. Eydis had asked her for information about the woman earlier, but she couldn't give much more than that.

"Ella said she was beautiful, but unremarkable," Eydis said.

Ella blushed in embarrassment. "I didn't put it like that."

"But it's what you meant," Eydis countered.

And she couldn't argue with that. It had been her impression of the woman.

"I'm sure Throthgar will introduce her soon enough; then you can form your own impression," Katherine said. "You Thorinsons are all involved in each other's lives, after all."

Eydis blushed, Ella was pleased to see.

And when she didn't counter, Katherine looked across the arena, and changed the subject.

"I can see Richard fidgeting from here."

"Have you seen his gladiator?" Ella asked.

"Lucius gave me a sneak peek when he was training." Katherine grinned, fanning herself with a hand dramatically. "I had half a mind to invite him over."

"Do you ever stop?" Ella asked, rolling her eyes.

"Why should she?" Eydis giggled. "And don't forget why you're here."

"That's different," Ella insisted. Her interest in Lucius wasn't just because of his rippling muscles. Or his intensity in the arena. It was because... It occurred to her that she wasn't quite sure what it was about Lucius that drew her in. She hadn't spoken more than a few words with him, so it wasn't as if she had much of a foundation for her feelings. Other than the romantic notion that the Maiden meant to guide them together.

"Not really," Katherine said. "There's not that much difference between lust and a crush. They're both just a desire for more. More attention, more contact, more intimacy."

"I never thought of it like that," Eydis said, looking down at the arena thoughtfully.

Before they could say more, a trumpet sounded to announce that the next fight would begin in a moment.

Ella pushed her thoughts aside, leaning forward in anticipation. Inside her boots, her toes curled in excitement. It had been weeks since she had seen Lucius in the arena, and she was more than ready now.

Finally, there was another blast on the trumpet. And her heart skipped a beat.

But instead of one of the gates opening to expose Lucius, she heard Marcus's voice.

"People of Cardea!" His voice boomed through the arena, which seemed designed to ensure his words reached every person there.

A hush fell over the crowd as they looked towards the Di Antonios' box.

Marcus stood at the front, Lucilla looking pristine on his right. If the heat bothered her, there was no indication of it. Richard was on his left, looking almost as impatient as Ella felt.

"For the final spectacle of our Summer Solstice games, Lord Galloborne and I have a special treat for you. My gladiator, Lucius Gaspari, the Lion of the Arena--"

He had to stop as the crowd cheered, and he nodded approval.

"Today, Lucius makes his return. And it is my honor to announce that his opponent will be Lord Galloborne's gladiator, in his debut fight."

There was a chorus of cheers, just at the idea of something new. A fighter they hadn't seen before.

The doors directly across from where Ella sat opened. She knew almost immediately that it wasn't Lucius. Even as he appeared through the shadows, she could see that it wasn't his walk.

Still confident, but not the same strut. His movements were more controlled and decided, with less of a sway. Then he came closer to the light, and she could see that his armor was blue, rather than red. Instead of a scutum shield and sica sword, he carried a net, and a golden trident. Not a unique weapon set in the arena. But it fit the nautical theme someone had chosen for him. As did the crest of his helmet, which looked like a horse rising from the waves, with a dark blue plume hanging down his back.

"From the Hvall Archipelago, here to test his mettle, I give you Lagan Stiggson, the Master of the Seas!"

There were a few cheers, but they were more from anticipation than anything.

Katherine purred her approval.

And then one of the other doors opened.

Ella sighed, frustrated that she didn't have as good a view as she had with Lagan's entrance. But this time, there was an eruption of cheers. Not quite as loud or enthusiastic as they had been for Aelia. But still enough to make the arena seem to shake from the excitement.

Standing up, without caring what anyone thought, she approached the railing.

Lucius' armor looked slightly different, having been updated in the off-season. His helmet was still a roaring lion, with a red plume that matched the rest of his armor.

Like Aelia, he played to the crowd. And Ella noticed she wasn't the only young woman standing at the railing. Some were commoners, but quite a few were noblewomen, both from the city proper, and from the Aurellian District. She felt a bitter tension in her chest as she watched them cheer and applaud her gladiator.

But she forced herself to take a deep breath, and looked back to where Lucius was reveling in it. Watched the visible planes of his chest, and the way his muscles rippled as he held up his sword, with its angled tip.

Both gladiators approached each other across the sand, moving with almost equal confidence.

The sica and the trident crossed in a brief, friendly salute before they took a step back, and began sizing each other up.

Lagan let go of his trident, adjusting his grip as he caught it again. A small but showy gesture that even Ella could appreciate.

With all the time she had spent in the arena, waiting and hoping to see Lucius, she had gained an appreciation for the games.

And a bit of expertise. She had begun to notice patterns, and the signs of a good gladiator—the difference between a good fighter, and a good showman.

Between Aelia and Lucius, even she could admit that Aelia was the better fighter. But Lucius was the better showman.

Ella leaned her elbows on the balcony's edge as she watched the two circle each other.

❧ CHAPTER 3 ❧

Richard and Marcus had used the fact that their gladiators had never fought as a selling point for this fight. And Ella could tell quickly that it was true.

They circled slowly. Sizing each other up. Both cautious, and reluctant to make the first move.

Lucius broke first, and feinted. Stepping closer with his shield, as if preparing to rush him. Then laughed when Lagan flinched backward.

Lagan didn't seem to find it funny, and he lunged with his trident. It wasn't a feint, and Lucius regained his shield just in time.

The trident's center tine glanced off the shield's curved edge. But despite the emotional attack, Lagan's movements remained controlled. He didn't let momentum carry him closer to his opponent, and pulled back quickly.

Lucius closed the space between them. Pressing with his shield, while swiping with his sword. But Lagan moved out of the way.

They were still sizing each other up. Learning how the other responded, and looking for weaknesses. None of the blows were meant to land. Just to see how the other would respond.

Lucius nodded as he stepped back, and Ella found herself smiling. Lagan was reactive, and easily shaken. In the arena for the first time, no doubt he was nervous, and Ella could appreciate that. But it didn't change that emotional responses were a disadvantage.

He might become a great gladiator, but he didn't yet have experience.

Unlike Lucius, who was in his element. He was the Lion of the Arena. A position he had earned through blood and sweat.

They circled each other again. And this time Lucius attacked. Not a feint. He kept the shield up to protect himself, the angled tip of his sword darting around the shield to slash at Lagan.

Lagan cast his net over the sword with a flick of his wrist. Lucius made a startled sound as the net trapped him, and pulled his arm out of the way. Adjusting his hold on the trident, Lagan stabbed it toward Lucius' exposed chest.

Ella felt her heart stutter in her chest.

But Lucius pulled his shield up in time, blocking the blow. Safely behind it, he surged forward. Putting the weight of his shoulder into the push.

Lagan was forced back. And Lucius pulled his sword free from the net as he took a couple of steps back.

Lagan retreated. His head turned, the plumb of his helmet swaying as he examined the arena.

He stepped back, into the shadow of one of the statues. The statue was one of Tallus Octavius Di Antonio's original gladiators. A male sword wielder. It was massive, the plinth taller than Lagan's head, shrouded in moonflower vines with white blossoms.

A few audience members jeered and laughed as he crouched down by the statue. But Ella found herself leaning forward in curiosity. So much so that she almost didn't notice when Katherine came up beside her at the rail.

"He's a hunter," Katherine murmured, leaning over the rail as well.

Ella looked over at her in surprise.

"Not a monster Hunter," Katherine clarified. "A game hunter. Though, coming from Hvall, he probably has some experience with monsters."

"How can you tell?"

"See the way he's looking around?" Katherine pointed out. "He's not hiding - he's calculating. I'm hoping he'll use the arena to his advantage. Then we'll get a show."

Lucius was stalking toward the statue. Almost lazily, his sword and shield were at ease

"Don't underestimate him, you idiot," Katherine muttered.

Ella bristled. "Who are you calling an idiot?"

"Calm down, lover girl. I've known Lucius a lot longer than you have," Katherine said. "Believe me, he has his moments."

In her indignation on Lucius' behalf, she almost missed the way Lagan's hold shifted on his trident as Lucius drew closer. His other hand adjusted the net. And he shifted his body weight.

Next to her, Katherine leaned forward to brace her elbows on the balcony rail.

As Lucius neared the statue, Lagan backed up, circling the plinth.

Lucius followed.

And Ella understood why Katherine had said not to underestimate him. Lagan was taking advantage of Lucius' false sense of security.

She felt her stomach quiver nervously as they moved out of sight around the column.

"Oh, come on!" Katherine hissed.

They heard a commotion, and there was a cheer from the people who could see what happened.

"Damn it!" Ella cursed, knuckles white as she clenched her fists in frustration.

The two gladiators came back into view, Lucius pressing Lagan back with his shield.

The Master of the Seas struggled to try and keep his ground. But Lucius bore down, forcing him to step back again, and again.

Ella bit her lip, fidgeting in excitement as she grinned. She had seen Lucius use this move to best his opponents multiple times. The fight was almost over.

But Lagan shifted. Still pushing back, but adjusting his hold on his trident. He jabbed it forward, around the shield.

Ella gasped as she heard Lucius grunt in pain, and he stumbled back.

She leaned forward, watching Lucius press a hand to the thick leather belt around his waist.

"He's fine," Katherine said. "His ego is more bruised than he is."

"I know," she said, trying to assure herself as much as Katherine. She knew the weapons used in the arena weren't sharp. But it didn't change the sense of panic every time a weapon struck Lucius. Accidents happened, as she had seen firsthand. Especially when it came to stabs.

Lagan gave Lucius only a moment to make sure there was no damage. Then he lunged again. Moving like a panther, he attacked with his trident.

When Lucius raised his shield in defense, the trident pulled back. And the net flew over the shield.

"Smart," Katherine murmured. "It won't work, but it's the right idea."

Of course it wouldn't work, Ella thought. Watching Lucius the summer before, she had quickly noticed that he favored his shield. If forced to choose between a weapon and a shield, he chose the shield. For good reason.

Lucius surged towards Lagan, and the shield collided with the other gladiator's armored shoulder.

As they were locked together, Lucius worked his other arm between them. Elbowing an unprotected spot on Lagan's ribs to force him back.

It gave him space to pull the shield free from the net as he stepped back. But he barely had time to recover before Lagan charged again.

He didn't give Lucius a chance to raise his shield this time. Instead, he wedged an elbow behind it, exposing Lucius' chest. He used his other hand to keep the sword at bay. While he bore down with his shoulder, pushing him back.

There was a flutter among the crowd as the two gladiators were locked together. Weapons and defenses were useless as they wrestled, trying to overpower each other.

Ella heard her heart pounding in her ears. While Katherine leaned further over the railing, trying to get a closer look.

She didn't see how it happened. But one of them surged, and Lucius' helmet was knocked off, falling to the sand and rolling away.

It was her turn to lean further over the rail. But Lagan was in the way, so she couldn't see more than Lucius' short-cropped dark hair.

There was a tug at the back of her bodice, and she looked back to find Katherine smirking as she held onto her collar.

"I wouldn't want you to fall in," Katherine teased. "More than you already have, I mean."

Ella huffed. But was distracted a moment later when the two gladiators pulled back. Neither had succeeded in overpowering the other. So they both stepped back.

But not before Lucius took a swipe at Lagan's head. She blinked in surprise. But it just knocked his helmet off.

"Fair's fair, sailor!" Lucius called.

"Are gladiator fights supposed to be fair?" Lagan asked.

Lucius laughed, while they once more circled each other.

Ella couldn't help but giggle.

Lucius was the one who attacked next.

As he lunged forward, his sword swept up. And when Lagan raised his trident in defense, Lucius swept it aside. With Lagan's chest exposed, he couldn't stop the shield from slamming into him.

He stumbled back, and Lucius refused to relent. Driving forward, his full weight behind the shield, he dropped his sword to put more force behind the shield.

Until Lagan lost his balance.

He tucked his body and rolled, so he didn't fall on his back. But he was on the ground.

The crowd burst into cheers, thinking the fight was now at an end.

∘≪ CHAPTER 4 ≫∘

The Stark's box in the arena was smaller than the Di Antonios', but still with space to fit twelve comfortably. In addition to a refreshment table, and the two footmen in attendance.

Their banner, a white Phoenix on a red background, hung over the railing to announce their presence. More than any other ruling family, they sometimes seemed forced to remind people of their existence, and position, in the city.

Runa had taken a seat at the end of the first row, with Aksel Stark on her right. Reinhardt Steinmann was behind her, Godric next to him. A perfect position for someone who knew nothing about the arena, or combat.

Aksel was well informed on all (or nearly all) of the gladiators. He could tell her who sponsored them, bits about their fighting styles, and even some of their lovers. Of all the Starks, he was the most suited to city life, and Runa had always been fond of him.

Though over the last few years, she noticed him becoming quieter. Ever since the war, and his regular service in the forts around the border. There was a deep sadness in him that hadn't been there before. Her father said it was inevitable when a man had seen war, and endless border disputes.

It was an effect she had grown used to in the last five years.

Ever since the Cimbrian war, she had noticed a change in the men she had known all her life. As if a light had been dimmed, or something had been lost. She saw it in Hammond, Godric, and so many others. But she hoped Aksel wouldn't grow as jaded as his cousin Jonathan, who always seemed lost in brooding thoughts.

It made her wonder if the older men she knew had once been less weighed down. Had her father, before serving with the

Starks? What had Reinhardt been like when he was younger? It was hard to imagine them as different from what she had always known. And she was almost afraid to ask, fearing what it would mean for Godric, and Aksel.

But for now, they were both in high spirits.

Reinhardt, unlike Aksel, was far less sanguine, and less familiar with the gladiators. But he knew fighting styles, strategies, and the advantage of different weapons.

Godric and Aksel listened respectfully when he spoke, while Runa listened in fascination.

As a young child, the mountain of a man had frightened her when he came to visit, which he often did. But despite his daunting exterior, he had always been kind. As she had grown up, he had a way of explaining things, especially military matters, in a way she understood.

Everyone in the box was enthusiastic about enjoying the fights. Wagers had been placed on all the fights, usually helped by Aksel's information on the fighters.

Except for Aelia's fight.

Aelia's victory had been regarded as a foregone conclusion. No one wanted to make a bet against her and take the inevitable loss.

Lucius and Lagan, however, were a completely different story.

"It will be Lucius," Aksel said confidently, as they watched him play to the crowd.

"Don't be so quick to write Lagan off," Tor said, from where he sat next to Godric. "I've met a few Hvall tribesmen, and they can be fierce fighters."

Aksel shook his head, and Runa tore her gaze from watching Lagan in the arena.

"I'll take that bet," she said. To the surprise of everyone in the box. It was the first time she had gotten in on the wagers today. But between intuition, and an itch to prove Aksel wrong, she couldn't resist.

"Weren't you just telling me that gambling is a bad habit?" Godric asked, quirking an eyebrow.

"Hush," she ordered, looking back at Aksel. "Forty silver, it will be Lagan."

"You don't waste time." Aksel nodded, and offered her his hand to shake. "You're on."

The rest of the box seemed evenly divided on their bets.

As the fight continued, Runa wondered if she hadn't been too quick to make such a steep bet. It wasn't that the forty silver would be much of a loss for her. Rather, she knew Aksel would never let her forget if she was wrong.

Sure enough, Aksel crowed as Lagan hit the ground. "So, Runa, did you bring the silver with you? Or will you send it over tomorrow?"

She shot him a glare. But only for a fraction of a second.

For most of the fight, she had resisted the urge to move to the railing, trying to hide how invested she was. Now she stopped resisting, and surged out of her seat.

"Get up!" She cried, clenching the rail as she willed the gladiator to get back on his feet.

She wasn't the only one. More than a few people in the crowd were calling for Lagan to get up. Despite their initial support for Lucius, he had won some of them over.

Her heart pounded in her ears as she watched Lucius stalk towards him. The cheering of the crowd was an obnoxious buzzing in the background.

Lagan stayed on the ground, shoulders propped up as he watched Lucius approach.

But she thought she saw his left-hand twitch–the hand with the net.

"Get rid of that bloody shield," she muttered.

Reinhardt had made clear that, in Lucius' arsenal, his shield was far more valuable than the sword.

"The scutum isn't like most shields," he had explained. "It isn't strapped to the forearm. Instead, he holds it from the center, like this." He had made a fist, with his palm down. "Even if he tossed the sword aside, he could use the scutum to push his opponent around. All while it protects him from oncoming blows."

She had now seen enough to make her loathe the thing.

"Come on," she whispered.

Lucius stepped closer.

One moment, Lagan seemed still. The next, he was on his feet. Casting his net in the same motion. It caught on the shield, and he tugged hard.

Lucius was so surprised by the force that, for a moment, Runa thought the shield might fly from his grip. But he clenched it at the last moment, and pulled it back.

Undeterred, Lagan dug in his heels as he continued to pull.

Lucius tried to free the shield.

But Lagan didn't give him a chance. He slammed his shoulder into Lucius' chest, knocking him off balance. Then he twisted the net, until Lucius was forced to let go.

Lucius screamed in frustration as the shield flew from his grip. And Lagan cast the net behind him, so the shield skidded across the sand, until it ended up partially buried.

The crowd gasped, and cheered at the turnaround.

With a growl of frustration, Lucius surged at Lagan. His sword slashed, only to become tangled in the net. But he took advantage of that. Grabbing the net, he yanked his sword, slicing through the ropes. Twisting the blade to catch more of it as he cut through it.

They were now left with just offensive weapons.

Runa felt her heart pound in her chest as she watched Lagan throw the scraps of net aside. The crowd cheered in anticipation.

Lucius raised his sword just in time to ward off a blow from the trident.

The exchange of blows was equal, each pushing and pulling as they swung and parried, without either gaining an advantage. Lucius stuck close to Lagan, ensuring he couldn't take advantage of his weapon's longer reach. And Runa found she was becoming exhausted, ready for the fight to end.

"Are you having fun?" Aksel asked, coming up to join her at the railing.

"No," she snapped, watching the two continue the back and forth.

Lagan was trying to get space, but Lucius wouldn't give him the opportunity.

Aksel laughed, and she turned to glare at him.

In the brief moment she did, there was a gasp from the crowd.

When she looked back, both gladiators were locked together. Wrestling, and trying to push the other back.

"If Lucius can get him to the ground, he can overpower him," Aksel grinned.

"He has to get him there," Runa reminded.

Lagan rammed an elbow into Lucius' chest. Getting space between them. Enough to push Lucius away, and make him stumble.

Another push fully compromised his balance. He fell to his knees. Then a kick to his chest sent him onto his back.

"Dammit," Aksel muttered.

Lagan stepped up to Lucius, bringing a foot down on his chest before he could attempt to get up. Then he brought the tip of his trident to point at Lucius' throat.

There was a moment of hesitation. And the crowd seemed to hold their breath. Waiting to see if Lucius would make a last moment escape.

But Lucius raised his hands in surrender.

Despite the crowds' clear favor of Lucius initially, they now cheered at Lagan's victory.

Runa laughed, smiling until her cheeks hurt as she watched Lagan lift his arms in victory, while the crowd roared.

The Master of the Seas had earned his place in the Di Antonio arena.

He turned towards their box, and Runa's heart fluttered. She might be wrong... but she thought his eyes focused on her.

She tried to dismiss the thought. From this far away, it was hard to tell.

But he only looked away as the priestesses draped him with the victor's garland. Runa tried not to glare at the priestess, who kissed his cheek as she set the wreath on his head.

Still, his gaze returned to her.

The Guard &

The Dancer

CHAPTER 1

From its position on the northern edge of the bay, the cheers from the Di Antonio arena carried across the bay. Past the docks filled with merchant and naval vessels, until the sound reached the Lotus District.

Only a few generations earlier, the land had been uninhabitable marshland, created by the deltas of the Silver River, and rainwater that rolled downhill from the main city. Until merchants from the Meishan Empire in the east asked for safe haven. It was unclear if they had asked for the marsh, or if the republic had given it in hopes of making them leave the city.

With a few years of hard work, the refugees had shocked everyone by draining the land, and building an island for themselves. Like the main city, canals helped create boundaries between the market, the poorer residences, and the more luxurious homes of the wealthy.

A few years later, refugees from the Yamato Empire had fled an orc invasion, and come west to Cardea. Despite their peoples' fraught history, establishing a tenuous alliance with the Meishan.

A wall surrounded the island, creating a clear separation between themselves and the rest of the city. While they were subject to the laws of Cardea, they had demanded the right to establish their own council, and their own city guard. Just as the Aurellian District had. Generally, they were left to their own devices, save for a delegate assigned to keep an eye on things.

It was no secret that the residents of the district resented any interference. They insisted on taking care of their own problems, and refused to admit when those problems got out of hand.

But they didn't mind when Cardeans came to spend money in their markets. While more than a few of the merchants had lucrative dealings with the main city.

While they worshiped the titan sisters, and the pantheon of gods, they did so under different names. They didn't have the loud parties that the Cardeans used to mark the Solstices, or the days of the gods - those were bizarre to the more restrained residents of the Lotus District.

To most of them, at least.

A few of the upper-class families, who had the most connection to the main city, had taken to celebrating on the eve of the solstice. Few of them threw in-home parties. Instead, they paid for the tea houses to stay open late, with buffets of food laid out, and dancers to entertain them.

Nuan Mei found the whole thing ridiculous. It was an attempt to be more like the Cardean nobility, and for what reason?

The solstice might be holy to the Cardeans, but it wasn't to the Meishan. It never had been. It was just an excuse for the wealthy to have a party, and try to imitate the Cardeans. As if they needed another excuse to do that.

The day before the solstice, she woke before dawn. It was her turn to dust and tidy the parlors of the tea house. Then pulled out the summer dresses to air them before the Solstice.

Then came the endless parties.

The day had devolved into a blur of tea leaves, polite conversations, and the flutter of dancing silks. There hardly seemed to be a moment to catch her breath from one dance before she was called to do another.

When it finally stopped, there was a soft glow on the eastern horizon.

Nuan Mei was sore and exhausted, the bottoms of her feet raw from dancing.

As she had watched Lian He carry a sleeping Xia Mei upstairs, she knew her small room upstairs was the last place she wanted to be.

Instead, she put her silks away, and slipped out into the predawn haze.

Outside, the air was cool and fresh, free from the flowers and perfumes of the tea house. She inhaled in relief as she walked down the empty streets. A few guards were on patrol, but paid no attention to her as she crossed the bridge into the market.

A few more blocks brought her to a small tea shop on the lower end. It was humble and run down - the opposite of the red and black tea house that she could still see above the other buildings. A familiar set of steps on the outside lead to the second floor, and the three rooms rented by lower-ranking members of the guard.

Nuan Mei made her way up, careful to avoid the ones that squeaked. Then slipped into Jun Su's room. Like the shop itself, it was small, and slightly rundown. But it was clean, and mercifully quiet.

Jun Su awoke as she came in, sitting on the mattress, which was unrolled on the floor.

"Nuan Mei," he breathed, almost in awe. "What are you doing here?"

She had shushed him softly, bending down to kiss his lips.

"I missed you," she said simply, as she shed her dress. The bed was hardly big enough for the both of them, but he made room for her to lay next to him.

As soon as she had curled against his side, exhaustion caught up with her, and she fell into a deep sleep.

She got a few hours of peaceful sleep. But it seemed the world didn't want to let her rest.

First came the merchants hawking their wares down the street. Calling out to potential customers, who came out to do their morning shopping. Then there were the food carts, with their clattering utensils, and rattling wheels.

She was a light sleeper, and the walls were thin. A loud conversation in the shop below was enough to wake her up.

Those few hours of sleep gave her enough rest that she didn't resist when Jun Su's hands wandered over his body. Instead, she rolled over to kiss him. Her back arched as his hand slid down her side, and traced the curve of her hip.

She reveled in their lovemaking, losing herself in it. Forgetting about cultures and customs in favor of passion.

But when the sun rose, they could feel the heat through the eastern wall. As it grew hotter, the air became muggy. Sweat beaded on her skin, and her hair clung to her face, neck, and back.

She and Jun Su wordlessly moved apart, trying to get as much space as possible.

They had talked about going to the temple of the Sun Empress in the afternoon. But neither of them had any interest to go anywhere in the heat of the day.

Save for late in the morning, when she begged Jun Su to get dressed, and bring her chilled noodles from one of the merchants down the street. She knew he couldn't resist her, and felt a little bad for taking advantage of that... but not enough to get dressed and go with him.

He also brought cool tea, which she rewarded with a kiss, before pulling away from the heat that radiated from his body.

Just before midday, a breeze came through the small window. Bringing with it the sound of distant cheers.

The noise only seemed to get louder as the hours wore on.

She sighed, still exhausted, but unable to get back to sleep. "Do they have to be so loud?"

"They should be almost done," Jun Su murmured, running a hand over her naked back.

The heat had at least started to ease, so the touch was more calming than irritating. Even if her skin was still damp.

Part of her wished she had stayed in the tea house. Where she had a bed raised off the floor, far less noise, and air currents created by mages to cool the rooms. If she were there, she could have enjoyed a breakfast of chilled fruit, a sweet roll, and milk tea.

Instead, she was in a rented room, waiting for a breeze to come through the single window. On a mattress on the floor, with thin, scratchy cotton sheets.

But Jun Su was there.

And she couldn't regret the time spent with him.

She looked over at where he lay on the floor, letting her have the bed. Smiling a little as she did. After getting food for them, he had stripped down to his pants, and lay on his stomach on the floor.

"What?" Jun Su asked.

Ignoring the stale air, and the uncomfortable heat, she rested a hand on his cheek as she leaned in to kiss his lips.

When she eased back, Jun Su smiled, brushing her hair off her forehead.

"I'm glad I came," she murmured.

Jun Su chuckled dryly as he sat up. "I'm glad you came as well. Though I'm not sure why you do."

Nuan Mei shrugged. "Because I wanted to."

He rose from the floor, stretching his back as he stood up. Nuan Mei watched, her eyes sweeping over his body, and the lean, defined muscle. Poor guard he might be, though it was easy to forget when he looked like that.

She watched as he went over to the washbasin in the corner, splashing water on the back of his neck.

Nuan Mei became aware that the sounds from across the bay had subsided. Leaving just the sound of the market outside. She could finally get back to sleep, before she had to return to the tea house.

She was starting to drift off when the sound of an aggressive argument outside broke the quiet.

Nuan Mei sat up, her heart skittering nervously in her chest.

Jun Su went over to the window, looking down into the street.

"What is it?" she asked, pulling the blanket up to cover her chest. Part of her wanted to go over to the window, but she didn't want to stand up.

"It looks like it's the gangs," Jun Su said, frowning as he looked down.

Nuan Mei couldn't hear the words, but she could hear the anger in the voices.

"What are you doing?" she hissed, as Jun Su began to grab his clothes and tug them on.

"I'm going to try and break them up before it turns into a fight," he said.

"Don't do that!" Nuan Mei stood up, putting her hands on his bare chest as he shrugged into his shirt.

"Nuan Mei, I'm a guard." He sighed as he rested his hands over hers. "It's my responsibility."

"No, it's not! It's the responsibility of guards who are on duty."

"It's my duty," Jun Su insisted. He brushed her hands off his chest to tie his belt around his waist. "I can't ignore them when they're right outside my window."

The argument grew louder, and Nuan Mei was sure they would soon come to blows. There were at least four voices, possibly more.

"I don't care," she said. "Stay here." She reached up to run her fingers through his shoulder-length black hair. "Please, Jun Su. Just stay with me."

He sighed her name, brushing his knuckles over her cheek. "I can't do that."

He stepped away from her, not noticing her annoyance as he went to grab his sword.

But before he could leave her in the room, they heard the sound of clattering armor outside. They both went over to the window to look down into the street.

Six guards had arrived on the scene, all fully armed. And Nuan Mei sighed in relief as they stepped between the gang members. There were four of them, posturing, and stepping close to antagonize each other.

"There," she said. "You don't have to go."

"I still should." But she could hear the hesitation in his voice even as he said it.

She wrapped her arms around his waist. "It's fine. See? It's already over."

The guards separated the gang members, forcing them to keep moving in different directions. A couple of the young men glared, but didn't dare try to disobey the guards ushering them along.

Jun Su sighed, and she rested her head on his chest as she hugged his waist. He returned the hug, kissing the top of her head.

"You know it's my job to deal with them," he murmured against her hair.

She ignored that, as she always tried to, and went over to the washbasin. Wetting a cloth to press against her forehead, and wiping down her upper body.

Jun Su sighed, but he didn't try to argue with her. He rarely did.

She watched from the corner of her eye as he put away his sword, and once more shed his shirt.

Knowing she had gotten her way this time gave her a sense of satisfaction. But it was hard to deny the sense of dread that was always hard to ignore.

Because she loved that he was a simple man. He wasn't one of the men who came to the tea house, who gave no thought to the people their decisions affected. He lived in a small, single room and didn't play with people's lives.

But he was a good man. A guard with a strong moral compass. And she knew she couldn't always convince him to ignore it.

In The Courtyard

⊶ CHAPTER 1 ⊷

While the Di Antonios might not be a ruling family, that didn't stop them from living like one.

When Callatis had been rebuilt, and the Aurellian District established, they had snatched up a sizable chunk of land. Situated on a bluff overlooking the sea, with an uninterrupted view of the sea. While the front gate looked out over the district, and the city beyond.

After Tallus Di Antonio had rebuilt the arena, in 1448, he had been so pleased with his success that he hired the same artisans to rebuild his villa. One that was just as much a work of art as the arena.

A volcanic stone wall surrounded the estate, the gold and iron gate flanked by two full-sized, winged marble horses. A long, tiled walkway led past manicured gardens, with clear pools, and towering marble columns. Past houses for favored servants, as well as sponsored artisans, and the gladiators.

The main house was in the classic Aurellian style—four stories of gilded marble and sandstone, columns, and high arches. Reliefs and murals on the walls and pediments depicted scenes from legend, and the family's history. Long hallways and airy chambers were filled with paintings, sculptures, and pottery.

Runa had visited the house many times since she was a child, even before Marcus had married Lucilla. So she knew much of the artwork had been there before. But after their marriage, they had remodeled the villa, and Lucilla had left her mark. Giving it a more feminine, welcoming touch. The main halls held fewer depictions of warriors, in favor of beautiful men and women at ease. Combined with lighter colors, and more open spaces.

As usual, the Sorensens were given the Peacock Suite to freshen up. It was one of the finer guest suites in the villa, decorated in the colors of a peacock's plume. Their servants had arrived that morning, preparing baths, and laying out their clothes for the evening. Gianna led Runa to a washroom, where the statue of a nymph poured water into a deep, hammered brass tub. Runa sank into the warm water to wash off the dirt and heat of the arena.

Once she had bathed, Runa dressed in a sky-blue gown, and Gianna styled her hair. Less grand than the ball the night before, but elegant enough for a Di Anotonio party.

The double doors at the back of the house opened onto a terrace overlooking the courtyard. A long set of stone steps led down to a tiled patio. In the center, a shallow pool sparkled in the light of the evening sun, surrounded by columns wrapped in garlands. In the center, a group of marble maidens splashed in the water, watched over by handsome, shirtless guards.

Four tables, covered in purple cloths, and ladened with refreshments, were set around the edge of the pool. Flanked by tall vases of sunflowers, hollyhocks, gladiolus, and larkspur.

A grassy lawn surrounded the patio, with scattered fruit trees, and a flower garden to the right. A pair of peacocks ambled across the lawn, unbothered by the guests as they arrived. Beyond the garden, a terrace provided a perfect view of the sea.

At the bottom of the steps, Marcus and Lucilla waited to greet their guests.

"I'm so glad we could have you here tonight," Lucilla said, kissing Pia's cheek. "It's an honor."

"Thank you, Lucilla." Pia returned the smile. "The courtyard is beautiful. You've outdone yourself."

"She always does," Marcus beamed, wrapping an arm around his wife's waist. "Galatea herself has truly blessed me."

"I do my best," Lucilla said, smiling at her husband.

"Did you enjoy the fights, Runa?" Marcus asked, giving her a knowing smile. "Or the finale, at least? Aksel mentioned you won a pretty sum from him."

"I did," she said, trying not to blush. "You know how Aksel is. He was so confident in the outcome, I couldn't resist challenging him. Just for fun."

"That's what the games are for," Marcus said. "A fun way to challenge each other. Next time you come, we'll have you in our box."

"It probably won't be long before she takes you up on that," Godric said. He poked her side before she could swat his hand away.

Runa glared at him, but tried to look unbothered by the teasing.

"Let me know anytime you want to come," Marcus said. "Any of you."

"Thank you, Marcus," Tor said.

Marcus bowed his head respectfully. "Enjoy the party, all of you."

They all murmured their thanks, before continuing into the courtyard.

The guest list was more pleasant than the ball the night before, Runa noted, as she looked around. While Richard had invited most of the ruling families, Marcus was under no such obligation. No doubt he had invited a few of the Aurellian District nobles out of obligation. But there was no sign of the Randells, or the Gerrods. That alone was an improvement.

Richard smiled as they approached, and came to greet them. More at ease than he had been the night before, since he didn't have the responsibility of playing host. "I wondered when the Sorensens would make their appearance."

He clasped wrists with Tor, before respectfully kissing Pia's cheek. Runa accepted a similar greeting, before turning to Hammond.

"I imagine you're ready for the parties to be over."

"I am," he admitted. But he kept his voice low so only she could hear. "It's been a long week."

Runa nodded sympathetically. "How did Richard take the victory?"

"I've never seen him so delighted," Hammond chuckled. "Even when we were children."

"He's waited a long time for this," Runa noted.

A footman bearing a refreshment tray came over, and Runa took a glass of sparkling white wine with pomegranate juice.

"Now that the solstice is over, I can finally get some work done," Hammond said, taking a sip of his drink.

"You're returning to the Rest for your birthday next week, aren't you?" She asked.

He nodded. "I'm looking forward to that, too."

As much as Runa enjoyed the society of the city, she was more than ready for a few days to rest, now that the solstice festivities were ending. But that didn't mean she wouldn't enjoy tonight.

"Is Eydis here?" She asked. Though she already knew the answer.

Hammond shook his head as he took a sip of his wine. "Marcus told me to invite her, but she, Ella, and Katherine all declined. I don't understand why she can't even pretend to interact with society."

Runa looked to where Graham Galloborne stood nearby, talking to Aksel Stark as she took another sip of her wine.

"Even Throthgar is here tonight," Hammond said. "Somewhere."

"Probably waiting for Phillipa and Carolyn," Runa guessed. "I believe they're freshening up here. And Phillipa won't come out until she's sure she looks perfect."

Hammond nodded, understanding.

"Don't worry about Eydis," Runa said. "I think she'll adjust to society eventually. Just give her time. Even Adrian doesn't make many appearances."

"Adrian is my second cousin," Hammond said. "He's allowed to be reclusive."

"What about Nikolas?" She countered.

Nikolas Lumina was Hammond's cousin on his mother's side. While the Luminas weren't a ruling family, they were nobility, and Nikolas held a position on the Council of Prefects. A position Runa well knew Hammond had forced him into after the war. An attempt for Hammond to consolidate power during his term as counselor, and beyond. But while Nikolas was far more sociable than Hammond, he hated formal events.

Hammond groaned, and gave her a look that begged for mercy. "Don't remind me."

Runa bit back a giggle, not wanting him to think his suffering amused her. Watching him try and keep his cousins in line was like watching him try to herd cats. And yet there was something about his reaction that she found rather adorable. Not that she would ever embarrass him by saying so aloud.

"If you can get Nikolas to a party, I'll help keep an eye on him," she offered, to compensate for her amusement. "I can't make any promises for Eydis, though."

"If anyone can keep her in line, it's you," Hammond said. "But I wouldn't ask that of you. Nikolas, on the other hand... I may have to take you up on that."

She inclined her glass towards him, and he gave her a wry smile as he tapped his against hers, before they both took a drink.

There was a commotion behind her, and she noticed Richard's attention turn toward the stairs.

"There they are," Hammond murmured.

Runa looked back to see Phillipa had arrived. She was dressed in wine-colored silk, her honey-blonde hair in an elegant updo.

Behind her, Carolyn was on Throthgar's arm, looking blissfully happy. Throthgar looked far more comfortable in a less formal outfit than he had worn at the ball. But still fashionable enough for Carolyn.

Richard excused himself from the others, and went over to greet Phillipa.

"All's right with the world, I suppose," Hammond said, as they watched the two.

"I suppose," Runa echoed. She sipped her drink as she watched Phillipa take Richard's arm.

It was strange to see Phillipa's satisfied smile, compared to Carolyn's happiness.

She wondered if the difference was obvious to everyone else, but knew better than to ask Hammond if he could see it. As intelligent as he was, she had learned that he tended to be blind to social cues. Part of why she had chosen to talk to him tonight was because she knew he wouldn't tease her about her Lagan.

The courtyard filled with more guests, who mingled around the pool, or strolled through the garden.

She sighed as she noticed Stefan Marszalek had arrived. He was chatting with Attecus Daneius, a member of Marcus's inner circle.

"What's wrong?" Hammond asked, noticing her annoyed look.

"Stefan is here," she said, taking another drink. "It looks like I'll have to be on my guard."

"He still hasn't given up?" Hammond asked.

"With Richard pushing William towards Birgitta, Stefan doesn't have many more options," Runa said. "Not unless he wants to take his chance with Emilie Holst."

Hammond shuddered. "Even he's not that desperate."

She hummed and nodded. "I should go say hello to Phillipa. Will you be alright on your own?"

"I'll stick with Godric," he said. "How much trouble can I get in with him?"

"Quite a bit," Runa said, looking at Godric, who spoke with Graham and Aksel. But she left him to his own devices anyway.

She didn't look at Stefan as she passed him, not wanting to give him any encouragement. Richard and Phillipa were chatting with Conrad Trevar, but Phillipa turned to Runa with a smile as she approached.

"You look lovely," Phillipa murmured, kissing her cheek.

"So do you," Runa said. "Have you been to the Di Antonios' before?"

"I haven't." Phillipa looked around the courtyard admiringly. "I'd heard about it, but it's so much more than I'd expected."

Runa nodded, looking around again.

"Ladies and gentlemen."

All eyes turned to Marcus, who stood on the steps so everyone could see him. Lucilla was beside him, a keen eye looking over the assembly.

"Thank you for joining us this evening. On this longest day of the year, we honor

Aurora, Titan of the Dawn. Who guides and protects us with her light, even as she gives us our harvest." He held up his glass. "To Aurora!"

"To Aurora!" The crowd echoed, Runa included, raising their glasses in the toast.

Marcus took a drink before nodding approval.

"I don't think Aurora will mind, however, if we take a moment to honor our champions of the arena." His deep voice filled with satisfaction.

Runa stood up a little straighter in anticipation.

This was what she had been waiting for.

"They require no introduction," Marcus said. "But allow me to present: Aelia Orsini, Panther of the Arena! Hero of the Battle of Delorway Hill, and our reigning female champion!"

Aelia appeared in the doorway, and descended the stairs with appropriate, panther-like grace. Her armor had been traded for a dark red, Aurellian-styled gown with gold embroidery. The silk was draped elegantly over her powerful form, while her braids were twisted into an updo. She glittered with gold jewelry, as was the Aurellian style.

The guests cheered to welcome her, and she raised a fist to accept it. Still a gladiator, even in silks and finery.

She paused by Marcus and Lucilla, who both kissed her cheek before sending her to join the party, where she was quickly surrounded by admirers.

It took several minutes for the crowd to settle, and turn expectantly back to Marcus. Runa noticed a few of the women edging closer to the steps, hoping to stand out when the next gladiator made his appearance.

"Lucius Gaspari, the Lion of the Arena!" If he was upset that Lucius had lost the fight, there was no sign of it.

The crowd still cheered as Lucius descended the steps. And while he didn't seem quite as confident as the night before, his posture or expression showed no sign of disappointment. Like Aelia, he wore red, the fabric belted around his hips, leaving his chest bare save for a swath over one shoulder, and gold jewelry. Just as comfortable at a party as he was in the arena.

Lucilla kissed his cheek, and Marcus clapped his shoulder, before they sent him to his admirers.

Runa felt her breath catch as she turned back to Marcus, ready for the next introduction long before the rest of the crowd were.

⊰ CHAPTER 2 ⊱

Finally, the crowd calmed down from Lucius' entrance. And Runa noticed Marcus exchanging a look with Richard.

"And of course, I am pleased to present Lord Galloborne's gladiator. Our newest champion: Lagan Stigsson, Master of the Seas!"

For a moment, Lagan was backlit as he stepped through the doorway. But she still recognized him in silhouette. He was dressed much like Lucius, but the fabric was the same dark blue as his armor. His dark hair was pulled back off his face, and he wore less jewelry than Aelia or Lucius. Only a gold cuff around his left wrist.

Runa found her breath shaky as she watched him clasp wrists with Marcus. Richard met him at the bottom of the stairs, clasping his wrist and clapping his shoulder.

She made her way back to where Hammond and Godric were still chatting.

They were near Byron and Graham, so it seemed like a safe guess that Richard would lead Lagan in that direction.

Godric saw her coming, and she couldn't deny his smirk irritated her.

"He didn't get to show his toy off last night, so now he's making up for lost time," Godric said.

Hammond shrugged. "Can you blame him?"

"I don't blame him," Godric said. "I'm just judging him for it."

"You and Runa are exactly alike," Hammond sighed, shaking his head.

"Well, Runa?" Godric looked at her. "Are you going to go meet him? You should thank him for winning you that forty silver."

There was enough of a challenge in his voice that made Runa want to rise to it. Only because it was what she wanted to do.

She gave her cousin a falsely sweet smile. "I think I will."

Sure enough, Richard led Lagan toward his family. They were soon swarmed by other nobles eager to meet the new gladiator.

Runa took a sip of her drink, observing how Lagan seemed to take everything in stride as he was introduced to the guests. If the crowd overwhelmed him, he showed no sign of it. Instead, he seemed to enjoy it.

Looking at her cousin, she held her hand out expectantly. Godric rolled his eyes, but offered his arm to escort her into the crowd.

Lucius had also joined the group, standing on Lagan's other side.

"You're from the Hvall Archipelago?" someone asked. An Aurellian noble Runa knew by sight, but not by name.

"I am."

"How did you end up in Cardea?" someone else asked.

Lagan started to answer, but their eyes met as he saw her approach. He recovered quickly, and returned his attention to his audience. But she saw the corner of his mouth curl in a smile, and his gaze returned to her as he spoke. He might be personable with the gentry, but she had still made him pause. And that caused a warm glow of satisfaction inside her.

"My father was a trader for our tribe, and I sailed with him from my twelfth summer. When I took over his ship, I was more interested in adventure than trading."

"A common tale," Godric chuckled.

Runa couldn't help but smile, remembering her father's stories of his days at sea.

"It is," Lagan said. "I'd been to Cardea several times and even met Tristan Galloborne a few times. So when I met Lord Galloborne, it seemed like Numitor's guidance."

Blinking in surprise, Runa looked at Richard.

He did his best to hide it, but she saw a flash of annoyance in his pale blue eyes.

Richard kept his family on a short leash. His siblings almost always traveled with him when he moved between houses. Byron and Caitlyn lived on an estate in the Galloborne territory, and came when he called. Even if Byron chafed at the call.

But Tristan was the wayward cousin even Richard couldn't control. While he had his own lands, and a comfortable living, he had always been drawn to the sea. He had chosen to apprentice under a respected ship's captain, with ties to the Smuggler's Guild.

Six years ago, he had left on a six-month voyage, and had yet to return to Callatis. Occasionally he would visit his property on the coast, accepting select dinner invitations when he did. But he never dared to set foot in Callatis. Knowing that the moment he did, Richard would find a way to keep him there.

Every time he was ordered back, something always came up. Storms would waylay him, or he would have to travel months out of his way. Until Richard would become distracted, and leave him in peace for a while.

More than a few people perked up at the mention of Tristan. While he might be a thorn in Richard's side, he was a fascination to others. Every mention of him included grand tales of pirates, or sea monsters.

Richard recovered quickly, forcing a smile as people asked questions about Tristan.

"We've run into each other from time to time in different ports," Lagan said. And Runa had no doubt he was enjoying the rapt audience. "He probably saved my life when he warned me about a storm above Caldona. I might not have made it home if I'd sailed into it."

Caldona was the Sorensens' ancestral home. A pair of islands off the coast of Cardea, where Godric's family lived.

"Then, a couple of years ago, we were both docked in Oceansong, in Vestra. We were talking in a tavern when word came about a scylla on one of the islands off the coast. There was a royal reward for the person who killed it, so we decided to team up. And it's a good thing we did."

"I heard about that," Godric said. "You and Tristan were the ones to take it out?"

Runa had heard about it as well. It had been impossible not to. The scylla had been on one of the most traveled routes between the Oenone Archipelago, and the Innogen continent. Its reign of terror had driven up the price of goods imported from Oenone. Olive oil in particular. There had been a collective sigh of relief when word came that the monster had finally been killed, and trade resumed.

"We were," Lagan said proudly.

Everyone listened in rapt attention, eager to hear the story. Lagan looked to Richard, who nodded approval. His irritation at Tristan had given way to interest.

"When we came within sight of the island, we saw another ship attacking from the sea. They tried to keep a safe distance, and I don't think they expected the scylla to come out into the water. But once the tide came in, it swam out and shattered their ship to splinters.

"We decided to sail around to the island's far side, which was mostly rocky terrain. But we found a place to anchor the ships, and scaled the cliffs. We camped out on the bluffs that night, and watched the scylla on the beach. It lived in a cave above the water, but seemed to spend most of its time on the boulders along the beach."

"How big was it?" Lucius asked.

Lagan considered, then looked around. "About the size of the pool," he said, gesturing to it. "With five heads, and four tails."

The pool was roughly twenty-four feet long, and ten feet wide. Far from the largest sea monster, but more than enough to be intimidating.

"Tristan and his crew came up on the right, while my crew and I came from the left, when it was napping. It woke up as we were trying to tie it down, and started to put up a fight. Its heads lashed around, breaking some of the ropes." Lagan pulled aside the fabric over his chest, showing a large bite scar on his shoulder. "One of the heads grabbed me when I couldn't get out of the way. But it dropped me when one of Tristan's archers shot it in the eye."

Runa's heart clenched as she saw the scar, her imagination painting the image in vivid detail.

"Sotiria, Tristan's first mate, got the killing blow. She jumped onto the creature's back while some of us distracted the heads, and plunged her spear into its heart."

"That was so brave." An Aurellian woman fluttered her lashes as she looked up at Lagan.

He smirked, and Runa had the sudden urge to yank hard on the woman's curls. She doubted they were all hers, anyway.

"It was fun." He gave Runa a smug grin. "And more than worth it."

"What made you give it up for the arena?" Attecus asked.

"We were shipwrecked in Breakwater Landing when a storm rose up, about a year and a half ago," he said. "I had nothing else to tie me to Hvall at that point, and I was always interested in the arenas. So I decided it was time to try something new."

Breakwater Landing was a coastal city in the Galloborne territory. Not far south from Sapphire Bay, Runa realized. He had been half a day from landing in Sorensen territory.

"I happened to be there on business, and decided to visit the arena." Richard returned to the conversation, once more basking in the situation. Even more so now that Lagan had gained a new level of respect from those listening. "As soon as I saw him fight, I knew I had found my gladiator."

Which wasn't entirely true. Richard had asked her father, and Kristoffer Thorinson, to see Lagan fight and give their opinion. Though her father hadn't been available at the time.

Lagan smirked, chest-puffing up a bit. "Did you enjoy the fight, Lady Sorensen?"

All eyes turned to her. Most politely curious, but she noticed a few of the young women glared with jealousy.

"Which one?" She asked, keeping her voice light. "There were more than twenty."

There was a polite bubble of laughter, though Lucius gave a hearty laugh as he clapped Lagan's shoulder. Beside her, she heard Godric snicker under his breath.

She was pleased to see Lagan was undeterred.

"Only one that mattered," he grinned. "Well, two. Aelia deserves some credit."

"She is a crowd favorite for a reason," Runa agreed, still dodging his question.

"Of course," Lagan said. "But I meant mine."

She liked his boldness.

"Well, I am pleased to see that I was right. You do use a trident."

She gave Richard a quick look, while Lagan nodded acquiescence.

"And I did win forty pieces of silver." She couldn't resist a triumphant look at Aksel, who looked away. Only then did she return her gaze to Lagan. "I suppose I have to say that I enjoyed it."

"Then I succeeded," Lagan said.

"Careful, Richard," someone said. "It looks like your gladiator is a charmer."

"Oh, Runa can handle herself," Richard said. Though the look he gave her said he was a bit taken aback.

Lagan's expression was very different. And the intensity of his warm brown eyes thrilled her.

A few more people, oblivious to the charge in the air around them, continued to question Lagan. They asked about his homeland, and his fighting style. Runa tried to think of something to ask, to insert herself into the conversation again. But she didn't want to ask a broad question.

None of the questions she could think of were appropriate for a group conversation.

After a few minutes, Phillipa leaned in to whisper to her. "Try wandering away from the group. I'm sure he'll follow you."

"Thank you," Runa whispered back. "I think I will." She might question Phillipa's feelings for Richard, but there was no denying her methods worked.

Phillipa smiled and nodded, taking a sip of her drink.

⋙ CHAPTER 3 ⋘

Once she had finished her drink, Runa left the group to set the empty glass on the nearest refreshment table. She glanced back, catching Lagan's eye briefly, before she turned towards the gardens.

Enchanted glass orbs created a romantic glow among the flower beds, low hedges, and decorative fruit trees. Enough to let her move along the path of colorful tiles with ease. She passed a bed of hollyhocks - the flower of Galatea the Mother, which Lucilla surrounded herself with.

She could see a handful of other people in the garden. Mostly couples in search of privacy. Throthgar and Carolyn sat on a bench under one of the pear trees, hands clasped, and leaned in close. Bubbling fountains throughout the garden covered the hushed conversations.

As she strolled down the path, she wondered what she hoped to gain. If Lagan followed her... then what? Would she find his arrogance off-putting in a conversation? Or even more charming?

If he charmed her, she could move beyond a light infatuation. If not, it could quash her interest before it took root.

If he followed her at all.

Doubt nagged at her as she stepped onto the small bridge across a brook running through the garden.

What if she had overestimated his interest?

This wasn't a feeling she was accustomed to. Her happiness, and the things she wanted, were usually under her control. To find them dependent on someone else was strange waters that she wasn't sure how to navigate.

"Did I bore you?"

Her heart fluttered as she heard his voice. His accent was unrefined, but not coarse. While his voice was deep, and a little rough.

She smiled, but fought it back as she turned towards him.

"Not at all," she said. "I just needed some air."

"So did I," he grinned, coming to stand closer.

"Is that the only reason you followed me?"

He looked into her eyes, one corner of his mouth tugging in a smirk. "No. I wanted to talk to you."

She couldn't hide her smile, and felt herself blush. It was nice to have him say so without any guile.

"That will make people suspicious," she pointed out.

"I think we already did that," he reminded, stepping closer. And his smile reminded her a little of the wolfish smirks the Thorinsons had. And it sent a shiver up her spine, even as she returned the smile.

"The social season is off to an excellent start for gossip," she said. "We've done our part to keep society amused."

Now that Richard and Phillipa had made two public appearances, with Throthgar and

Carolyn making no attempt at concealment, and Runa herself walking off with a gladiator, there would be no shortage of gossip for the next week at least.

"I thought people didn't like being talked about," Lagan said, cocking his head as he watched her. His look reminded her that Reinhardt had said Lagan moved like a hunter. She could see it now. In his controlled movements, and intense focus.

But she felt safe under that gaze. She had walked among wolves and lions all her life. She was used to predators.

"I've been a topic of conversation all my life," she said. "There are worse reasons for people to talk."

She was hardly the first noblewoman to flirt with a gladiator.

"And here I thought you would be a well-behaved lady," he chuckled.

"I'm well-behaved for a northern lady," Runa corrected.

"Is there a difference?" It was a genuine question.

She started walking again, and Lagan followed without hesitation.

"The north is still regarded as a backwater, and a bit savage. You could say there are lowered expectations when you're a northern noble. Most of us don't care to correct that."

"Hammond seems fairly civilized."

Runa smirked at that. "That's what he wants people to think."

She saw him mull that over.

"We are civilized." She slipped her hand around his arm, and was pleased that he bent his elbow to accommodate her. "But some of us still call the gods by the old names, and we're prone to having tempers." She flashed him a smile.

"They don't know what backwater is," Lagan scoffed. "Otherwise they would know nothing about you is uncivilized."

"That's a bold assessment." She couldn't help but laugh a little. "You might be disappointed if you get to know me better."

"I doubt that," Lagan said.

They ascended the steps up to a terrace on the edge of the property, looking out over the sea.

The setting sun lit up the sky in brilliant shades of lavender, peach, and warm pink, as Aurora brought the day to a close. Callista and Larissa were already in the sky, both in their fullest phase.

Below them, the tide was out, leaving an expanse of white sand beach in the Di

Antonios' cove. Waves rolled in to lap gently at the shore. Further out, the water looked calm, the sun flashing off the shifting surface. Consus was calm, it would seem.

"This is one of my favorite spots," Lagan admitted, bracing his elbows on the smooth marble railing.

"So this is where Richard's been hiding you?" she guessed.

"I've been here for training, and trying to civilize me." He gave her a playful, toothy grin that made her giggle. "Richard gave me a townhouse in the city. But it's easier to go unnoticed when I'm not dressed like this."

The Gallobornes owned several townhouses, which they either rented out, or used for people they sponsored. Runa tried to reason which one Richard would use for his gladiator. The one on Garnet Avenue, perhaps?

"Not after today," she said. "You may have a little longer before people start to recognize you in trousers and a proper shirt. But not long."

The thought conflicted her a little. The Aurellian style showed his body off so well, she enjoyed the view. But at the same time, she wanted to see him in the Cardean style. Not as fancy as Richard, or other nobles, with embroidery and decorations. But the simple style, like what Godric favored, would suit him well.

"Doesn't sound too bad," he smirked.

Runa rolled her eyes. Even as she did, she knew she found his arrogance charming. May the Maiden help her, but she did.

"You enjoy the attention." Her tone was accusing, but playful.

"I do," he said. "I spent years fighting pirates, dragons, even a kraken, and yet--"

Runa's eyes widened, and she leaned closer without thinking. "You fought a kraken?"

Lagan was momentarily surprised at the interruption. But he quickly recovered, and gave her a satisfied smirk. "I did. But if I tell people that, they think I'm making it up."

"Are you?" she asked.

"I wouldn't lie to you," he said.

She found she believed him.

"But some people claim I made up fighting the scylla."

"If you made that up, you wouldn't have given someone else the killing blow," Runa reasoned.

"I did kill the kraken." He gave her a smug smirk.

She didn't rise to it, though.

"So you'd rather pretend to fight in the arena, and have all Callatis fawn over you for your prowess." It wasn't even a question, and she smiled as she said it.

"Nothing in the arena was pretend," Lagan insisted.

She laughed. "It is safer than fighting a kraken."

He nodded, though she suspected he was reluctant to admit it. "That's an advantage, though."

She certainly liked the idea of him fighting in the arena far more than the thought of him fighting monsters.

"Do you miss the sea?"

"I did say this was my favorite spot," he reminded, nodding towards the water.

Runa looked out to the horizon, and the sea seemed to stretch without end. Somewhere beyond that line, there were islands and continents—the rest of the world. But somehow, she and Lagan both stood together on the Di Antonio's terrace.

"My father used to be a sailor," she said. "A smuggler, to be precise."

She had grown up on her father's stories of the sea, and almost wished she could see it the way he did. To feel the call that pulled sailors back to it. But no matter how much time she spent near, or on the water, she only felt admiration for its power and beauty.

Lagan's brow arched. "A smuggler's daughter?"

"I told you I wasn't as civilized as you might think."

"I'll try to remember," he said. He looked back at the party, letting out a small sigh. "I'm still getting used to all this."

"The pageantry of it?"

"Is that the word?"

She nodded.

"The pageantry," he repeated. "And all the social rules."

"You're allowed some leeway," she pointed out.

He met her eyes. "Lowered expectations?"

"Exactly."

"You were telling me about your father," he said, after a moment.

"Yes." She looked out at the sea again, debating exactly how much she should say. "He was a soldier by the time I was born, so I don't know if I'm technically a smuggler's daughter. But he loves the sea, and will take any excuse to sail."

"You must be familiar with a ship, then." He seemed to like that idea.

"A little," she smiled.

That was an understatement. Her father had made sure she understood a ship. Enough so that she could take command if the need arose. But she had learned from Hammond that not everything needed to be public knowledge.

"What about you?" she asked, shifting the conversation.

Lagan looked out at the water, and she saw a shadow pass across his expression. "My mother was a healer. Several years ago a sickness ravaged our tribe, and she wore herself out treating the sick. She wasn't able to recover."

"I'm sorry," Runa said, her heart twisting in sympathy. "What was her name?"

"Ada," he said. He shrugged, but she could see it still affected him. "My father died in a storm at sea a couple of years earlier. Once my mother was gone, I didn't see any point going back up north."

"Was there anything else to keep you there?"

He shook his head. "I'm an only child, and my grandparents are gone, too. When my ship wrecked at Oceanbreak, I felt Atta -

Consus, as you call him here - was telling me I had been at sea long enough."

"My father said he had a similar experience," Runa admitted. "After he met my mother, he got caught in a storm, and felt it was a warning. He says it's unwise to stay at sea when Consus tells you to return to the land."

Lagan nodded. "My father taught me the same thing."

"I'd ask if you regret it, but I think you already answered that," Runa said, smiling a little.

Before Lagan could answer, something caught his attention behind them. Runa followed his gaze to see Lucius coming toward them.

"There you are," he said. "You can't keep him all to yourself over here, Lady Sorensen. Not at his first party."

"I put in an appearance," Lagan said.

"That wasn't an appearance," Lucius insisted. "That was a tease!"

"You did say you wanted people to fawn over you," Runa reminded him.

"Exactly." Lucius grinned. "You've earned this. So come enjoy it."

Lagan looked towards the party, almost as if remembering that it was for him.

Lucius and Aelia as well, of course. But as it was his debut, and his victory, he was the novelty everyone was interested in.

Runa touched his arm lightly, trying to ignore the thrill of his warm skin, and the solid muscle beneath.

"You should enjoy this," she said. "It's yours. And the only way to get used to the pageantry is to be a part of it."

"I'd rather talk to you," he said.

Lucius hesitated, looking between them as if he only now realized what he had walked into. He settled on giving Runa a look that asked for help.

But the words had affected her more than she would have expected, and found herself unable to speak.

"There'll be time for that later," Lucius said, realizing he was on his own. "She's not going to disappear at midnight. Now come on, before Lord Galloborne comes looking for you."

"He's right," Runa said. "We'll see each other again."

Lagan caught her hand, his touch gentle, even as she felt the calluses on his strong hands. "Is that a promise, Lady Sorensen?"

"Runa," she said, horrified at the way her voice quivered. "And yes, it is."

"I'll hold you to it." He lifted her hand to kiss her knuckles. "Runa."

The simple move took her breath away.

Lagan straightened up, offering her his arm, which Runa accepted. While she had made the same motion with plenty of men in the past, this one felt right. As if it was where she belonged.

⌘ CHAPTER 4 ⌘

Runa could feel the gaze of nearly half the party on them as they stepped back into the courtyard.

"I'll see you again soon?" Lagan asked, as she slipped her hand off his arm.

"Soon," Runa agreed, smiling at him.

"C'mon." Lucius clapped a hand on Lagan's shoulder, leading him toward where Aelia was talking to a group of Aurellian District nobles.

Now on her own, Runa looked around to see where everyone was. As she did, she made eye contact with Richard. Even as children, she couldn't remember ever seeing him so upset at having one of his toys taken away.

No, that wasn't true, she realized. She remembered a time as children, when Throthgar had tried to take a toy from him. And his immediate response was to swing a fist at Throthgar. An untrained, sloppy punch. But a punch nonetheless.

Only for Throthgar to tackle him in retaliation.

Runa remembered Eydis cackling in delight as they watched the boys struggle. She had been too shocked to respond.

Now, his look hardly phased her. She simply shook her head in bemusement as she approached the nearest refreshment table. A footman offered her a small gold plate with sliced fruit, and strips of grilled meat flavored with a mixture of strong Aurellian spices.

"Well, now I know why I couldn't catch your attention."

Runa sighed in frustration, recognizing that smooth, deep voice.

"No," she corrected. "You couldn't catch my attention because I knew I wasn't what you cared about."

She turned to face Stefan Marszalek, not bothering to hide her disdain.

Stefan was lean, polished, and handsome, with black hair and intelligent blue eyes.

After the war, with the Council of Prefects desperate to fill seats, he had easily claimed a position, after being put forward by the Lofgren family. The younger son of a lesser noble family, he made no secret of his ambition. If anything, he wore it as a badge of honor.

He was now the Counselor of the Council of Prefects, having won the position a year before, at the end of Hammond's term.

To most people, that was all he was. But she knew he was a sorcerer, with an impressive level of power. A fact he kept even more closely guarded than Hammond did.

Richard had requested she not wound his ego by turning him down too harshly. Stefan was a swing vote on the council, though his interests tended to align with Richard's. And he wanted to keep it that way.

Granted, he hadn't been as obnoxious as men like Pierre Clement, or Brendon Rathdrum. But he still tried her patience.

"At least I never tried to fool you," he said.

Runa was forced to acknowledge that was true. While he had made his interest clear, it had never been with false professions of love.

."No. But you were only interested in me after you realized you didn't have a chance with Meiriona Llewellyn."

"How was I supposed to know she wasn't interested in men?" Stefan muttered.

"Everyone knew," she said. "No one told you because you don't have friends - you only have people you use for your ambition. And no one trusts you, because even your allies know you'll turn on them as soon as it's in your best interests."

As she saw shock, and what might have been pain cross his face, Runa faltered for a moment. Just for a moment. More than a year's built-up irritation made her stand her ground. Richard might want his allegiance, but Runa had no respect for someone whose loyalties were so fickle.

It took a moment for Stefan to recover. "And is the gladiator more loyal?"

"That's beside the point," Runa countered, meeting his eyes.

He held her gaze for a moment. But then looked away. "I came to offer an olive branch," he said. "I know when I'm beaten."

"There was never a competition," she said.

Stefan finally seemed to realize he had been dismissed. His jaw worked for a moment, as if he wanted to say something. But then he took a deep breath, and bowed. "Lady Sorensen."

"Master Marszalek," she said coolly, before sweeping away.

She made her way over to the pillar where Hammond was doing his best to avoid attention. He was the safe choice, and it would give her a moment to collect herself.

"You're having an eventful evening," Hammond said as she approached.

"You're not going to lecture me on impropriety, are you?" She bit into a piece of spiced lamb, then held her plate out to him.

"Hardly." He snorted, taking a slice of peach from the plate. "Then I would have to lecture Throthgar about the same thing. Thank you."

They both looked towards the garden, where Throthgar and Carolyn strolled the paths hand in hand.

"I am glad I got to see you put Stefan in his place," he added. "I've been waiting for you to stop playing nice."

"Richard asked me not to," she said.

Hammond shrugged. "Richard values him as an ally. And I know he was the deciding vote when I became counselor, but

I still don't trust him. Maybe you'll get through to him."

"I doubt it," Runa sighed.

"Time will tell." He took a piece of meat from her plate. "You did surprise me though."

She paused as she chewed a piece of meat, considering. "Lagan surprised me."

"Life has a way of doing that," Hammond agreed.

His tone was pointed, as if he were thinking of something specific. But she wasn't sure it was enough to question him. After debating for a moment, she decided not to. She had come to him because it would be safe from questions, and she owed him the same respect.

Another thought resurfaced. "Do you remember when Richard punched Throthgar for stealing a toy from him?"

Hammond looked confused for a moment, but then his eyes widened in recollection. "I do remember that! Throthgar tackled him."

They both looked over to where Richard once more stood with Lagan and his admirers.

Runa fought back a surge of irritation as she saw the Aurellian woman from before fluttering her lashes at Lagan. She rested a hand on Lagan's arm as she responded to something he said. But Lagan immediately shook her hand off.

"I suppose none of us have really changed," Hammond said. "Throthgar still takes what he wants, and Richard can't stand to share his toys."

"And Eydis still revels in the chaos," Runa reminded.

"That's a given," Hammond sighed. "As a child, I remember telling my mother I thought Eydis might be a changeling."

"Oh stars." Runa giggled. She could easily picture young Hammond, unnerved by his sister's cackling, bringing his concerns to his mother. "What did she say?"

"She said I was being silly. But Aunt Düsana threw salt on her, just in case."

"She would," Runa giggled.

"Nothing happened, of course," Hammond said. "Eydis just laughed."

That was exactly what she would have guessed.

"You should probably make the rounds before people think *you're* a changeling." He gave her a wry grin.

She sighed as she bit into a slice of peach, the sweetness refreshing after the spicy meat.

She was still chewing when Richard stepped away from his conversation and came over to them.

"Runa," he said coolly.

"You still don't know how to share your toys." She couldn't help a wry smile. Richard's annoyance didn't particularly bother her. If he were angry, that would make her careful. But a childish tantrum deserved to be teased.

"Have you lost your mind?" Richard asked. "First you disappear into the gardens with my gladiator, then you insult Stefan to his face?"

"You know he deserved it," Hammond said.

"Of course he did. But that's beside the point." He turned back to Runa. "What were you thinking, going into the gardens?"

"You say that as if I took his hand and dragged him away," Runa said. "I just wanted to speak with him, and we were visible the whole time. I'm not Bronwyn dragging Corion into a dark corner for a tryst!"

"Keep your voice down!" Richard hissed.

"They can't hear us," Hammond said. "I already masked our voices."

"Thank you." Richard nodded, then rounded on Runa again. "You know that's not how the gossips will tell it."

"Why does it matter? People talk about me no matter what I do. It will hardly reflect poorly on Lagan's reputation."

"She did exactly what Phillipa's been doing to you," Hammond countered, before Richard could respond. Runa appreciated the support. "And it worked just as well. On Phillipa's advice, I suspect."

"It was," Runa confirmed. "She suggested it."

Richard glared at Hammond, but it was clear he knew he couldn't argue with that. "You didn't have to take her suggestion."

Runa sighed in exasperation. "Honestly, Richard."

"I hope you don't have any other surprises," he said finally.

"I promise, I'll be on my best behavior for the rest of the night," she said, even as she rolled her eyes.

"You should probably tell that to your father," Hammond said. He reached to take a piece of meat off her plate. "But maybe with less sass."

That caused her shoulders to sag. "You're probably right."

She handed her plate to Hammond. "Enjoy your evening. I should make the rounds."

❧ CHAPTER 5 ❧

In Breakwater Landing, Lagan had earned plenty of attention for his exploits in the arena. He had enjoyed the parties, and the attention. Enjoying a life that was safer, and far more comfortable, than the one he had grown up in. As well as the praise and adoration that had come with his success.

Lucius' stories of the fame and attention gladiators received in Callatis had only reaffirmed his decision. He had looked forward to this night for months.

But now, he found he couldn't enjoy it fully. Even as he spoke with the nobles, their attention focused on him, he was distracted. His eyes followed Runa, her hold on him even stronger than it had been before.

Now he knew the curve of her lips when she smiled. The melodic cadence of her voice as she spoke, with strength and self-assurance. The light in those beautiful green

421

eyes when she teased. The floral scent of her perfume. He kept remembering the exact way words and turns of phrase had sounded from her lips.

Even when he could shake her from his thoughts, he became aware of Richard standing beside him.

Richard's moods seemed to ebb and flow faster than the tide. There would be flashes of annoyance, quickly replaced with a satisfied smile a moment later.

He had seen the way Richard glared at Runa. The animosity had been painfully obvious when they spoke. He had been in enough risky business dealings and shady taverns to recognize a fight when he saw one.

Runa seemed to hold her own. But he still hated the idea that Richard might give her a hard time because of him.

After a while, the group around him dispersed, and he was able to slip into a quieter space with his thoughts. Richard spoke with Marcus and Attecus, while Runa giggled with a group of women he didn't know.

"You shouldn't look so worried. People will think you're not enjoying the party."

He looked over to see Lucilla Carrera coming towards him.

In his time on the Di Antonio property, he had spoken to Lucilla a few times. She was a proud woman, but she carried it well, and could be almost friendly at times. Lucius and Aelia had a strong respect for her, and she checked in on them often. Lagan wasn't sure if it was from genuine concern for their comfort, or for her husband's investment. Maybe it was both.

"I can't tell if Richard is angry," Lagan admitted.

"He's not," Lucilla assured him. "He's just throwing a tantrum. He'll get over it."

Lagan blinked in surprise at the bluntness.

Lucilla took a sip of her wine. "If you had walked off with anyone but Runa, he wouldn't have batted an eye."

"I thought the Sorensens were allied with the Gallobornes." He had checked the night before.

"Oh, they are," Lucilla said. "They're close friends. But Richard is unaccustomed to people who aren't intimidated by him."

Lagan looked over to where Richard was laughing at something someone had said.

The disagreement certainly hadn't stopped him from enjoying the evening.

"He's not the one you should be concerned with," Lucilla said.

Lagan followed her pointed nod, and took a deep breath as he saw a couple approaching him.

The man was tall and broad. His hair was the same dark red as Runa's, with green eyes that sized Lagan up shrewdly. The family resemblance was impossible to miss. Beside him, hand tucked in the crook of his arm, was a slender, dark-haired woman. Her brown eyes were softer, but no less appraising.

He didn't need Lucilla to tell him who they were.

"Tor, Pia, may I present Richard's gladiator, Lagan Stigsson," Lucilla said, her tone deferential. "Lagan, this is Lord Tor Sorensen, and his wife, Lady Pia Sorensen. Lady Runa's parents."

Lagan bowed his head respectfully.

"It's a pleasure to meet you," Lady Sorensen said. Her voice was softer than Runa's, not quite as self-assured, but with similar inflection. "Congratulations on your victory."

"Thank you, Lady Sorensen."

He looked at Tor, and for the first time in longer than he could remember, he felt nervous.

The older man was a little shorter than he was, but not by much. And despite the finery he wore, he was an impressive presence. Made all the more so by his critical frown. Reminding Lagan that he had been both a smuggler, and a soldier.

Pia squeezed her husband's arm pointedly.

"It was an impressive fight," Tor said, and there was grudging approval in his voice.

"Thank you," Lagan said, ensuring his tone was respectful.

"You're from Hvall, correct?" Tor asked.

Lagan nodded. He was entirely out of his depth.

He had handled the press of questions well enough - that had been easy. But the Sorensens were different. He knew it was important to make a good impression, but was sailing without stars to guide him. He wanted to glance around and see where Runa was, but didn't dare.

"I am," Lagan said, squaring his shoulders. He would be respectful, but he wasn't going to cower.

"What brought you south?"

He hesitated a moment. He had told Runa about his mother almost without thinking, wanting to be honest with her. Despite how many people had asked the same question, he had only told them he had wanted a new adventure.

"I realized there was nothing for me in Hvall after my mother died," he admitted. "And I felt Consus was telling me it was time to find my own path."

"I'm sorry for your loss," Pia said, her sympathy genuine.

Lagan nodded his thanks, then looked back to Tor. "When I was shipwrecked in Breakwater Landing, most of my crew went back north on another ship, and I decided to try my hand in the arena."

"Not a bad choice," Tor said. "You seem to have done alright."

"I like to think so," Lagan said, shrugging one shoulder.

Pia made a small sound that he thought might have been a laugh, but he wasn't sure.

"And do you like it here?" she asked, composed in less time than it took him to blink.

"I do," Lagan said.

"Clearly," Tor muttered.

Lagan met the man's challenging gaze. But didn't dare return it.

"Tor," Pia murmured.

Her husband sighed, shoulders sagging a little. He glanced to the side, and Lagan followed his gaze to where Runa was still talking to several women. She laughed at something one of them said, leaning in to say something. And Lagan wished he could hear it.

As if sensing them, she looked over. Meeting first her father's gaze, then Lagan's. She took a sip of her drink, clearly considering the situation. But then turned back when one of the women touched her arm.

"She's not going to rescue either of you," Pia said, her tone playfully scolding. "Lagan, we're having a dinner party next week. Why don't you join us?"

Lagan and Tor both stared at her in surprise.

When Lagan collected his thoughts, he started to say "yes", before remembering that he wasn't supposed to accept any invitation without Richard's approval. He cursed inwardly.

"Richard and his siblings have already confirmed," Pia said, seeing his hesitation.

"I'll tell him you're invited as well. I'm sure he won't pass up an opportunity to show you off again."

"I'd like that," Lagan admitted.

"Excellent," Pia said, with a kind smile. "It will still be a rather large party, but we'll have more time to get to know each other. Don't you think, Tor?"

Lagan looked to the older man, hoping for some glimmer of approval. Something to work with, at least.

Tor looked at his daughter again, then nodded. Lagan could tell he wasn't thrilled, but he seemed to decide not to fight back. "We look forward to seeing you there, Lagan."

"Where are we seeing him?" A young man with the Sorensen coloring came over to join them.

"I've invited him to the dinner party next week," Pia said. "Have you met Lagan, Godric?"

"Not yet," Godric said, giving Lagan a similar appraising look.

"Lagan, this is our nephew, Godric Sorensen."

He bowed his head at the introduction.

"You certainly didn't disappoint today," Godric said. "You even got Runa to come to the arena. That's saying something."

"I'm glad she enjoyed it," Lagan said.

Godric quirked his brow, seeming a little amused, but not disapproving, which was probably a good thing.

"It would seem he's usurped your homecoming," Pia said, smiling at her nephew.

"You're welcome to it," Godric said. "I have more than enough attention." He turned back to his aunt. "Speaking of, I was thinking about going home, but wanted to see how long you planned to stay."

"I wouldn't mind making our excuses," Pia admitted, looking around at the party. "I don't think Lucilla will mind. Godric, why don't you have a footman fetch the carriage? Tor, would you tell Runa we're leaving? She may choose to stay, but I'd like her to make arrangements before we go. Lagan, would you keep me company while they're busy?"

"Of course, Lady Sorensen," Lagan said, a little confused.

Tor kissed his wife's cheek before going over to his daughter, while Godric went to fulfill his assignment.

"This way." Taking Lagan's arm, she nodded toward where Lucilla was lounging on a chaise in a corner of the patio. "You seem to be adjusting to all the attention."

"I like attention," Lagan admitted. "It's the pageantry that takes getting used to. They didn't stand on ceremony so much in Breakwater Landing."

"I suppose you can't be a good gladiator without an ego." Pia laughed lightly. "As for Breakwater, it's a northern city. In Cardea, people tend to value social rules more the further south you go."

They reached the corner Lucilla had claimed, and she rose from her chaise when she saw them. With a wave of her hand, her companions moved aside. If she was surprised by Lagan's presence, she gave no indication. "Are you leaving, Pia?"

"Yes." Pia smiled at the younger woman. "The excitement of the day is catching up with me, I'm afraid."

"I understand," Lucilla said. "Thank you for coming. It was such a pleasant surprise."

"Thank you, Lucilla," Pia said. "Your hospitality never fails to impress."

Tor and Runa came over, and Lagan caught a small smile from her before she turned to Lucilla.

"Thank you for having us," she said, as they exchanged kisses on the cheek.

"You know you're always welcome." Lucilla let Tor kiss her hand.

As they chatted for a moment, Lagan tried to think of something to say to Runa. But he was acutely aware of the people around them.

Before he came up with anything, Godric arrived to say the carriage was ready. All too soon, the conversation wrapped up.

Lagan looked to Runa, and she met his gaze.

"We'll have to speak again soon," she said. "I enjoyed our conversation this evening."

"So did I," Lagan said. It felt like far too little. He wanted to say more, but wasn't sure what.

She smiled, and the expression seemed genuine, rather than polite. Before Godric offered her his arm, and she let him lead her after her parents.

❦ CHAPTER 6 ❧

The Sorensens arrived home a little before midnight.

Despite the fact Aurora herself had completed her daily journey, the city's Solstice celebrations wouldn't truly end for several hours yet. But their house was quiet, a few windows lit to welcome them home.

A footman opened the door with a bow, and Pia sighed in relief as she was greeted by the familiarity of home.

"I look forward to sleeping in tomorrow," Runa said, as they made their way toward the staircase.

"So do I," Pia agreed. "Do you have any plans for tomorrow, Runa?"

She shook her head. "I may call at the Gartners, and visit Azalea. But that's all."

"You're not going to stalk the gladiator yards to see if you can catch sight of Lagan?" Godric teased.

Runa scoffed. "Hardly."

"What about you, Godric?" Pia glanced back at her nephew, he trailed behind the rest of them on the stairs.

"I have to report to the Stark headquarters later in the morning, and I'll run some errands," he said. "But I should be home for dinner."

Pia nodded. "Just let us know if your plans change. We're not expecting anyone for dinner."

Very few people made plans for the day after the solstice, let alone a dinner party.

Beside her, Tor was uncharacteristically quiet. No doubt he was tired from the day's excitement, but she knew his thoughts weighed heavy on him. She turned her head to press a kiss against his arm as they reached the landing.

Tor adored their daughter - Runa had been the jewel of his eye even before she had been born. And while she had experienced a few crushes as a child, she hadn't expressed genuine interest in anyone as she reached adulthood. So Tor had been spared watching another man sweep his daughter away. Instead, he had been pleased each time she spurned an inferior suitor.

Today had caught them all by surprise, but none more so than him.

Godric bid them a good night as he turned down the side hallway to his room.

As they reached the end of the hall, Pia squeezed Tor's arm.

"Speak with her," she whispered.

As they turned back, she saw Runa looking between them. She had grown into such a confident young woman, it was the first time in a while that Pia could remember seeing her look nervous. It made her heart twist, remembering how Runa had looked up at them as a child. So precocious, but so sweet.

Tor hesitated. "Runa."

"Yes, Papa?"

Pia watched as Tor looked at Runa, his expression softening.

"Your mother invited this gladiator--"

"Lagan," Pia corrected, squeezing his hand.

He sighed. "We've invited Lagan to the dinner party on the 26th."

Runa looked between them, giving Pia a questioning look.

"I trust your judgment, Runa," Tor went on. "And if Lagan has caught your attention, then... the least we can do is welcome him into our home." The words came out pained, but both women overlooked that.

Runa threw her arms around her father's shoulders, hugging him tight. And Tor didn't hesitate to wrap her in his arms.

"Thank you, Papa."

"Do you truly like him, Runa?" Tor asked, as they stepped back.

"I think I do." She seemed a little surprised at the idea herself.

"I don't see how he can be good enough for you," Tor sighted. "But I suppose I can give him a chance."

"That's all we can do," Pia said, smiling at them.

Runa hugged her. And once again, Pia's heart twisted as she was struck with just how much her baby had grown. She reached out to twist a stray curl of red hair at Runa's temple. "Sleep well, Runa. We'll see you in the morning."

Runa bid them both a good night, before turning towards her own room.

"I'm proud of you," Pia told Tor, as they turned down the opposite hall.

He grumbled gruffly, opening the door for her.

She squeezed his hand again before retreating to her dressing room to prepare for bed.

When she was younger, Pia had loved the city. She had enjoyed balls, and parties that ran late into the night. Every year she had counted the days until her family would return to Callatis for the social season. She had been grateful for any chance to escape from her family, which was easier in the city.

But as she had gotten older, she had found she had less energy for late nights, and the constant drama of society. Her pregnancy with Runa had weakened her, while at the same time drawing her focus more toward the family she had made for herself. She still enjoyed it, but in smaller doses than when she had been younger. She had extended their visit to Sapphire Bay a few extra days so they would have an excuse to skip the Galloborne ball.

Now, however, she wondered if that had been a mistake.

She certainly couldn't have foreseen that Richard's gladiator would catch Runa's attention. But perhaps Tor wouldn't have been so surprised by Runa's interest if they had been there for that first sight. According to Lucilla, Runa's interest was clear almost from the moment Lagan had been introduced.

When she returned to the bedroom, Tor was ready for bed, but stood at the window, looking out over the gardens behind the house.

She ran a hand over his back, kissing his arm.

"You know why she likes him, don't you?"

He didn't respond right away. "Why?"

She tried to stifle a giggle, but failed. "He's you, Tor."

He looked at her, clearly confused. "What's that supposed to mean?"

She smiled as she went over to the bed, climbing under the light summer blankets and settling back amongst the pillows.

Her husband watched her, waiting for an answer.

"He's tall, handsome, a sailor, and a fighter." She looked at him through her lashes. "He's almost exactly like a certain smuggler I met in a ballroom once. Long ago."

He didn't respond, but she knew he was considering it as he climbed into bed beside her. She watched him as he lay back, his arms behind his head.

"You know I'm right."

"That doesn't mean I have to like it," Tor muttered.

Pia laughed, reaching over to stroke his hair.

After a moment, he caught her hand, bringing it to his lips to kiss her palm.

They were both very different than when she had first seen him walk into that ballroom. When her father muttering about having to share a party with a Sorensen had motivated her to approach him.

"At least she isn't trying to spite you," she said. "That's a better start than we had."

Spite was far from a solid foundation to build a relationship on. But Tor's patience had helped them heal over their initial mistakes.

"Do you think he's sincere?" Tor asked.

"I think you'd be a better judge of that than I am."

He sighed, and she knew the answer he didn't want to say.

"I'm almost more worried Runa might lose interest and break his heart than I am that he'll hurt her," Pia admitted.

Tor gave her a dubious look. "I doubt that."

"I hope not," Pia said. "I rather like him. He's certainly a better option than any of these social climbing idiots that flock around her."

Over the last few years, she has grown increasingly frustrated with the options available to her daughter. And even more so with the ones who actively tried to pursue her.

"A gladiator," Tor reminded her.

"She doesn't have many options," Pia pointed out. "The Thorinsons are either taken, or see her as a child. The Gallobornes and Arnons are taken, or she's uninterested in them."

Richard had attempted to talk Runa into a political marriage, but Pia was glad Runa had been too stubborn to agree.

"What about Graham?" Tor asked. "He's still unspoken for."

Pia shook her head. "Eydis has been in love with Graham since they were children. Runa would never do that to her. Besides, she needs someone strong enough to support her, and level out her temper."

"And you think this gladiator is the one?" Tor asked, still doubtful.

Pia smiled at him softly. "I think Runa is sensible. Which is why, when he comes for dinner, we're going to be polite and welcoming. We'll let them get to know each other, and see what happens. And you-" she rested her pointer finger on his chest "-will give him a genuine chance."

Tor chuckled dryly, catching her hand again and lacing their fingers together as he rolled onto his side to look at her. "Is that an order, Lady Sorensen?"

"Yes," she said primly. Then leaned in to kiss him. "Now try to sleep. It's not worth worrying about tonight."

"If you say so," he sighed, rolling onto his back once more.

Pia moved closer to rest her head on his shoulder as she lay down. "I do."

Tor hummed, kissing her forehead as they settled into sleep.

To be continued in

Volume 2

SONG W. ERETSON

Song W. Eretson is an American author, artist and force of nature, who has been writing for more than two decades. She's also a culture analyst, and co-host of the podcast "Two Women Talking". She used to write Disney princess fanfiction, which is still a decided influence to this day. When not writing or drawing, she can usually be found crafting, watching Disney movies, or dreaming about fantasy ballgowns. Her inspirations include Jane Austen, and Robert E. Howard.

Links to Song's work, and her social media, can all be found at linktr.ee/songweretson

Printed in Great Britain
by Amazon